Bombshell

Also by Alison Clifford

White Rose Series

Roses

Retribution

Deception

New London Books

Seeing Red

Secrets Within

Bombshell

White Rose Series Book Four

by

Alison Clifford

http://alisonclifford.net

Morandoo Press

This work is copyright. Apart from any use permitted under the Copyright Act 1968, no part may be reproduced by any process, nor may any other exclusive right by exercise, with the permission of the author.

All the characters in this book are fictitious, and any resemblance to actual persons living or dead is purely coincidental.

Copyright © Alison Clifford 2017

For Amanda,
my long-time best friend.

Who knew a chance meeting at RAAF recruiting would lead to Macca's on pay night, long phone calls, and a friendship I'll always be grateful for.

Love you, you old hag.

Chapter One

"Ready?"

Jerry's heart went into overdrive. He wiped his sweaty palms on his trousers and checked the empty bag was tucked through his belt. "Ready," he confirmed.

"Guns prepped…and GO!"

Jerry waited for the black-clad man beside him to exit the car before moving to follow. He fumbled his shotgun, wedging it between his knees before heaving it up and scrambling out.

The other guys were at the entrance of the bank as Jerry sprinted across the sidewalk. They raced in, the door closing behind them as Jerry reached it, and he yanked it open again in time to hear Matty bellow an order to those inside.

"Hit the ground, NOW!"

A deafening gunshot followed by a rain of ceiling plaster almost drowned the cries of those in the bank and the yells of the gang members. Jerry joined Peter, his shotgun waving in the air as he shoved and kicked people to the ground while Matty and Reuben confronted the cashiers. He took point as instructed, the barrel of his gun swinging in a wide and flowing arc, covering those lying on the floor. The mask he wore made the job hard; his peripheral vision reduced to an oval around his eyes.

Jerry heard the low growl of Matty's demands for cash and glimpsed the hasty movements of the cashiers. It was going according to plan. He kept his gaze moving over the customers, waiting to see if Matty needed the extra bag.

The woman at his feet whimpered, grabbing his attention.

"Shut up," Jerry snarled. She stole a quick glance at him and he lashed out with his boot, the point of his steel caps connecting against her arm. She groaned, her eyes screwed up against the pain. "Don't look at me!"

A sudden move to his right, and Jerry swung the barrel of his shotgun round. "Stay down, old man," he yelled. "Don't be stupid if you want to go home to Grandma!"

More demands were being made of the cashiers, Matty telling them to hurry. The woman whimpered again. As Jerry glanced at her, she became rigid and began to jerk. Her eyes were wide open and unseeing as her legs thumped into his feet in a violent pulse. Ice ran through his veins as he stared down at her, his mind blank, not understanding what was happening.

"What the hell is going on?" Matty demanded from the counter.

"I don't know!" Jerry yelled.

"She's having a seizure," a man called from the floor nearby. "Let me help her, please?"

"Stop her," Matty commanded.

"You can't. For pity's sake, let me help her."

"No." Jerry had no clue what to do, but he couldn't allow the man to move. He kicked at the woman, rolling her onto her back.

"Don't," the man yelled, pushing himself up from the ground.

"Get down!" Jerry yelled, swinging his shotgun around. His chest squeezed in on his heart, his brain spinning as control slipped away. The man ignored him and lunged towards the woman still thrashing on the floor.

Jerry reacted. The explosion from his shotgun reverberated around the room. The man hit the ground. There was red everywhere. Someone screamed, and Jerry noticed through the surrounding haze that the woman at his feet had stopped jerking and lay still, her eyes half open and empty like the blood-splattered man now lying beside her. Matty's voice screamed in his ear. Something pulled at his clothes, dragging him across the floor, stumbling over people and to the door. The pulling on his clothes continued, guiding him towards the car. A shove from behind and he was sprawling on the rear seat. A hand pushed him over and he hauled himself upright. The car moved and swerved under him, his head bouncing off the side window, but he barely noticed.

Jerry could only stare at the back of the driver's seat. His ears rang from the gunshot and the screams, and his mind saw only the man lying on the floor with his chest blown open.

A sudden and violent change of direction slammed his head against the window again, bringing him out of his trance. With that came feeling. The burning in his chest made him gasp for air. His probing fingers found no holes, but his chest felt open and exposed, as though his ribs had shattered, and blood pumped from his heart. He retched, bile burning as he leaned forward and emptied his stomach on the floor.

"Pull yourself together," Matty snarled from the front. "We're not out of this yet, and they'll look hard for us because of what you did."

Jerry wiped a shaking hand over his mouth and pushed himself upright as he tried to control his racing heart.

Reuben pulled into an alley and stomped on the brakes. "Everybody out."

The car shook under Jerry as the others escaped.

"Get a move on, or you'll be left behind," Peter said from beside him.

"Don't leave me!" Panic rose, propelling Jerry out of the car and through the open door of the nearby garage.

They ran through the abandoned workshop and out a back door. They didn't slow as they raced across the small parking lot behind the garage, weeds pushing up from cracks in the ancient concrete, and around a corner to a waiting truck. The truck seemed out of place; neat and tidy, bright flowers painted on the sides, standing amongst rusting iron and broken windows.

The four robbers piled in the back of the truck as the driver headed for the cab. Reuben pounded on the divider between the cargo area and the driver's cab, telling the driver they were set, and the truck rolled away. Jerry lay on the cold and unforgiving floor as the truck swayed out onto the city streets. There was a long silence. No one spoke. It was the rule. No talk while they were still in the city. Talk could lead to arguments, which could lead to someone hearing them. Not worth the risk. Jerry didn't care. His body shook, tremors flowing through his limbs, chattering his teeth. The sound of the shotgun, the jerk of the man as the round struck him. The blood, the screaming; it all crowded in his brain, a cacophony of chaos. The monotonous rumbling of the truck over the roads eased his terrors. The tremors subsided and the silent darkness enfolded him.

A sudden hammering from the driver's cabin started Jerry out of his haze, giving them the signal they were clear of other traffic.

"What the hell were you thinking?" Reuben said, lashing out at Jerry and connecting with his backside.

"He wasn't thinking," Peter said. "He reacted. The guy was going for him."

"It will have them hunting us even harder now," Matty said. "I say we dump Jerry."

"Don't be stupid. Even if we kill him first, he'll lead them straight to the rest of us. We have to cover our trail and make sure our story holds tight if they come looking."

"Reuben's right," Peter said. "We have to stick together. I'll take the shotgun and destroy it. Jerry." Peter's boot nudged him. "Jerry!"

"I'm listening," he said. "Tell me what to do and I'll do it."

"We'll stop on the way back home and burn your clothes. If we leave the ashes miles away, they won't find them. Did you get much blood on you?"

Bile rose in Jerry's throat. He swallowed, fighting it down again. "I don't know. Some."

"We'll stop by a stream or something, and you can wash yourself while we burn the clothes. Got it? Every damn inch of your body, okay?"

"Got it."

"Reuben, get Mac to stop. We'll fill him in on the plan."

Reuben hammered on the wall again, a prearranged sequence that had the truck swerving off the road and coming to a stop soon after. The truck shook as Mac climbed out of the cab, followed by a dull thud of the cabin door being slammed. Footsteps crunched outside on the dirt and as Peter opened rear door, Mac's face appeared.

"What's up?"

"Need somewhere to clean up," Peter said.

"Right. I know a place not far from here." Jerry saw Mac glance at him and then look away again. "We can deal with the clean up there."

"Not that kind of clean up," Peter snapped. We don't need a body leading the feds straight to us."

Jerry's heart hammered in his chest, sweat breaking out on his forehead as he took in the implications of the conversation. Mac was prepared to kill him, as was Matty. His bowels cramped. Jerry clenched his butt. If he crapped himself in fear, even Peter might change his mind about not doing him in.

"Find a forest track somewhere. We need to burn Jerry's clothes, and he needs to wash up."

Jerry looked from Peter to Matty. Matty stared at Reuben and they nodded. The back door closed and moments later the truck trembled as Mac climbed back into the cab. The truck started and jerked back into motion.

"You screwed up Jerry, but we'll see you right," Peter said. "You need to keep your mouth shut, right? No caving because you shot a guy. You've got more to lose than any of us, and if you do anything to set the feds on our trail, I promise you'll regret it."

Jerry's hands clasped together in front of him. His body was like ice, but his hands were slippery with sweat. "I won't say nothin'. I swear." He swallowed hard on the bile that rose yet again. How long would it take for that man's image to fade? He'd killed a man, and Jerry thought a part of him had died too. As if a chunk of his soul had gone with the man. The feds would find him, they would find him, and he'd have to pay for what he'd done. Jerry's bowel cramped again. He wasn't scared of the feds—he was terrified of going to jail.

"I need a crap," he said.

"Hold it," was the unsympathetic reply.

"I don't know if I can."

"For God's sake…" Reuben pounded on the cabin wall, and the truck slowed and stopped. Peter eased open the door, peering out to see where they were.

"Right," he said, looking at Jerry. "Over behind them bushes, and make sure you can't be seen."

Jerry bolted out of the truck, past a curious Mac, and then into the edge of the forest. A thick screen of bushes lay ahead. He skirted them at a run and reefed down his jeans before his bowel let go.

"Oh Jeez," he whispered. The cramping eased with the evacuation, leaving Jerry trembling with the aftermath of the force of it. He scanned the ground and then reached for a clump of wet leaves. He gave his butt a wipe and then stood and pulled up his jeans again. His hands still trembled, and his brain couldn't work out if he was cold or scared.

"Hurry!" Peter's voice reached him from the truck. Jerry wiped his damp palms on his jeans, trying to block out the blood spattered across the fabric, and headed back for the truck. For the first time he noticed where they were. It was a small country road cut through a forest. There were no buildings, or other cars, in sight. It wasn't so bad. He couldn't remember hearing any cars, either. No one would have seen them.

Jerry shuffled back to the truck as Mac returned to the cab. His bowels weren't cramping anymore, but he was drained. He caught a foot on the step up into the truck and sprawled headlong onto the floor.

"Get up, loser," Reuben snapped as Peter slammed the door shut. Jerry just made it onto the bench on the side of the truck when Mac, obedient to Reuben's hammering, jolted the truck back onto the road.

"Mac reckons he knows a good spot about five miles up the road," Peter said. "We need to be quick, so no dawdling."

Jerry nodded as he stared at the floor between his feet.

The truck made a sharp left, bounced its way for another few minutes before another left turn, and then it pulled up. They waited in the back for Mac to give the all clear. A thump, and then the door opened.

"Everybody out," Mac called. "We should be all right here—not a soul in sight."

Jerry stumbled out of the truck and glanced around. They were in a small clearing, a turning circle at the end of a narrow dirt track.

"Jerry, get over here," Peter called from the far side of the clearing. A small walking trail, visible amongst the grass, led away from the clearing. "I can hear a stream that way." Peter pointed. "Strip off your clothes and then get down there and get clean."

Jerry peeled off his top, the blood drops turning brown as they dried. The reminders of his action dropped to the ground, taking some of the strain with them. His mind felt lighter as his jeans joined the pile.

"Keep your boxers," Peter said. "But we'll need your boots and socks."

Jerry added the items to the pile. The air was cold, but he didn't care. Then he looked down at his scrawny chest. A few tiny red spots blotched his pale skin. Some of the blood had soaked through his top. An overwhelming urge to rub them off was smothered by the gruesomeness of what had caused them, leaving Jerry panicked.

"Get down to the stream, and don't come back until you're spotless, and that goes for your hair too."

Jerry's hand flew to his head, his fingers running over his short blond spikes. He couldn't feel anything out of the ordinary. A chuckle from Peter made him look up at him.

"There's no blood there, idiot, I just wanted those damn spikes of yours flattened."

The grin on Peter's face relaxed Jerry, so much he found he could even grin back.

"Now get your butt down to the stream and get clean," Peter said, pointing down the path.

Jerry turned and picked his way down the path in his bare feet. The stones dug into his feet, but the stream came into view before any broke his skin. Jerry dropped his boxers on the ground and waded into the water. He gasped, the icy flow making him hesitate, but the sounds of the others' voices reached him, encouraging him to go on. Five minutes later he again stood on the bank of the stream, this time dripping with water as he tried to hug warmth back into his body. The sun, filtering through the trees, provided little in the way of warmth and the breeze across his wet skin made it worse. Jerry struggled to get his boxers up his legs, the fabric clinging to his damp skin and making the simple task slow and frustrating. The faint smell of smoke, mixed with gasoline, drifted down to him. He picked his way as fast as possible to the clearing. Dirt and bits of tiny sticks clung to his feet, but his focus was on getting to the fire and warming up.

"Ah, there you are," Peter said as Jerry joined them. "We're almost done."

Jerry stopped by the fire, holding his hand out to the warmth. There was no sign of his clothes—only the remains of his boots lay in the flames. He sighed. He'd liked those boots.

"Here, put these on."

Jerry caught the overalls Reuben had thrown at him. They were covered in oil, but Jerry didn't care—it wasn't blood.

"Thanks."

"See that you give them back."

"I will." Jerry stepped into the overalls and pulled them up over his shoulders and fastened them up.

"Right, let's get out of here," Peter said. He kicked soil over the dying fire, the boots destroyed now. "There, that should do it." He gave Jerry a shove. "Back in the truck."

"I think you have a fantastic lesson planned," Beth said as she followed the two teachers down the forest trail. "The locations all have great examples of what you want to show them."

"Thanks Beth," Rennie, the shorter of the two, replied.

"We appreciate you taking the time to run through it with us," Mike added.

"You two know your subject, so I don't think I added a whole lot."

"But at least we know we have the plans for the day well mapped out." Mike sniffed the air. "Can you smell smoke?"

"I can," Beth replied, picking up her pace to hurry down the trail after the others. Her heart pounded as the smoke grew stronger. *Not another fire.* They emerged at a clearing just in time to see the back of a white truck disappear down the track.

"A picnic lunch?" Rennie suggested, looking around the clearing. "Fires aren't allowed here, and there are no signs of it."

"Over here." Beth was already heading to a track she could see leading from the clearing. She kicked at the ground, a few yards into the forest. "Someone's had a fire here and they haven't fully doused it. See?" She nudged the soil with the toe of her boot, exposing embers. "They've chucked dirt on it and left it."

"Sounds like there's a stream down here," Mike said, from farther down the track. I'll fill up our water bottles and we can put it out."

Beth passed her bottle to Rennie, who accompanied Mike to the stream. Beth moved a few small twigs away from the edge of the smouldering fire as she waited for the others to return. Nothing serious, luckily.

Rennie came back into sight, followed by Mike. "Someone's been down there and it looks like they had a swim." She upended a bottle over the embers, passing a bottle to Beth to do the same.

"A swim? At this time of year? No frozen people down there? Turned to ice cubes?"

Mick shook his head and laughed. "No frozen people. Maybe they went down for water, like us." The three watched as steam hissed from the remains of the fire, filling the air between them.

"Not to put out the fire, though," Beth said. She stared down at the ashes. "What's this?" Beth crouched by the remains of the fire and reached to pluck a blackened piece of leather from the coals. "Looks like they were burning more than wood." She dropped the leather again and stood up. "Pass me your bottles and I'll get more water."

It took another two trips to the stream to get enough water to extinguish the fire to make it safe.

"I think that should do it," Beth said as the last splashes of water evinced no hissing. She frowned down at the piece of leather and then glanced down the track leading from the clearing as if she might still see the truck. "All a bit weird," she muttered to herself.

"What's that, Beth?"

"Nothing," she replied. "We'd better get going." The others pulled on their backpacks as Beth grabbed her cell phone and took a couple of photos of the dowsed fire, focussing on the leather.

"Do you think something's wrong?" Rennie asked, watching as Beth stuffed her phone into her bag.

"No, I wanted photos," Beth replied. She didn't add it was in case something cropped up. It was probably nothing to worry about, but it never hurt to take a photo or two. She swung her bag onto her back. "Let's go."

Chapter Two

"How did your morning go with Rennie and Mick?"

Warren's voice drifted in to Beth from the bedroom where he was getting dressed for their dinner date.

"It went well. They have everything under control by the looks of it. All the plans are ready to implement, so they can get moving on them now." Beth inserted the diamond studs Warren had bought for her to celebrate their fourth wedding anniversary into her earlobes. She twisted her head from side to side to appreciate the sparkle from the stones before continuing. "We found something unusual near a small track."

"Of course you did." Warren's voice came closer as he spoke. He appeared in the doorway to the bathroom and leaned against the wall. Beth looked at him in the mirror, his handsome face serious as his brown eyes stared into hers in the reflection. "What was this unusual thing?"

"Someone had lit a small fire and not put it out properly."

"Is that all?" Beth detected relief in Warren's voice. Not surprising, really. She had a knack of finding things in forests, and not nice things either.

"No, that's not all. We doused the embers with water and I found a piece of leather in the middle of the ashes."

"Leather? It could be from anything."

"It seemed a strange thing to find there."

Warren continued to stare at her in the mirror. "It's not what you would usually find in a campfire, true. Was there anything else with it?"

Beth shook her head, the diamonds catching her eye as they flashed in the mirror. "No. I didn't see anything else unusual." She shrugged. "Just thought I'd mention it."

"It's been noted," Warren said, smiling and tapping the side of his head.

Beth returned his smile and then stepped back from the mirror, sliding her hands over her hips to smooth the soft fabric of her dress. A movement caught her eye, and she looked up to meet Warren's gaze again as he came to stand behind her.

"You look beautiful," he said, his deep voice melting through her like warm chocolate. She smiled at his reflection, the glow in her eyes matched by his.

"I have a hot date tonight, so I want to look my best."

The corner of his eyes crinkled as he returned her smile. "Who's the lucky man?"

"An incredible, handsome, and intelligent man, who looks just like the man I married four years ago."

"He looks like me?"

"Yes, the spitting image." Beth's head tilted as she pretended to consider him. His smile grew as did hers. "I wouldn't want to have anything to do with him if he wasn't exactly like you."

"Just as well there's only one of me then."

"It is." She turned into his waiting arms. "Only you."

Beth watched as his smile died and the glow in his eyes deepened. "My Beth, my love," he whispered, a finger trailing down the side of her face to her chin. He lifted it and touched his lips to hers. She surrendered to him, the warmth of his kiss, and the sense of being home in his embrace.

He broke the kiss. "We won't make it in time for our reservation if you keep distracting me."

"Hey, you started it."

He grinned. "Are you complaining?"

She snuggled against his chest. "No. No complaints here."

His laugh rumbled under her ear. "Me neither, but we need to get going."

Beth pulled away and turned back to the mirror. With a quick twirl of her finger she twisted the loose tendrils of hair hanging down near her ears into loose spirals and then reapplied lip colour. She caught sight of Warren watching her and turned to face him.

"Hold still." Her thumb brushed across his lips, removing the trace of gloss that lingered. His hand caught her wrist, and he lifted it. The soft touch of his kiss on the sensitive skin shot a delicious tingle through her. It would be a night to remember.

Warren took her hand and led her out of the small restaurant after they'd finished dinner. He paused on the sidewalk, drawing her into his arms. Beth laid her head on his broad chest and listened to his breath entering and leaving his lungs, the momentary quietness enveloping them.

"What do you want to do now?" she asked, feeling his light kiss on her hair.

"Why don't we walk for a while?" he suggested.

Warren released her, and her hand sought his, their fingers intertwining as they moved away down the sidewalk. They didn't speak, just walked in a comfortable silence. Beth felt her arm brush against Warren, relishing the closeness they shared. A hint of his aftershave tantalised her nostrils and she leaned close to enjoy the scent of him.

"Are you cold?" he asked.

"No, you smell nice."

He smiled down at her and released her hand, wrapping his arm around her shoulder instead and pulling her into his side. Beth sighed, smiling, and slid her arm around his waist as they crossed the street and headed for the path leading around the Washington Memorial. The great pillar grew in magnitude as they approached, towering above them. The national flags of the USA circling the base like sentries fluttered in the slight breeze. Beth tilted her head back to see the top of the massive pillar. As monuments go, it was impressive, and Beth loved the solidity of it.

"Beth?"

"Hmm?" Beth replied, her eyes still focused on the top of the monument. She brought her gaze back down to meet Warren's when he didn't continue. "What is it?"

He looked away towards the circle of flags. "Do you ever regret..." he hesitated, as if unsure whether to continue.

"Do I ever regret becoming an American citizen when I could have kept my Australian citizenship and stayed a US resident?" she asked, watching his face.

His lips pressed together for a moment, and then he brought his gaze back to meet hers. "Do you?"

She smiled, surging tenderness making her pull him close, into her arms. "No, I don't. I don't regret it, never have, and I never will. I'm a dinky-di, true blue American, one hundred percent."

His chest vibrated against her as he chuckled. "Dinky-di?"

"Absolutely." She sighed. "I will admit to missing Australia a little." A tiny shadow of sadness lingered in her heart. She didn't think of Australia often, but when she did the pull of her memories brought with them a tinge of sadness.

"I am grateful you feel that way, and I will always love my Aussie wife."

Beth stared at the stars and stripes fluttering in the evening breeze. She had no regrets—Warren was worth it. She turned and smiled at him and he took hold of her hand again as they continued around the memorial, emerging onto Constitution Avenue. They crossed the street and strolled in companionable silence down to the World War II Memorial.

Warren slowed their pace as they approached the bowl of the memorial. He stopped at the entrance, Beth standing beside him, staring at the beauty of the space.

Two fountains rose in arching sprays, one at each end of the large pool. They were lit from under the water, golden light illuminating the cascades. Smaller arches of water rimmed the pool, also lit up with the same light. Providing a backdrop to all of this was the wall, covered in over four thousand gold stars.

"I've never seen it at night—it's beautiful," she whispered.

Warren's arm tightened around her for an instant. "It is." He led her forward, and they circled the pool until they stood in front of the stars. Beth stayed quiet, sensing in Warren's stillness his connection with what the stars represented— lives lost, sacrificed in the line of duty. His whole life had been dedicated to serving and protecting others, first as a Marine, and then with the FBI. Beth didn't have the same connection, but she felt grief at the loss of so many lives. Memories of ANZAC Day marches she watched as a child filtered through her thoughts like a ghost. War wasn't something to celebrate, but it should be remembered and the sacrifices made honoured. The wall of stars, to her, was a suitable way of doing that. It conveyed the enormity of the loss of life in a haunting, but beautiful way.

Warren's head had bent, his eyes closed as he paid respect, before turning to draw her into his arms.

"I'm glad we came here," he said. "It's a remarkable place."

Beth kept silent, listening to the sounds of his life in his chest, feeling the warmth of his body seep into hers as her fingers rested on the muscles of his back. She closed her eyes, absorbing him through her senses, living with him in this moment.

"Yes," she whispered. "This is a remarkable place to be."

Chapter Three

Warren looked down the long row of targets set ready for the morning's assessments. Crisp morning air filled his lungs, its freshness sharpening his mind, ready for the task ahead. His sidearm, holstered at his side, grew more noticeable as the instructor approached. The formality of the blue FBI shirt and cap with the yellow embroidery took Warren back to his training days. He felt as ready now as he was then.

"Morning, sir."

"Morning, Special Agent Buchanan." Warren shook the man's hand and moved to the rear of the firing range. His pulse quickened as he watched other agents who were preparing for their firearms assessment as he was. He loved the challenge of the test: the accuracy, the speed, and the control. All right up his alley.

"This one sir," Buchanan said, waving at a position on the range. Right in the centre of the row where everyone would see him. Fine by Warren. "You have your sidearm?"

Warren lifted his jacket and grasped the familiar butt of his pistol, withdrawing it for the instructor's inspection. Warren's gaze didn't lift from his weapon as the instructor checked it. The crafted metal in the instructor's hands was his final line of defence; letting someone else touch it seemed wrong, regardless of their qualifications.

"Do you have enough clips, sir?"

"Yes," Warren said.

"Excellent. You know the drill. Start at three yards. Three shots, a pause of three seconds, and repeat. Then three shots, switch hands, and three more shots, all in eight seconds."

Warren nodded and turned to face the target. The caress of a cool breeze on his cheek registered in his mind. Not enough to affect the bullet's trajectory—nothing he needed to compensate for. He relaxed his shoulders, his hands hanging by his side and brushing his suit jacket. The assessment required he show that he could access his weapon when wearing the clothes he wore every day. No agent wanted to be fumbling with a coat when faced with a loaded shotgun pointing in their direction.

Warren breathed and waited. A beep sounded and he reacted, flicking his coat aside and drawing his pistol. As the sight on his sidearm lined up on the target, he fired three controlled shots; the weapon jerking as it discharged each round, the sharp cracks echoing down the range. A pause as his eyes scanned the target for the holes and then he holstered his weapon before dropping his hands to his side once more before the process was repeated.

"Good," Buchanan said. "This time switch hands."

Warren nodded and stilled his body in preparation. A beep and he pulled his sidearm out and fired three rounds. His left hand took over, less comfortable, but still familiar with the feel of the gun, and he fired again. He allowed himself a moment of satisfaction as he checked the holes in the target. It was going well.

The process continued. The distance increased by increments up to twenty-five yards. Silence prevailed over the range between the sporadic gunfire of Warren's assessment. He was aware of the presence of others as they stood watching his performance. If Warren knew anything, he knew they would judge him, and harshly.

"Okay, sir. This post is your cover." Buchanan slapped a wooden post set in the concrete floor. "Move to cover and fire two rounds. Then kneel and fire another three rounds, all in fifteen seconds."

Warren nodded and took up position. The slight breeze blew again; still nothing to worry about. Warren's eyes, wide and unblinking, fixed on the target. The beep sounded. He ran to the cover, his muscles controlling the movement of his arm as he found the target and fired. His knee hit the firm ground, he waited a heartbeat for the vibration of his contact to ease, and fired once more.

"Once more, then that's it," Buchanan said as Warren rose to his feet.

A stab of disappointment shot through him as if he were a kid who'd been told to stop playing and come in for dinner. He was enjoying himself. This was better than sitting in endless meetings, day after day. He relished the challenge of his job, but he missed the hands-on aspect of being a special agent.

Warren took up position and went through the drill one last time. He checked his sidearm and holstered it as Buchanan retrieved the target. The agents behind him rustled to life as they too waited for the result. Judgement time.

Buchanan's still face told them nothing as he walked back up the range. Warren felt the tension rise behind him with each step the instructor took.

"Not a bad effort sir," Buchanan said, as he reached Warren. He held up the target, neat round holes filling the central space. "All sixty rounds are within the target. A perfect score. Again." The instructor grinned at him. "Good to see you haven't lost your touch, sir."

Warren's eye ran over the grouping on the target. "I'm not past it yet."

"Not even close."

Warren suppressed the smile of satisfaction that tried to break through. He had a game to play yet.

"So, who won?"

Buchanan's eyes widened. "Who won?"

"Yes, Buchanan, who won?"

Silent stillness hung over the range, and then Buchanan grinned. "I did, sir."

Warren smiled back. "Good to see you haven't lost faith in me."

"No way. I knew you would be on target." Buchanan jerked his head at the door leading out of the range. "They all thought you'd be out of practice by now."

Warren kept the smile in place despite the annoyance that crept in. "They should know better."

"The arrogance of youth, sir. They have yet to understand the value of experience."

"Let's hope they don't leave it too long to learn." His gaze slid to where instructors stood at the end of the row. "I need to reload before I leave."

"Ammo's in the usual place, sir. I'll leave you to it while I sort this other lot." Buchanan's eyes narrowed as they ran along the row of waiting agents.

"Thank you. I'll see you next time."

"Always a pleasure, sir."

Warren's brow creased as he shot a look at the instructors hovering beyond the range boundary. It was all a part of the game, but Buchanan's comment had stung. Out of practice? Him? As Warren seethed, the truth hit. The comment stung because he feared it was true. Empty suits. That's the name the agents gave to the management sitting in their offices at headquarters. It had been a while since Warren had taken part in any field activities; his practice and assessments on the range the total sum of all he'd done in recent times. He clenched his fists and flexed his biceps. Okay, so he was still in good physical shape, but that didn't mean his skills were in the same condition. When he'd accepted the promotion to Executive Assistant Director, it was with the full knowledge that meetings and desk work would dominate. At first, he'd ensured there was time to join agents conducting investigations, to keep his hand in, so to speak. Warren thought back. It must be a least six months since he'd done anything like that. Maybe it was time to make it more of a priority. As a leader, he should be out with the agents under his command, working with them, experiencing what they experienced. How did he let it escape him?

"EAD Pearce."

Warren brought his mind back to the present and focused on the thin man who'd hailed him. His counterpart in the science and technology branch half walked, half shuffled to catch up with Warren, the frown on his face clearing as he reached Warren's side.

"Morning Anton." The arrangement had been for them to meet in the conference room of the lab building, and Warren had hoped to sneak a few minutes with Beth before the scheduled meeting started.

"Good to see you Warren," Anton said as he shook Warren's hand.

"You too."

"I thought I'd come down and meet you. There's something I want to talk to you about before we get started."

"Right." He wouldn't be snatching that ten minutes with his wife first. *Damn.*

Anton turned and fell into step beside him. Warren sighed to himself. He'd make sure he dropped in on Beth before he left the Quantico complex. Sure, he'd see her tonight, but she'd be waiting to hear how he'd gone at the range, and watching her work always spiked his interest.

"Fill me in, Anton…"

"Next item on the agenda—the increased number of bomb hoaxes. We all have a copy of the report. Pearce, can you brief us please?" Deputy Director Toovey looked over his glasses at Warren, the image of a school teacher springing to Warren's mind as he looked up at him.

Warren leaned forward. "You will all be aware of the dramatic increase in bomb hoaxes being called in to government buildings. No devices have been found, nor have we been able to locate those calling in the threats. The targets have been all over continental USA and the increase has not reflected in civilian buildings. There is no concentration relating to any particular branch of the government either. The targets have ranged from schools, to libraries, and right up to military bases and our own facilities. The only building that hasn't been targeted is the White House."

"Saving it for later?"

"We don't know, but security is operating at a heightened alert."

"What is being done to find the culprits?"

Warren gave the speaker a long look, searching for signs of sarcasm. The speaker, head of the Human Resources branch, wasn't looking at him. Warren gave him the benefit of the doubt and continued.

"The calls have all been made on prepaid cell phones. Not untraceable, despite what some people believe, but the phones seem to have been used once and dumped." His gaze swept the people sitting around the polished table. "Two of these devices were located, due to the cooperation of the IT and Investigative branches." He sat back in his chair. "Forensics have been over the phones and found no traceable evidence.

The cell phones themselves were purchased at stores without working cameras."

"That's a lot of planning for a bomb hoax," Anton said, his eyes fixed on Warren. "Do you think it's the swatters?"

"That's always a possibility. The cyber guys are monitoring the known groups, but there's nothing we can tie it to." Warren's lips pressed together for a moment as he thought. "I'm not convinced all of it is them. The swatters' main objective is to force the call out of the SWAT team and as many other emergency service personnel as possible. Not all the hoaxes fit into their normal attention-seeking pattern."

"Do you think attention-seeking is all that is behind the swatters' activities?"

"Nobody knows what their motives are, so all things must be considered. And that includes who is behind all the bomb threats. As I said, there's no real indication it's the actions of swatters."

There was a moment's pause and then the Deputy Director spoke. "What are your conclusions, Pearce?"

Warren shook his head. "The information we have doesn't support any conclusions at this point. There are several groups working on this issue and for now, we are treating all hoaxes called into government buildings as potentially being connected. The bomb squad are always on standby and we will continue to investigate each call."

"Real bombers don't usually call in the threats, though, do they? They set them off with no warning at all." Head of Human Resources again.

"Statistically that is correct. Are you prepared to risk a genuine incident occurring and not evacuating the threatened building?" Warren's eyes narrowed as he looked at the speaker.

"It's disruptive."

"It is, but have you heard the story about the boy who cried wolf?"

"Have you considered it may be purely to frustrate government services?"

Did they think he was stupid? "Yes, we have. There are a lot of theories and a lot of avenues to follow. We are investigating all possibilities."

"Thank you, Pearce. Keep me informed," Toovey said.

Warren nodded, and the meeting continued.

Chapter Four

Warren closed his portfolio case and pushed his chair back from the table. His gaze remained on his file before flicking to his watch. A quick glance down the table at the others, and he rose and strode for the door. The avoidance method, he called it. No eye contact and head for the door. Post-meeting discussions were pointless. It was beyond him why they kept re-hashing all that had been gone over. A waste of time, and time that was better spent with his wife.

Down the hallway, right turn at the end, open the door, and into the stairwell. The cold concrete echoed his steps as he took them two at a time. He wasn't past it by any stretch, no matter what anyone thought. Another door, opening into a corridor identical to the one below, but this one led him down its length to Beth's lab.

Warren stopped at the open door. The room, quiet and still, was an oasis of peace in the humming activity further down the hallway. Beth stared into a microscope, intent on what she examined and oblivious to his presence. He could see her lips moving, talking or counting—he couldn't work out which. A plant press stood on a bench on the far side of the lab, several of its layers folded over as if Beth had been reading it like a giant book. She had been reading it, Warren reflected. Her work as a forensic botanist meant she would be reading what was in the press, analysing and assessing it.

A sigh from Beth drew his attention away from the press. She sat back from the microscope, and said something. Probably a plant name, but it sounded like a magic incantation to Warren, and then she made a note on the paper on the desk. He moved, shifting his weight on his feet. The movement caught her eye and she flicked him a glance, and then a second as she realised who her visitor was.

"How long have you been standing there?"

Her smile drew him into the room, his lips curving to match hers. Her pen clattered on the desk as she abandoned it to rise from her chair. In a second her smile disappeared as she swayed, grabbing for the bench. Warren darted forward, his arms reaching for her waist to support her. Beth's hands clutched his shoulders, her breath coming in short gasps. His heart pounded as he held her close, looking at her face to work out what was happening. As she leaned against him, her breathing slowed to its usual tempo. After a few more moments, she straightened, her strength returned. The whole thing had lasted a few seconds, but it had seemed like minutes to Warren.

"Do you need me to call someone? The first aid officer?" he asked as she pulled out of his arms. Beth lowered herself into her chair again as he stared down at her. Dark shadows bruised the skin under her eyes, ramping up his concern.

"Just a slight dizzy spell. I must have stood up too fast." Beth's hand still gripped Warren's arm. "I'm okay."

"You sure? You look tired." Warren traced the shadows under her eyes. "Are you feeling all right?"

She smiled. "I'm fine Warren. Perhaps a bit tired, but that's it."

He searched her face for clues she was hiding something, but saw nothing and accepted her answer. "How about you pack up and I drive you home? There's bound to be an agent here who would be willing to drive the pool car back to HQ for me."

"I need to finish this." She released her hold on his arm and waved at the microscope. "I can't stop in the middle."

Warren sighed. "I guess not." He frowned down at her. "I'll stay while you finish up and then take you home. While you do that, I'll check in with Lisa."

Beth's tired smile did little to ease his concern. She turned back to her work, her hands on the microscope as she peered into it once more. Warren watched her for a moment, but she seemed okay. He walked across the small room to the bench on the other side and propped himself against it where he could see Beth's face while he called his professional assistant.

"Checking in, Lisa," he said when she answered. "Anything exciting happen while I've been out of the office?"

"The Director wants to see you, sir."

"Now?" Warren kept his eyes on Beth, once again absorbed in her work. He didn't want to leave her alone—not until he could be sure she was okay.

"No sir, first thing in the morning. His PA will email you."

"Good. Anything else? I won't be back in today."

"Nothing that can't wait until morning."

"Thank you." He had a gem in his assistant. She could tell important from over-dramatised in seconds and made sure he never had to deal with trivialities. Worth her weight in gold.

Warren frowned again as he watched his wife. Her pallor bothered him, but there was no sign of the giddiness returning. Satisfied, he turned his attention to back to his phone, accessing his emails. The one from the Director's office was at the top of the list. Warren opened it and scanned through the message. The Director wanted a briefing on the bomb hoax issue. The President's wife had been evacuated from the charity function early in the day due to a bomb threat and the White House wanted to know what was being done about it. He grimaced, flicked over to his contacts list, and called Jed Jones, head of the Critical Incident Response Group.

"I've only just found out myself, sir," Jed said when he answered. "The agent in charge of the Bomb Disposal Squad is filling me in right now."

"I need a report emailed tonight, and I want you to join me at HQ first thing in the morning. The Director wants a full briefing on what's going on and what's being done about it."

"Yes, sir."

Warren could almost hear the man wilt. Too bad. In their line of business, time mattered. Late nights and early mornings were the norm for people in their position—it was all part of the job.

"Briefing is at eight."

"Yes sir."

"Coffee in my office at seven-thirty."

"Yes sir." A brighter response that time. They always perked up at the offer of coffee.

"By the way, do you know an agent who lives in DC that can return my pool car?"

"I can do that, sir. I get a lift down here with a friend each day."

"Thank you. I'll leave the keys at the lab reception desk for you."

Warren hung up the call and turned to see Beth removing the slide from the microscope.

"Finished?"

"Report is complete. Just have to pack up now."

Warren nodded and leaned back against the bench. He wanted to help, but knew better than to offer. The evidence chain could be challenged in court if the defence counsel found out people outside the nominated examiners had touched the items, and the evidence could be rendered inadmissible.

Beth methodically replaced the sample and locked the evidence away, noting her actions on the log. She made final notes on her computer, and then shut it down before casting one last look around the room.

"Okay. Everything's done—we can go."

Chapter Five

"Jerry! Someone's here to see you!"

Jerry's heart lodged in his throat as he braced himself to flee. The pounding of blood thumped in his ears as he tried to swallow the lump in his throat.

"Who is it, Pa?"

"Peter."

Jerry's knees wobbled, dangerously close to losing all rigidity and dumping him on the ground. "Okay."

Peter appeared around the side of the greenhouse where Jerry had been working.

"How goes it?" he asked, relaxed, as if nothing had happened the day before.

"I'm all right," he muttered, bending to pick up a bale of hay to mulch his mother's plants.

Peter shot out a hand and grabbed Jerry's arm. "You need to keep it together, Jerry. We're counting on you."

"I told you I'm fine," Jerry said, pulling away. "I'm not going to be the one to squeal, am I? I've got more to lose than the rest of you."

"You have, Jerry, you have. But if you lose, I do too. You know that."

Jerry stalked into the greenhouse and dropped the bale by the end of the middle row of flowers. He reached for a knife, resting on the ground, and with a couple of quick flicks released the hay from its bonds.

"Nice flowers," Peter said from behind Jerry. "What are they?"

Jerry picked up the first chunk of hay from the bale and pulled it apart. "Orchids mainly, but these here are roses." He scattered the hay amongst the rose bushes.

"Orchids are hard to grow, aren't they?"

"Yeah," Jerry replied, glancing at Peter.

"Quite a business your mom has going here. You never told me how well she did."

Jerry straightened. "What are you getting at, Peter?"

"Nothing, buddy, nothing. Just interested. Where's Matty? Doesn't he work here too?"

"Out doing a delivery, most likely," Jerry replied. "You want to talk to him too?"

"Nah, just asking."

Jerry eyed Peter for a moment, then turned back to his task. He heard the rustle of the hay bale and turned to see Peter following him with more hay.

"More hay?"

"Yeah, thanks." Jerry took the offering, but didn't turn back to his work. "What do you want, Peter? There's more to it that just checking on me."

"I need to know you're okay."

Jerry nodded. "I am."

Peter reached out and laid a hand on Jerry's shoulder, giving it a gentle squeeze before dropping away.

"What did your folks say?" Peter asked, nodding his head toward the other greenhouse where Jerry's folks were working.

"Didn't say nothing. They didn't see me get home, so all good there." It had been terrifying, sneaking into the house. His pa would have known something was up, and he wasn't the kind that left things alone. There had been no comment about missing boots, clothes, or extra miles on the truck. They'd noticed none of that. "I told Mom I wasn't feeling good. They bought it, and Mom sent me to bed for the rest of the day. She even made chicken soup for me." He couldn't help grinning at how easy it had been to dupe his parents.

"Don't get cocky, Jerry," Peter growled. "That's when you'll slip up."

"I ain't going to slip up. They noticed nothing."

Peter scowled at him for a moment, then reached out and clapped Jerry on the shoulder. "You'll be all right then. I'd better get going."

"It was supposed to be a bit of fun. An adrenalin rush, something exciting, and with the reward of the money afterwards." Jerry swallowed hard, forcing down the sudden nausea. "Didn't turn out that way." He shook his head as if to remove the memories. "What about the money?"

Peter swung around. "The money's hidden for now, like the rest of the stuff. It's too dangerous to use, especially when everyone knows we earn almost nothing."

"But—"

"No buts, Jerry. We all agreed. We gotta use our brains to stay safe."

Jerry went back to spreading the hay. "I guess so."

"Good." Peter glanced at his watch. "I have to go. Tell Matty I dropped by to say howdy."

"Yeah, sure."

"And keep your lip buttoned."

Jerry watched Peter leave. Peter's attitude disturbed him. It was as if they were almost strangers now. And as if he would talk. Nausea rose in Jerry's throat as the memories flooded back. They were always with him, always sitting in his mind. His folks had believed he was sick because he'd looked it. And he still did. This morning he stared at the man in the mirror, seeing his face not as it was, but splattered with blood. His chest ached—he could still feel the hollowness, as if he had a gaping wound there. Jerry's hand clutched at his shirt, the heel of his hand rubbing up and down his chest, reassuring him it was still intact.

"Jerry!"

He dropped his hand and hurried back to collect more hay. His mom appeared in the doorway of the greenhouse.

"Jerry, have you seen my bag? You know, the one I use to collect the plant rubbish?"

Lights flickered in Jerry's eyes as his body ran cold. The bag. He'd forgotten about the bag. Where was it?

"Son, are you feeling sick again? You look awfully pale."

Jerry felt his mom's warm hands clutch his arm. He looked down into her worried eyes.

"I...maybe a little." Or a lot. The bag. He couldn't remember seeing it after the robbery. Maybe one of the other guys had it, or had they burned it with the rest?

"I think you need to go and lie down." His mom laid the back of her hand against his sweaty forehead. "You don't feel hot, but you're all sweaty."

Jerry took hold of his mother's wrist. "I'll be fine, Mom."

"You sure?"

"Yeah, I'm sure." He would be after he'd figured out where the bag was.

"Okay Jerry. Let me know if you get worse."

Jerry nodded and watched as his mom left the greenhouse. At least she'd forgotten about the bag.

Jerry stood staring at the plastic side of the greenhouse, trying to remember when he'd last seen the bag. He could remember shoving the end of it into his jeans, but after that, he couldn't be sure. It hadn't been hanging out of his jeans when he'd stripped at the clearing, so he'd lost it sometime before. But where?

His hand reached for his cell phone and then stopped. He couldn't call the other guys and ask them. If they hadn't seen it, he'd be in a heap of trouble with them and that wouldn't end well. The icy coldness swamped him again and he swallowed hard, fighting the panic. Okay, so maybe he'd left it behind. Was there anything about the bag that would lead the feds to him? The bag had no markings, and he didn't think they would get fingerprints from it. Or could they? He'd never had his fingerprints taken, so there was nothing they could match to. The tightness in his chest eased and he sucked in a deep breath. The bag would mean nothing. It had nothing to lead the feds to him. He let the breath out. All he had to do was keep his cool, and he would be okay.

Chapter Six

"So how are things going at headquarters?"

Warren narrowed his eyes, watching his best friend lounge back in his office chair. Sam's casual pose didn't fool Warren; a relaxed Sam meant an alert Sam. Sam Dalton, private investigator and ex-FBI agent. And he was up to something.

"You're no good at hiding from me, Dalton. I know you too well. What have you heard?"

Sam grinned, tipping his seat forward and resting his arms on his desk. "I hear lots of things. I hear a certain high-ranking FBI executive is restless, I hear murmurs the FBI is worried about an increase in bomb threats, and I hear there's a lawyer looking to hire a reliable firm of investigators to assist with criminal cases."

"A legal firm wants to hire you?"

Sam's chair tipped back again, his smug smile irritating Warren. "That's what I said."

Warren mimicked Sam's pose, his muscles tensed instead of relaxed. "And you're going to take it on?"

"If I can. I'll enjoy doing that level of investigation again."

Warren's jaw clenched. "Do you remember how to?" His hand waved in the air. "Sorry, I know you do, it's just…"

"You're jealous, right?"

"No."

"You want me to call you out, buddy?"

Warren looked up from under his creased brows, debating the wisdom of accepting Sam's challenge.

"I take it from your silence I'm right." Sam's mocking smile had changed to understanding. "I find it interesting that you've dropped in to see us instead of enjoying your morning break at the office."

"Stop being so smug." Sam's observations hit close to home. The briefing with the Director had been a waste of both his and Jed's time and he'd come to see Sam to get away from office politics.

"And you should stop being so stubborn." Sam's chair rocked as he abandoned it to round the desk and stand by Warren. "Quit the FBI. Come and join us at the agency. Have some fun again. I know you want to, deep down, so let go and take the plunge." Sam propped his hip against the desk. "We can use you. Sarah doesn't want to work full time now she and Aden have baby Logan, and Aden spends half his time teaching self-defence classes. If I take on this contract with the lawyers, either something else will have to go, or I will have to hire someone to help with the load." He leaned forward. "I want you to join us. You're a damn good investigator and I trust you. Will you consider it?"

Warren's fingers drummed a tattoo on the arm of the chair. Real investigation work again. Few meetings, more action, and more control over his hours. And what had Beth said to him once? He was a man of action.

"I'll think about it."

"Good," Sam said, resuming his seat. "I'll make space for you at the office."

"Slow down, I haven't said yes yet."

"You will."

"You're pretty sure about that."

Sam grinned. "I am."

"And you seem sure that the FBI is concerned about bomb threats."

"If I were the FBI, I would be."

"What do you mean by that?" The line between friend and FBI agent was a fine one, especially given Sam's business.

Sam's nonchalant pose dissolved, along with his grin. "I've heard the bomb squad is being called out a lot and a bit of research soon showed me the numbers are increasing. If the FBI isn't concerned, they should be."

"You know I can't discuss FBI business with you."

"So it's true then. Swatters?"

If Warren heard that word again it would be too soon. "Investigations are proceeding."

"Nice line there, buddy. I use it a fair bit myself so I know how to decode it." Sam's lifted eyebrow and twitch of a smile drew a similar response from Warren. "Are you concerned?"

"I am, but I'm not sure what's behind it, nor are any of my people. It could be swatters, but there's no firm evidence it is. That's the most frustrating part." He leaned in towards the desk. "And how you always get me to talk is beyond my understanding. This is all confidential, of course."

"You talk to me because you trust me." Warren heard the sincerity in Sam's firm voice, and understanding too. "I'm one of the few people you do trust completely." Sam's chair rocked as his weight lifted from the back to the front. "And you can. No conflict of interest between friends."

Warren's shoulders dropped, releasing the tension he hadn't realised was there. "I know. I don't like to worry Beth with the things I know, but you…"

"Have seen it before and you know I can take it," Sam finished for him.

Warren's thoughts went back to Beth's giddy spell the day before. "I don't want to burden her."

"So, you really are concerned about the bomb threats?" Sam's brow furrowed as he stared at Warren.

"I've got a bad feeling about it. I'm not sure why, but I do. It feels as if it's leading up to something, but no one can see any danger looming." His shoulders rose with his sigh. "I hope I'm just being paranoid."

Sam stared at Warren, his mouth pressed into a thin line. "I'd go with your gut feeling. It's always done you right in the past."

"That's what worries me."

"It's worrying me too."

Silence fell, each man lost in his thoughts.

"I'm worried about Beth, too," Warren broke the silence.

"Because of her workload?"

"I don't know."

"There's a lot you don't know at the moment."

Warren glowered at him from under his brows. "I know enough." His fingers drummed another tattoo on the arm of the chair. "It probably is stress. She's still on her own at the lab."

"Gut feeling?"

"Only that she's not as fine as she says she is."

"Do you want me to ask Heather if she's noticed anything?"

Warren's brow creased and his fingers ceased their rhythm. "No. Not yet, anyway. I'll see how she goes for the next week or so." His frown turned to the window. "The weather's been nice the last few days. Maybe I'll take her out this weekend for some fresh air; it usually does her good."

"You're making her sound like a blanket, or duvet, or something."

Warren's lips twitched. "She certainly keeps me warm."

"Keep it clean, buddy." Sam sat back in his chair. "But you're right—she has made you warm up, and it's good to see. You're a happier man these days."

Warren smiled as he contemplated Sam's comment. It felt disloyal to his first wife to agree with Sam, but it was true. He'd come alive since meeting Beth and falling in love again. She was the axis around which his world spun.

"I'm right, aren't I?" Sam dug.

"For once, yes. You're right."

"And if you join the agency, you'll be able to spend more time with Beth."

Warren chuckled. "You're not going to give up, are you?"

"Not a chance." Sam leaned forward, his gaze intense. "Tell me you're not tempted, tell me you like sitting at a desk or in meetings all day, and I'll back off."

Warren met the direct stare. "I said I'd think about it," he said.

Sam sat back, grinning. "Let me know when you're ready, and we can talk salary."

"What about the others?"

"Right behind me all the way. We'd make a great team—you, me, Sarah, and Aden."

Warren grunted. "I'll let you know."

The office door flew open and Aden strode in with Logan in his arms, stopping when he saw Warren.

"Sorry, didn't realise you had Warren with you, Sam," he said, backing out.

"No, don't go Aden," Sam said, rising and circling the desk, his arms held out to take the baby. "We've finished."

Warren saw the quick raise of Aden's brows followed by Sam's tiny shake of the head in response. They had indeed been talking about him.

Aden relinquished his son to Sam. "Can you watch him for a few minutes? I need to call a client and Sarah's gone out."

"Never a problem, Aden. Take your time."

Warren stood as Aden left the room. "I'd better be going."

"Think about it, Warren."

"I will."

Warren made to leave, but stopped as Logan leaned out of Sam's arms, holding his own little ones out to Warren.

"Hey, looks like you have a fan," Sam said, smiling at the baby's determined effort to reach Warren. "Here, hold him."

Warren found himself with an armful of baby before he could decline. He'd never held Logan, never feeling the urge to, and he couldn't remember the last time he'd carried a child. He shoved a hand under Logan's bottom and felt the weight of the little body snuggle into his chest as he supported Logan's back with his other hand.

A little pair of green eyes peered up at Warren. "Yayayayaaa."

Warren had no idea what to say in response to Logan's babble and a swift glance at Sam's beaming smile gave him no clues.

"Yayaya bababa."

A small hand reached up and wandered across Warren's cheek to his nose.

"Babababa."

"It's a nose, Logan."

The green eyes fixed him with a solemn stare. "Bababa?"

The questioning eyebrows lifted over the baby's eyes charmed a smile out of Warren. Logan's soft hand moved to Warren's cheek and then dropped as Logan plonked his head on Warren's chest and heaved a great sigh. Warren lifted his head to meet Sam's gaze.

"I think he likes you, buddy," Sam said.

"I don't know why." The little, warm body in Warren's arms wriggled and sighed again.

"He can pick the good ones from the bad ones in the blink of an eye."

"Then maybe you should hire him."

Sam chuckled. "I've thought about it, but this line of work is a bit hazardous for babies."

Warren eased Logan into Sam's arms. "The whole world can be hazardous for babies."

Sam settled Logan in the crook of his arm, directing his penetrating gaze on Warren.

"Bad case?"

"They're all bad when they involve children."

"True." Sam glanced down at Logan who had shoved a thumb in his mouth and sucked it with small movements of his jaw. "This little one will be all right. His mom and dad will make sure of that."

"No one can make sure of it."

"Then you have to do the best you can." Sam's eyes bored into Warren's. "You are worried about Beth, aren't you? She'll be okay—she has you."

Warren's lips twitched into a brief smile. "Thanks Sam. I'll be in touch."

"I'm here if you need me."

Warren nodded. Sam's help was nothing to be underestimated, and he felt reassured knowing he had such a good friend he could rely on.

"Thanks again, Sam. See you."

Chapter Seven

Beth was greeted by her boss's assistant as she answered the summons she'd received via email that morning. As he was Assistant Director of the Laboratory Division, she'd headed straight down, curious as to why he's requested the meeting rather than issue directions via the normal channel. A sensitive case, maybe?

"Good morning, Beth."

"Good morning. Kamal wants to see me."

"He does. You can go in now—he doesn't have anyone with him."

Beth knocked on Kamal's office door and waited for his invitation to enter. The soft scent of lavender wafted through the air as she walked into his room, a friendly greeting, except she knew why she could smell it.

"You have a headache already?" she asked.

Kamal's frown answered her question. "Still got the one from last week."

Beth peered into the diffuser from which the lavender essence drifted, and then picked up a small bottle, reading the label. "Have you tried paracetamol? I hear it helps with headaches."

"As a botanist, I thought you'd be all for herbal medicine."

"I am, but I'm practical too." She put down the bottle of essence and took a seat. "I guess you didn't call me down here to discuss herbal medicine, so what do you need me to do?"

"Did you hear about the bank robbery on Friday?"

"On the news, yes. A man was shot, wasn't he?"

Kamal sighed. "And died this morning from the wound. The suspect that fired the shot dropped a bag on the ground as he fled. The forensic team at the scene found plant material inside the bag which they collected. They also tape-lifted the inside for any seeds or pollen. I want the evidence processed pronto."

Beth nodded. "No problem. I'll need to look at the bag too. They may have missed something—it won't take long to check."

"Absolutely."

Beth nodded. "Right. I'll head to the evidence store now."

"Beth."

"Yes?"

"Before you go. I've heard from John Bennett. He's resigning his position."

Beth's heart sank. She missed the company of her fellow botanist though she couldn't blame him for not wanting to return after the injuries he'd sustained in a fire the year before. "I'm sorry to hear that."

Kamal nodded. "I want you to consider moving to full-time and taking up the extra days."

"You're not going to replace him?"

"Not in the short term. Will you consider it?"

Beth nodded. "I'll think about it. In the meantime, I'd better get moving on this evidence."

"Morning Beth. The boss said you'd be down to check the bag—it's over there."

"Thanks Anne."

Beth walked to the bench where the bag lay. It was about the size of a standard pillowcase and made of hessian. She pulled on gloves and slowly examined it. She found no visible plant evidence on the exterior;

cross-contamination from contact with the ground could mean that pollen samples might be misleading, anyway. The tape-lifted samples from the inside, collected by the attending forensic team, would give a clearer picture.

Next, Beth folded back the lip of the bag.

"Can you please pass me a magnifying glass?" she asked Anne.

Glass in hand, she examined under the folded seam. Nothing there. She continued to work her way down, her attention focussed on the side seams.

"Ah," she breathed.

"Found something?" Anne was by her side, already armed with a camera.

Beth pointed out the tiny fragment and leaned back so Anne could photograph it. That done, she eased it out of the seam and placed it on a piece of newsprint lying ready on the bench. Beth continued to search the bag, examining it by eye and probing with her fingers, but found no further plant material.

"That's it," she said, laying the bag down.

"I'll add the photo to the others so it's ready for you," Anne said, moving to her computer.

"Thanks." Beth completed an evidence sheet and folded the newsprint up to protect the sample.

"Do you ever worry someone will mistake an evidence pouch for a scrap piece of newspaper?" Anne asked, returning to the bench.

"No," Beth replied with a smile. "It's marked well enough. I've seen stranger things used to collect botanical evidence. A group of agents once put samples in the only magazine they could find lying around—Penthouse."

Anne laughed. "Red faces?"

"Just a dull crimson. I didn't let them forget that in a hurry."

Beth completed the evidence log, sealed the sample and removed her gloves, tossing them in a bin. "Thanks for your help, Anne. I'll get the rest of the samples and get to work."

Beth walked the long hall to the evidence store at the far end of the building, taking the collected sample with her. The agent in charge of the store had the other samples waiting for collection. Within minutes Beth had completed the chain of custody procedures and was bearing the load back to her lab.

"Right," she muttered, setting the collection down on a long bench. "Leaf fragments first."

Beth opened the folded paper that contained the leaf fragment that had been found in the bag by the team processing the scene. It was a small section, not the entire leaf, probably only about a quarter of it. She examined it, her eyes taking in each detail, one at a time: the shape of the fragment, the ridges on the outer edge, the texture and colour. She reached for a hand lens to examine the fragment for plant hairs, and to look for any other marks.

"I've seen you before," she said when she'd finished her inspection. "But where?" The leaf fragment was almost black in colour, with deep red veins that faded to almost white in places. "Think, woman." Beth stared at the wall, seeing only the leaf pattern in her mind. "I can see you," she muttered, then closed her eyes. The darkness focused her vision. "A hothouse growing…orchids!"

Her computer soon confirmed the identification. A quick search and the image of the leaf appeared on the screen.

"That's it." She examined the leaf fragment again, to be certain. "*Anoectochilus chapaensis*, a jewel orchid," she said, writing down the information. She flicked through the details that had come up during her search. "Not a common one. That might be helpful, or it might not." She glanced at the fragment, giving it a half smile, half grimace. "Not my problem, thank goodness."

Beth completed the notes and placed the fragment back in a small press to begin the drying and preservation process. She clamped it and moved on to the tiny fragment she had found that morning. This one wasn't so easy.

"Hay of some sort." She sighed, made a note, and placed the sample in the next layer of the press. The type of grass could be identified, but it depended on the importance of identification. The cost involved in lab time would probably not be worth it. Pollen was next. Again, a more involved process, but more worth the effort. Beth completed the paperwork on the two evidence samples already dealt with and prepared to process the pollen. It would be a lot easier if John were here, or even if another botanist joined the team to help out, but that wasn't going to happen. She wasn't sure if she wanted the extra hours, but she'd promised she'd think about it, and that's what she'd do.

"Dr Pearce."

Beth looked up to see a lab technician come in through the door with a file in hand. "Yes?"

"Can you help me with this, please?"

"Sure." Another day, another pile of evidence waiting for processing. "What have you got?"

Beth curled up beside Warren as they sat watching television that night.

"I spoke to Kamal this morning, and he told me that John isn't coming back. He wants me to consider working full time."

Warren moved beside her, his arm around her shoulders pulling her closer. "Do you want to?"

"I don't know."

"You like having the time off to do other things, don't you?"

"I do, but perhaps I should give it a go. The workload isn't getting any lighter and there's a limit to what the technicians can do."

"It's going okay though?"

"Mostly."

"Well, it's up to you. Don't feel you have to," Warren said. "You don't owe him any favours."

"Thanks. I guess I'll think about it for a while and see how I feel."

"Don't overdo it."

She sat up. "You're thinking about my dizzy spell, right?" The crease between his eyebrows confirmed it. "Stop worrying, I'm fine."

"If you say so, but I reserve the right to worry."

"There's no need to," she replied and snuggled into his embrace again, not noticing the frown deepening on her husband's face.

Chapter Eight

Special Agent-in-Charge Burns stalked into the investigation room. The agents that noticed their SAC enter sat up a little straighter, nudging the arms of their fellows who hadn't. Arms folded over his chest, he read the information on the large whiteboard at the end of the room. Silence fell, the agents waiting for him to complete his review. Finally, his arms dropped to his side, and he turned to face them. A roomful of eyes stared back.

"EAD Pearce is joining us today to work on the investigation."

A muttered comment about 'empty suits' grabbed Burns' attention. "You should be happy he's interested in what we do and wants to help out. Any more complaining and you'll be manning the phones for a month." No further comments reached his sharp ears. Satisfied his point had gone across, Burns continued. "Some of you have worked with him before, so fill him in and keep going on the investigation."

Burns nodded to the lead agent and strode from the room. He wasn't sure if he agreed with Pearce's desire to work on investigations, but he respected the man for it. Empty suits; not a respectful nickname, but one many of them deserved. Pearce was different though. He'd kept in touch with the real FBI world, taking a hands-on role with investigations when he could. Not a complete surprise when it came to Pearce; the man had earned the reputation for being a maverick in the past—one reason Burns had always looked up to him. Maybe his team could learn something from the EAD, but he was never around long enough to be a part of it. Burns swiped at a sheet of paper hanging from a noticeboard, tearing it from its pin and sending it floating through the air. He snatched it before it hit the ground, scrunching it into a ball and launching it down the hallway. To do any real good, Pearce should join the team for a week. He didn't have long enough to immerse himself in an investigation in the space of a day. That wouldn't happen though. There was no way he could take the time from his role. Maybe he was an empty suit.

"Special Agent Burns."

Burns spun around. Pearce walked up the hallway to where Burns stood, his firm step seeming to emphasis the powerful build of the man.

"Where am I assigned today?"

This was the part Burns hated. He never thought he'd be telling EAD Pearce what to do. The world could turn on its head and feel more comfortable. Burns saw the glimmer in Pearce's eyes and let go of the breath he held. If the EAD appreciated the humour of it, then so could he.

"Bank robbery sir. One fatality, four men still to be found, plus the driver. The team is working in that room." He pointed to the open doorway of the investigation room.

The gleam of amusement turned into enthusiasm. "Right. Thank you for having me, Burns."

"You're welcome, sir."

Burns watched as Pearce headed into the room and listened as he greeted the other agents. He swooped on the paper ball as he passed, flinging it against the wall. It ricocheted away down the hallway, Burns frowning after it. Damn it, he wanted to work with Pearce, not sit in the office doing his job as SAC. A burst of laughter from the investigation room chased him as he stalked back to his desk. Sometimes, being the man in charge sucked.

"What do you want me to do?" Warren asked the lead agent and bank robbery specialist, Zonardi. The joke he'd told had had them roaring with laughter; the agents now relaxed and lounging in their chairs. Perfect. If they were going to take him seriously, he needed them to forget his position and see him as a fellow agent.

Zonardi's gaze slid to the whiteboard and back to Warren. "Well, sir, I was hoping you might have a contact we could call to see if the plant fragment has been identified yet."

Warren's lips twitched. He appreciated someone who didn't hesitate to ask for favours when it came to solving crimes. And someone who had the balls to ask a person who held a position in the FBI such as Warren's, too.

He leaned back in his chair, meeting Zonardi's challenge without expression.

"You want me to call my wife and tell her to hurry up?"

Zonardi's wide open eyes almost caused Warren's professional façade to crack. He relented.

"I'll see what I can do," he said.

If they wanted him to call his wife, who was he to object? The only objection might come from Beth. While he wasn't her boss, he ranked above her in the organisation and she performed work for his division. Any communication relating to work always passed through the formal channels, not direct from his office to her. Anything resembling a direct command from him would only land him in hot water at home. There was still enough of the independent Aussie in her for Beth to resent high-handed authority. The cell phone in his hand, smooth and compact, didn't feel dangerous. If he phrased his request in the right way, she wouldn't take it as a command and he would be unscathed. He felt the eyes of those nearby watching him as he dialled Beth's number.

"Hello Warren."

As usual, hearing her voice made his day better. "Hi Beth. How's things at the lab?"

"Busy, as usual."

Warren could almost feel the waves of suspicion flowing through his phone. "I can believe it. I'm calling to ask a favour." Better to be up front right from the beginning.

"You're at the DC field office, aren't you?"

He needed to be careful here. Her tone wasn't telling him anything right now. "I am."

"And you've been assigned to the bank robbery case?"

His breath rushed out in a silent sigh of relief hearing the resignation in her voice. "Yes."

"And you want a favour?"

His gaze caught several others watching. He rose to his feet and turned away from them and their listening ears. "Do you want me to beg?"

Her chuckle spread a warm glow through his heart. "Now there's a thought." Her voice had dropped, low and husky.

Better put a stop to this conversation before it turned into something he definitely didn't want others listening in on. Warren cleared his throat of the tension Beth's comment had caused. "So, ah, have you been filled in on the case yet?"

"You're not alone, are you?"

"No."

"I'll play fair then. I've started examining the evidence and so far, I've identified the plant fragment as being from the orchid family. The particular plant is called anoectochilus chapaensis, known more commonly as a jewel orchid."

"Can you spell that out, please?" Warren asked, his hand diving into the top pocket to extract his pen. A helpful agent slid a notepad onto the desk next to Warren.

"Sure." Beth spelled it out as Warren wrote it down. "It's not a common orchid, which may help with your search."

"Where?"

"Well, before I put forward any suggestions, I also found a small fragment of what looks like dried grass lodged in a seam."

"Hay?"

"I would say so. The ends of the fragment look cut, not torn. As to the type of hay," he could picture her shrugging as she paused, "it's too hard to identify without a much deeper analysis. It would need someone with more specialised skills than I have, and may not be worth the effort if you don't need it."

"So, we're looking at somewhere with both rare orchids and hay."

"It would be a start."

"Where, Beth?"

She sighed. "Botanical gardens, specialty gardens, orchid clubs, nurseries."

He scribbled down her list and pushed it towards one of the waiting agents. "Thanks Beth, you've been incredibly helpful."

"I love you too."

He smiled, his eyes not seeing the room around him as his mind focussed on his wife. "Right back at you. When will the report be ready?"

"When I've finished it."

It was his turn to chuckle. "That put me in my place."

"I can only hope."

The phone clicked as she rang off. He gave the agents a quick run-down on what Beth had told him and several agents typed on their laptops. Within a few minutes they had a list of potential locations.

Warren joined Zonardi by the whiteboard.

"There was a report of a truck parked behind a disused workshop on the day. It was white with flowers painted down the side. The woman couldn't remember the name of the business, but she gave a good description of the artwork."

"She couldn't remember the name, but could remember the flowers?"

Zonardi smiled. "Apparently they reminded her of her wedding flowers."

Warren shrugged. "Better than nothing."

"Excuse me," an agent said. "I found something that may be of interest."

Warren followed the agents over to a laptop.

"I found this on a nursery website."

The laptop showed the front page of a website. In the foreground of the image was a white truck with flowers painted down the side.

"It matches the description," Zonardi said, looking back at the board and then at the laptop.

"And they grow the orchid we're looking for. In fact, they're the only nursery we can find that does."

"Okay. I'll get started on the paperwork for a search warrant. You keep looking and see what else you can find." Zonardi called over to another agent. "Call for a forensic team to be on standby, and request Dr Pearce join them—we'll need her expertise." He smiled at Warren. "Thank you, sir."

"Glad I could help." Not that he had, really. All he'd done was marry Beth. He watched as the agent continued looking through the website. It was good to be a part of what the agents did, but he wouldn't be going with them to the nursery. He would have to stay behind. It was investigation, but not in the field. Sam's offer floated into his mind, tempting him, but he pushed it away. Now was not the time to think about what could be. There was still work to do here before he returned to his office, and Beth could tell him about it later.

Chapter Nine

"Listen in." Zonardi moved his gaze around the gathered agents and the forensics team. "There is a nursery not far from DC where the correct plant specimen is available, according to their website. The site also shows a truck matching the description of the one seen near the location of the abandoned getaway car in the foreground of one image." He paused, allowing time for the information to settle. "The business is owned by George and Daisy Cole, a middle-aged couple with no criminal record. They do have a son about the right age, and his description matches one of the robbers—the one who shot the now deceased customer. The son doesn't have a criminal record."

"Only means he hasn't been caught yet," one agent muttered.

"There are no firearms registered to the address, but that doesn't mean there won't be any. I want the forensic team to wait until all is clear before moving in." He waited until they had all nodded their understanding. "We have Dr Pearce with us." He looked at the EAD's wife, who met his look with a straight one of her own. "All plant material collection is to be left to her as it's our main evidence at this point and I don't want any mess ups. Also, I want those doing the initial search and arrest in bulletproof vests. If this is our guy, we know he's killed before and he may be armed. Be prepared."

Zonardi eased the black SUV into the entrance of the orchid farm. Another vehicle followed, peeling off to the left, the two vehicles blocking the exit to the drive. Agents exited the second car and disappeared around each side of the premises. Zonardi pointed at two agents and then the home standing to one side of the property. His gaze caught the other agent who nodded in response, and followed Zonardi as he approached the greenhouses. The agents sent to the rear of the premises had by now had enough time to take up position.

Zonardi tensed as a man emerged from the nearest greenhouse. He took in the greying hair and wrinkled face and relaxed. This wasn't the suspect. Father, maybe?

"Can I help you?" the man asked.

"Morning, sir. Special Agent Zonardi, FBI." He held his credentials out for the man. "I'd like to speak with Jerry Cole. Is he about?"

Zonardi watched the man's gaze slide to one greenhouse and the agent behind him moved away in the direction of the man's glance.

"What do you want with him?" the man asked as Zonardi followed his agent.

Zonardi ignored him, intent on finding the suspect.

The two agents approached the open flap of the greenhouse. Behind them the old man yelled out.

"Hey!"

They had to get there fast before the suspect realised something was happening. Zonardi withdrew his sidearm, holding it down at his side, and slid through the opening.

A young man crouched at the far end of the greenhouse, black agricultural tubing on the ground beside him. He gave no sign he'd heard the agents' arrival and continued with whatever task occupied him.

The two agents crept up to him, wary of any reaction. As they grew close, Zonardi noticed wire coming from the man's ear. To confirm Zonardi's guess, the man began humming, his head nodding rhythmically.

Zonardi stepped forward. "Jerry Cole."

The young man whipped around from his crouch, overbalanced and sprawled on the ground in a heap. Zonardi stepped forward, ready to act, but the young man made no attempt to rise. His hands were visible and empty, so Zonardi holstered his sidearm and pulled out his credentials.

"Special Agent Zonardi, FBI." The credentials went back into his pocket. "Are you Jerry Cole?"

The man nodded.

"We'd like to ask you a few questions, Mr Cole."

Cole's hand lifted to remove the buds from his ears, but not before Zonardi saw his face tense. Zonardi readied himself for attempted flight, but Cole made no move to stand. He unplugged his ears and sat on the ground.

"What do you want?" he asked. The voice was surprising; warm and melodious.

"Not here," Zonardi said. Not on the boy's own territory. "Come outside."

Cole's eyes narrowed before relaxing once more. He shrugged. "Okay."

The agent with Zonardi assisted Cole to rise and stayed close as they left the greenhouse. They guided Cole towards one of the SUVs.

"Dr Pearce," Zonardi called out to a group waiting near the other vehicles. "All yours now."

"Who's that?" Cole asked, staring after Beth as she and a photographer headed for the greenhouse.

"That is one smart woman. She will prove you were involved in a recent crime."

The comment didn't seem to worry Cole. A cool customer.

"I've got no idea what you're talking about."

"Really?" Zonardi asked. "We'll let the plants do the talking then."

"Huh?"

"Dr Pearce is a renowned forensic botanist and she can get plants to tell her the most amazing things."

Zonardi watched with interest as fear flickered through Cole's eyes. He smiled.

"Jerry Cole, you have the right to remain silent…"

"There." Beth pointed at the raised flower beds of orchids. Several jewel orchids stood in a line at one end. Beth waited as the photographer captured images of the plants and showed other areas she wanted recorded as they continued their search of the greenhouses.

Emerging from the last greenhouse, she lifted her evidence kit and went back in to the first greenhouse to start the sample collection. Beth pulled on gloves and began with soil samples. She crouched, and using a metal spoon, scooped a sample from the ground and deposited it into a small bag she held open in her other hand. She sealed the bag, labelled it, and set it aside. An alcohol wipe cleaned the spoon ready for the next sample, and she repeated the methodical process. The bedding around the flowers, samples of the straw and compost, all joined the first sample in a pile. She moved carefully, wanting to avoid disturbing the area or set her head spinning. Tumbling head first into a flower bed and contaminating any evidence wasn't on her to-do list. Once satisfied she had collected enough, Beth returned the spoon and bags to the kit and took out a roll of sticky tape and a clear acetate sheet. She placed a section of the tape onto the plastic wall of the greenhouse, then removed it and stuck it to the sheet. Once labelled, she added it to the evidence collection. Last of all, Beth approached the orchids. The leaves were identical to the one in the lab. She examined the plants, but found no torn leaves. Not conclusive. If the bag had been used to hold cuttings or trimmed leaves, there wouldn't be anything to find. She selected and collected specimens of the plants growing in the beds. There were a range of different flowers, standing still and serene, protected by the greenhouse. She paused for a moment, enjoying their beauty before she collected further samples. These she laid flat and sealed in a small portable plant press. Then it was onto the second greenhouse and a repeat of the process before sampling the outside of the property. With the pollen samples developing, she needed a full range of evidence to work with. This was her one chance to collect all she might need.

With the samples stowed in containers, Beth approached Zonardi who was with the suspect, now in handcuffs.

"Dr Pearce?"

"Special Agent Zonardi, I'd like to collect samples from Mr Cole."

"Certainly."

Beth extracted the tape from her kit and approached Cole. She avoided his gaze, aware of the hostile tension of his posture.

"It won't hurt," she said, and pressed the tape to his clothing, quickly taking samples from each item. Packing the tape away she then took out a small brush and plastic container.

"I need to take samples from the boots," she said to a place between Cole and Zonardi.

A moment of hesitation, and then Cole lifted a foot off the ground, allowing Beth to brush around the boot, collecting the soil in the container. The sample was small, the boots almost clean. There was barely a mark on them; they looked new to her. Her gaze remained on the boot now lowered to the ground.

"Anything else?"

Beth looked at Zonardi, making sure their eyes met, and then flicked hers down at Cole's feet, and back up. A tiny nod from the agent and Beth was reassured he had noticed the nice new boots Cole wore too.

"That's the lot. Thank you, Mr Cole, Special Agent Zonardi."

"Thank you, Dr Pearce."

Beth left them, returning with the samples and packing up her kit. She stood and surveyed the scene again: greenhouses with spaces between each one, parking space out the front, a home to one side. Her eyes scanned the flower beds around the home; not many, luckily, or any analysis of pollen would be a long and laborious task. They documented all the beds well, along with photographs of the surrounding area. She turned to look at Zonardi and the suspect. It looked as though Zonardi was getting ready to leave. She had the samples she needed from Cole, so her work was complete. Her gaze rested on Cole. He wasn't a big man; weedy, and he barely topped Beth at five feet nine inches. There was something about Cole though, something Beth couldn't put her finger on. He was slight in build, but there was an attitude of toughness and resilience around him, as though what he lacked in physical strength he made up for with mental.

She shrugged and turned away again. Zonardi would have to deal with that, and he was more than capable. Beth picked up her kit and headed for the vehicle she'd arrived in. It was time to head back to the lab.

She'd taken two steps when her subconscious kicked in and a memory surfaced. A quick pat of her pocket reassured Beth her cell phone was present, and she hurried to the SUV and pushed her kit into the back.

"Back in a minute," she said to the agent there and headed back towards Zonardi.

The agent was supervising the loading of Cole into another vehicle. Beth waited until the door closed before she approached him.

"Agent Zonardi," she said, attracting his attention.

He turned to her. "Yes?"

"Could I have a word please? It may be important."

"Sure, Dr Pearce. What is it?"

"Can we talk over here?" Beth asked, walking away from the vehicles, hoping he would follow. She didn't want to talk where the suspect might hear.

He followed her. "Okay, Dr Pearce. Spill."

"I was out walking with some friends on the day of the robbery and we found a small fire that hadn't been put out properly. We poured water on it to take the heat out of the coals, and we found this in the ashes." She pulled out her phone and showed Zonardi the photo she'd taken of the leather. "The location of the fire is not far off the road between here and DC." She looked at Zonardi, who'd grabbed her phone and had zoomed in on the image.

"This looks like it could come from work boots."

"Yes."

"And he has new boots," Zonardi said, peering at the photo.

"It may be nothing."

"Or it could be something. Did you see any vehicles?"

Beth thought back. "I can remember seeing a white vehicle through the trees as it drove off. I can't say more than that. Perhaps the people I was with could tell you more."

Zonardi clicked his tongue, his gaze focussed on the distance. He nodded and brought his gaze back to Beth.

"Map," he said, and headed back to the vehicles, with Beth following.

Zonardi signalled to two agents standing around waiting and they joined him in front of an SUV. "Change of plan. We will make a diversion on the way back to DC. Dr Pearce has notified me of a potentially suspicious campfire, discovered on the day of the bank robbery. There is a possibility that the campfire was used to burn evidence related to the crime." He looked around at the group, all staring at him. "We will process the scene on the assumption it is part of the crime. Dr Pearce, can you show us where?" He spread open a map on the hood of the car.

Beth examined the map, locating the general area before homing in on the track leading to the clearing. "Here," she said, pointing to the spot. "The track opens to a small clearing, like a turning circle. We found the fire close to lunch time, near a small path leading to a stream." The agents nodded their acknowledgement, and the drivers leaned in to examine the map before referring to their cell phones.

"Got it," one of them announced and read out the coordinates.

"Right," Zonardi said. "Let's move."

Beth slid into the middle of the back seat of an SUV and was flanked by two agents. Within moments they were bouncing back down the track to the main road. The mini convoy accelerated towards the forest Beth had nominated. The closeness of the others in the car, the warmth of the day, and the hum of tyres on tarmac, all took their toll. Beth's eyes grew heavy, her brain lethargic. She filled her lungs with air and sat up straighter, focussing her mind on the task ahead and refusing to allow her tiredness to take over. Her eyelids didn't want to play, and she battled to keep them from dropping.

"We boring you, doc?" one agent asked, nudging her with an elbow.

"I'm having trouble keeping up with your scintillating conversation," she replied, relieved as his question jolted her out of her fatigue. The surrounding agents chuckled.

"Sorry doc. We'll use small words so you can keep up."

"Thanks guys. No more than two syllables, please."

Her shoulders shook as the agents beside her laughed. "You got it."

The car slowed and turned off the main road onto a dirt track. Within minutes they were pulling up at the entrance to the clearing. The agents climbed out, Beth following.

"This the spot?" Zonardi asked as he stopped next to Beth.

"It is," she confirmed. "The fire was over there." She pointed, Zonardi following her gesture.

"Right." He turned to the assembled group. "Watch where you walk. We need tyre prints, shoe prints, anything else you can find. Photos first."

The agents nodded and began their careful examination of the area. Beth followed Zonardi as he led the way towards the fire site. They spotted it, the blackened ashes visible through the dirt Beth and her friends had piled onto the fire before they'd left.

Zonardi waited until the photographer had taken the required images and then moved forward. After donning a glove, he poked a careful finger into the fire's remains and dug around, emerging with a piece of charred leather.

"Bingo," he said as he held it up.

Chapter Ten

George Cole stood in the doorway of the kitchen watching his wife, Daisy. Her hands twisted, fingers bending and flexing in a constant struggle against her grief. The accusations against her son, the invasion of her home and property by the FBI, had taken its toll. The longer George watched her, the deeper his scowl creased his brow. Her outward display mirrored his inner turmoil. Thoughts fought with each other, whirling like a hurricane of words in his brain. His son. Accused of robbing a bank and killing a man. It didn't match up with what he knew of Jerry. His son was gentle, not a killer. He'd raised orphaned kittens when he was ten, waking all hours to feed the poor mites. Then he'd joined the family business and had treated his mother's flowers with the same care. Jerry had always been the quiet boy, the one who sat in the background, doing as he was bid. Maybe that was where the answer lay. Jerry had always been a follower, not a leader, and he must have followed some of his no-good friends into this whole thing. George shook his head as the thoughts continued to tumble and collide. It was one thing following someone, doing something stupid. It was another to rob a bank armed with a loaded shotgun and pull the trigger. What had happened to his son? What had lured him to do such a thing, to even contemplate it, let alone do it?

Jerry had not spoken to the FBI agents during the questioning. The agents had told George of the accusations against his son—Jerry wouldn't look at anyone and had been silent the whole time. Jerry had also refused to name those he'd been with during the robbery, but George had a good idea who they were. Matty had disappeared when the black SUVs had pulled into the drive. George was sure he knew where to find him, and who Matty would have run to tell. Another dilemma. Should he tell of his suspicions? Or would that be buying more trouble for his son, trouble of a more brutal and unyielding kind? The chaos in his mind was nothing compared to the pain in his body. His gut was hollow and achingly empty. His chest was the opposite. Hot anger he couldn't direct mixed with cold fear for his son. Who should he be angry with? Jerry? The others he'd been with? The FBI? Or was all of this somehow his fault? George couldn't bring himself to think of what would happen to Jerry now. The coldness in his chest radiated round his body with each beat of his heart.

"I can't stand it," Daisy said, rising to her feet and sending the chair scudding back from the table. "I need to do something." She turned her head to and fro as if a task would appear before her. "I know. I'll bake a cake for when he comes home."

George squashed the urge to tell Daisy their son wouldn't be home soon. It wouldn't help, and the last thing he needed was for her to start blubbing. He hated crying women.

"I'll go feed the hens while you do that," George said, and turned to head out the back door of the house.

George trudged across the small garden and through a metal gate to the barn. He kept his eyes moving for any sign of Matty's return, but there was no movement around the greenhouses or in the surrounding fields. The barn door swung open without a noise—a testament to George's rigid maintenance routine—and he caught a flash of movement behind the hay pile.

"Get your butt out here, Matty," he snarled. "I want answers."
Silence.
"I know you're there. Don't make me come and find you!"

He heard the dry rasping of straw and then Matty shuffled out from his hiding place. George took five fast paces, grabbed Matty by the front of his sweater and slammed him into the side of the barn.

"You were a part of this, weren't you?"

Matty's chest heaved under George's hand. "I don't know nothin'," he muttered.

George eased his grasp and then rammed him against the wall again. Matty's head bounced on the wall and he groaned.

"Tell me!"

"Go to hell. I just came to get my things and I'm outta here."

"Not until I get the truth!"

"You won't get nothing from me."

George's eyes narrowed. "Maybe I'll just hand you over to the feds then."

"Not if you want Jerry to live, you won't."

"What the hell do you mean by that?"

George's grip loosened and Matty twisted himself free. "One of the others has friends on the inside. If they find out someone has grassed, Jerry will cop it."

George reacted, the back of his hand smacking against Matty's cheek, sending the younger man crashing into the wall once more. "You bastard! You dragged him into this, and then you threaten me!"

"He didn't need dragging, trust me. He went willingly. And yeah, he pulled the trigger." Matty felt the side of his face as he clambered to his feet. "You might want to consider how far Jerry will be dropped into it if you say anything. He'll cop the beating of his life, and if anyone else goes down, we'll make sure Jerry doesn't get away with anything. We'll tell the lot."

"How do I know you haven't already told them? How do I know you didn't send the FBI here?"

"Why would I do that? Why would I risk Jerry dragging the rest of us down with him? No, you want to blame anyone, blame the feds for knowing too much. They have all those fancy ways of finding clues and tracking people down. I've seen it on the TV show." Matty's lip curled. "It's those scientists that tracked down Jerry, I'll bet. They're the ones who found clues and tracked him." Matty spat on the ground. "Now, you need to let me go, with no noise, no fuss. Or else."

George's hands clenched and unclenched over and over at his side as he took in the threat to his son. His hands were tied.

Matty's lips curled into a sneer. "That's right. You need to let me go or your boy won't ever come home to you."

"Get off my property and never come back," George managed through the rage that tried to take over.

"You got it. I'm outta here."

George watched as Matty slipped out through the rear door of the barn. His shoulders slumped as the full impact of Matty's words hit. Jerry was a killer, a murderer, and he'd gone into the robbery willingly, or so Matty had said. The rest of the gang were busy covering their own butts, and they were letting Jerry take the fall for all of their actions. George's hand clenched again. He wanted to tear them apart, but he couldn't ignore the threat to Jerry. He needed to be smarter than that. His hands unclenched. The lawyer they'd called for Jerry could tell him what evidence the FBI had. Once he knew that, he would find a way to beat it down.

George dipped a bucket into the barrel of chicken feed and stalked out to the coop. His mind boiled as he tossed the feed into the pen. The hens fought and pushed until they had sorted out their own particular order.

Just like humans. There were those who had the best of everything, who ruled the roost, and then there was the rest, who had to fight to get enough to live. He knew which end of the order Jerry would be.

His chore complete, George stalked back into the house to see Daisy scrubbing the counter tops in the kitchen.

"I can't stand it," she said, her voice wobbling. "They come into my home and destroy it. I can sense them here still and I have to clean them away."

"Daisy, sit down and I'll make you a cup of tea," George offered.

"No!" Daisy spun and confronted him, her cheeks flushed. "I want them gone. I need to erase them." Tears flowed down her cheeks, and she stood glaring at him. "They've taken my boy, and they've taken my home."

George placed an arm around her shoulders. "Come and sit down. We can finish the cleaning later." He patted her shoulder. "We'll hear from the lawyer soon. Maybe Jerry will come home."

She pulled out of his embrace. "Don't treat me as if I'm stupid! The FBI won't let him go. They'll never let him go!" Her shoulder shook as she sobbed. "The FBI have taken my baby, and I'll never get him back. They'll hurt him. I know it."

George lowered her into a chair at the table. His hands trembled as the fury took over his mind again. His family had been attacked, and he had never been one to sit back and let things happen.

George walked out of the kitchen, leaving Daisy crying at the table. He opened the fat directory sitting on a table by the telephone and looked up a number. With a finger resting on the entry, he picked up the handset and dialled.

"Good afternoon, Quantico Base…"

Beth closed the evidence locker in the lab and turned the key, securing it for the night. The sounds of running feet on the linoleum in the hallway reached her and she turned in time to see one of the security guards appear in the doorway.

"We've received a bomb threat, ma'am. I need you to get your bag and evacuate the building immediately. Please notify security outside if you notice anything unusual on your way out."

The guard disappeared before Beth could reply. It wasn't the first threat they'd received, so Beth knew the drill. She pocketed the key and reached down for her bag, sitting on the floor under her desk. As she straightened, the room spun and pitched, sending Beth off balance. She flung out a hand to grab the bench and missed, the momentum carrying though and tumbling her to the floor.

"Damn it," she muttered. The room still moved around her as she pushed herself up until she sat, the cold metal of the desk leg pressing into her back, providing stability. Beth kept her hands on the floor. The solidity of the hard surface helped her head slow down and restored equilibrium.

"Slowly this time," she muttered as she turned onto her knees. She tossed her handbag up onto her desk and then pulled herself up using the desk as support.

"All good," she reported to herself as the room remained steady. She grabbed her bag again and with a hand still resting on the smooth surface of the desk top, turned to the door.

"Excellent. One foot after the other," she encouraged, and walked to the door. The room remained steady around her and she let out a sigh of relief. Staying close to the wall in case the giddiness returned, she walked to the end of the corridor and the stairwell. She pushed open the door and began to descend. Her steps echoed in the empty concrete space.

"Last one out by the looks of it. Slow and steady wins the race."

Beth kept hold of the handrail as she descended. The dizziness stayed away, but she wasn't going to take any chances.

As she reached the bottom step, the exit door flung open, startling her. Beth stepped back and stumbled against the bottom of the stairs, losing her balance again and hitting the concrete with a painful thump.

"Ow!"

"Dr Pearce, I'm so sorry. We were just coming to find you." One guard reached down a hand to help her stand up again. Beth held her breath, but the world stayed still.

"Sorry to be so slow," Beth said, rubbing her backside. She would have a nice bruise. "I tripped up in the lab, and wanted to make sure I didn't stumble again on my way down the stairs."

The guard frowned down at her, keeping hold of her arm. "Are you all right?"

Beth nodded. "I'm fine."

The second guard piped up. "Maybe one of the medical staff should check you over, ma'am, but for now, we need to get you out of here."

The first guard kept his hold on Beth's arm. "Come with me ma'am. I'll take you to the medics."

"I'm fine," Beth protested as he marched her out of the building. "Honestly."

The guard didn't answer. He kept walking until they reached the rest of the evacuated staff.

"Dr Pearce needs to see a medic," he announced.

"I'm fine," Beth repeated, annoyed at the attention.

"We'll check you over, anyway," a medic said, taking over from the guard. "Can you tell the Assistant Director where Dr Pearce will be?" she said to the guard.

"Will do." The guard strode away.

"Great," Beth muttered as the medic led her away. Kamal would be on the phone to Warren to let him know within minutes, and then she'd be in for questioning when she arrived home. That's if Warren didn't come down from DC to fetch her.

The medic helped Beth onto a bench behind the crowd of staff waiting for the all clear.

"Tell me what happened?" the medic invited.

Beth sighed. "I straightened too quickly when I picked my bag up off the floor. My head spun, and I fell over. That's all."

"Hmm," the medic said, staring up into Beth's eyes. "How long did it take for the dizziness to fade and do you have any trace of it now?"

"It took only a few moments to fade, and I'm not dizzy now."

"Any light-headedness?"

"No."

"Have you experienced any similar symptoms recently?"

Beth's brow creased and her lips compressed. She would have to be honest. Too much found its way back to Warren, regardless of confidentiality. He had a way of hearing about everything.

"I had some dizziness a few days ago," she muttered.

"How long ago exactly?"

"Three days."

"How long did it last?" the medic asked, reaching for the blood pressure cuff.

"Only for a moment," Beth answered, holding her arm out for the medic. "This is a lot of fuss over nothing."

"I'll decide if it's nothing," the medic said, eyes on the reading. "Eighty over fifty. That's low."

"That's pretty normal for me," Beth replied.

"What's normal, if that's pretty normal?"

"Ninety over sixty."

"It's lower than normal. Do you have any other symptoms?"

"No." Her blood pressure should read higher by now, if the annoyance she felt was anything to go by. "Can I go now?"

"I'd like you to wait for a few more minutes so we can be sure the dizziness doesn't return."

Beth bit back her anger as her cell phone buzzed in her bag. She pulled it out and glanced at the caller ID. Warren. She had to take it.

"Excuse me." The medic nodded. "Hello," she said into the phone, trying to sound bright.

"Are you all right?" Warren's voice sounded sharp. He'd heard.

"Good news travels fast."

"I heard you became dizzy and had a fall."

"You're making me sound as though I'm your granny. I'm fine, honestly. Yes, I had a dizzy moment and stumbled, but I'm fine." All traces of lightness disappeared, and she almost snarled the last words down the phone.

"I'm sorry, Beth, I didn't mean it like that. I'm worried, that's all."

She lifted her hands to cover her eyes. She should appreciate his care, not snap at him. "I'm sorry too, and I shouldn't have growled at you. I guess I'm a bit annoyed by the fuss."

"They're just doing their job."

"Reporting my every move to you?"

"That's not fair, and you know it. I'm your husband. Kamal would make sure the next of kin was notified if there was a problem with any of his staff."

"And my next of kin happens to be sitting in FBI headquarters."

"It certainly doesn't slow him down."

Beth's annoyance faded into tiredness. "I guess not."

"Do you want me to come and get you?"

The sudden tenderness in his voice quashed the last remnants of her bad mood. "No, I'll wait for the all clear from the medics and then come home."

"The all clear? What does that mean?"

"They want to make sure the dizziness doesn't return. I should be good to go soon." She could almost hear him debating in his head; the silence on the line was loud.

"You sure you don't want me to come down and get you?"

"I'm fine Warren, I don't need you to come down."

He seemed to get the message. "Okay. Take it easy, and I'll see you at home."

Warren hung up the call with Beth, and immediately his phone rang.

"Pearce."

"Sir, it's Jed Jones. I wanted to let you know we found nothing. The lab building is clear."

The knot of tension lodged in Warren's gut eased. "A hoax then?"

"It looks that way, sir. Have the techs come up with a number for the caller?"

Warren grunted. "They have. There are agents already on their way to pick up the caller. He didn't think to disguise his number."

Jones chuckled. "Love it when they're nice and easy."

"Agreed. Thanks for the update."

Warren tapped his phone against the palm of his free hand. Locating the caller had been child's play for his agents. George Cole, the father of the bank robber they had in custody. A revenge call? Taking his anger out on the FBI? It was the most likely explanation, but Warren didn't like to assume. He also didn't like knowing Beth's building was the target of the call. He glanced at his watch—he needed to head home if he was going to be there when Beth arrived. There was nothing more he could do tonight—the relevant agents were more than capable of doing their jobs. The pang of not being involved more in investigations shot through him, a physical longing to be more active. Sam's voice, offering him the chance to be active in investigations again, drifted into his head. Now was not the time to contemplate that. Warren needed to get home and look after his wife.

Special Agent Morris rapped his knuckles against the wooden door of the Cole home. The door opened and Morris resisted the instinct to take a step back as a scowling face thrust at him.

"What do you bastards want now?"

"Mr Cole?"

"Go away."

Morris held out his credentials. "Mr Cole, my name is—"

"I don't give a damn what your name is. Go away."

"Sir, I can't do that until we talk. May I have a few moments of your time?"

Morris' polite demeanour seemed to have the effect he hoped for. The aggressive posture of Mr Cole relaxed.

"Say what you want to say, then leave," Cole said.

"Mr Cole, I'm here about a call received at the FBI Laboratories earlier this afternoon. Do you know anything about that call?"

"I know nothing about that. I never made the call."

"Then may I speak to your wife? The caller identification number indicated it came from your home telephone. Maybe your wife knows something about it?"

Morris kept a close watch on Cole. The man's eyes flickered from the agent to the hallway and back. The FBI knew the call had been from a man, but Cole wouldn't know that. If he didn't want his wife questioned, there was a good chance he'd admit to the call.

"My wife doesn't know nothing about it."

"How do you know?"

"It was me."

Morris only just caught the mumbling words from the man. "Sir, is there somewhere private we can talk?"

Cole glanced into the hallway and then around the front yard "Not in the house," he said. "We can talk out here."

Cole stepped out of the door and closed it behind him. Morris turned and followed Cole off the front porch and towards a clump of rose bushes. He stopped when Cole did and waited for the man to begin.

"It's been one hell of a day," Cole said. "My son's been arrested for a crime I can't believe he committed, my house and property searched, and my wife keeps crying."

Morris said nothing. He needed Cole to come clean, and he didn't want to interrupt whatever train of thought was passing through the man's head.

"I got mad."

Another silence.

"Did you make the call?" Morris asked.

"Am I in trouble?"

"Did you make the call?"

Cole plucked a rose off a bush and crushed it in his hand before releasing the mangled bloom and allowing it the fall to the ground. "Yes."

Morris sighed to himself with satisfaction. Now it was up to him what to do. He had no specific instructions to arrest Cole despite the law saying he could. What he needed to do was find out if the man posed any real threat.

"Are you aware of the penalties for making a bomb threat?"

"It was only a hoax."

"Bomb threats are a felony, so that's at least a year in jail. On top of that there are fines, often in the thousands."

Cole's mouth flopped open and shut, like a fish gasping for air, his eyes wide and staring.

"Are you…am I…"

Morris grabbed the stunned older man by the arm, steered him to the porch steps, and lowered him onto the wooden planks. He crouched in front of Cole, catching the man's gaze.

"Whether I arrest you depends on if I think you pose a risk to the community, and if you can convince me you won't do anything similar in the future." Morris was relieved to see colour return to Cole's cheeks.

"I was angry."

"That's understandable, but making threats is not."

The front door opened a crack. Morris looked up to see a woman appear, her eyes wide and her face tense.

"Is everything okay, George?" Her voice, thin and wavery, barely reached Morris.

"Everything is fine, Daisy. Go back inside. I won't be long."

The woman backed into the house and eased the door shut.

Morris stood up, relieving the cramped muscles in his calves. "Mr Cole?"

Cole stood up from the porch step and looked Morris square in the face. "I assure you I have learned my lesson and I promise I won't make any hoax calls again." He pulled his shoulders back and puffed out his chest. "My word is good."

Morris ran his tongue around his teeth as he considered the man standing in front of him. The call had been made on the spur of the moment. The lack of thought and planning, such as leaving his caller ID visible, backed that up. Cole had no criminal record either—not so much as a speeding ticket.

"All right, Mr Cole. I will accept your word that you won't do it again. Consider this an official warning though. You make any further calls similar to the one today and you will be arrested and charged. Are we clear on that?"

"Yes."

Morris watched Cole as he climbed the porch steps and went back into the house without a single backward glance. He sighed. Did he make the right decision? Only time would answer that question, but Cole had been shocked by the penalties. With luck, that would keep him in line.

Morris walked back to his car and climbed in. He checked his phone for messages, and then started up the car and drove away, his mind already on his next task.

George watched him leave from behind the net curtains in the sitting room.

"Bastard," he muttered.

Chapter Eleven

Beth stood in the shower, her hand resting on her lower abdomen. She'd thought she was putting on a little weight, but there was more to the swelling of the waistline than that. She could feel it; a solid lump under her probing fingers, not the softness of an extra layer of fat. Unwelcome tears joined the water cascading from the shower head. She couldn't have children, and she hadn't strained a muscle or hurt her belly, so it wasn't swelling from any injuries. Cancer. It had to be cancer. Uterine or ovarian, judging from where the lump lay. The bloating she'd noticed that morning that had sent her fingers probing her tummy was a symptom she could remember reading about, also that ovarian cancer was generally incurable. Dread and despair almost sent her into a panic.

"Beth, are you all right in there?"

Warren's voice startled her out of her thoughts. There was no point in wallowing in her emotions yet. The diagnosis might be something else. A tiny ray of hope blossomed, giving her the strength to pull herself together.

"I'm fine. I'll be out in a minute."

"Okay."

Beth drew a deep breath, forcing her fears to the back of her mind. She turned off the water and stepped out of the shower, reaching for a towel. As she dried herself, she planned what she had to do. A visit to her GP was paramount. She would try to get an appointment for today. Until she knew for certain what was wrong, there was no point in worrying any further. Her hand came to rest over the swelling once more.

"Stop it," she whispered, angry at herself.

"Stop what?"

Warren's voice startled her again. She'd had no idea he was still outside the door.

"Nothing wrong with your hearing, is there?" she snapped.

Warren's head appeared around the door. "What's wrong? What do you want to stop?"

She closed her eyes for a second and then opened them to look at his worried frown. "It's nothing, I was just getting mad at myself over something of no importance." She held the towel over her belly in case Warren saw the swelling. It wasn't that big, but she wasn't taking any chances.

"So long as you're sure," he said. "Can I make you a cup of tea?"

Her bad mood drained away; he was only looking out for her. "Yes please. I'll be down shortly."

Warren smiled and withdrew his head. Beth heard his footsteps disappear and breathed a sigh of relief. She finished drying herself and went out to her wardrobe, opening the door to pull out some clothes. The full-length mirror hanging inside the door caught her eye. Beth turned sideways and ran her hand over her belly, looking to see how big the swelling was. There was a difference—not much, but it was there. More of a thickening than a definable lump. She sighed again. No matter what she told herself, the dread sat heavy in her heart.

"Tea's ready!"

Warren's voice drifted up the stairs and Beth grabbed some clothes and put them on. She chose a loose top to disguise the change in her shape, but her jeans, more snug than usual, reminded her of what she was trying to hide.

She joined Warren in the kitchen, aware of his gaze searching her face.

"Are you sure you're okay?" he asked, his voice so gentle she almost crumbled.

"I'm a little tired." Beth swallowed some of her tea. "I'm going to take it easy today. Read a bit and relax."

Warren reached over and took her mug out of her hand, placing it on the bench before pulling her into his arms. She snuggled against his broad chest, feeling it rise as he breathed, and relaxing in the security of his embrace. *It will be okay, everything will be fine.*

Beth felt the light kiss Warren dropped onto her head and lifted her face up so he could kiss her lips.

"Call me if you need me," he said.

"Okay." He knew her too well and he would be able to tell something bothered her, but he didn't push her for answers. Not yet anyway. She needed to change the subject, fast. She caught his gaze and smiled. "What would you like for dinner tonight?"

"Something simple."

Beth didn't miss the relief in his voice at her smile. "Okay. Spaghetti?"

"Sounds good." He glanced at his watch. "I'd better get going. I'll see you tonight."

Warren kissed her again, and she followed him out of the kitchen to where his briefcase stood by the door, giving him another smile as he left the apartment.

Beth walked back to the kitchen to where her cell phone lay on the bench. Her hand went to her stomach once more. *It's better to know. Call the doctor.* She scrolled through her contacts and dialled.

"Good morning. This is Beth Pearce, and I'd like to make an appointment to see Dr Malik…"

"So, Beth, tell me what's wrong."

Beth's hands shook as she stared at Dr Malik. She'd come for answers, but hearing the truth would make it real. No chance of denial once the words were spoken.

"I've been thinking I was putting on weight and this morning I felt bloated. I had a feel of my stomach and found a lump," Beth laid a hand over her swelling.

Dr Malik's eyebrows drew close over her dark eyes. "Any other symptoms?"

Beth shook her head. "No."

"How long have you been noticing the swelling?"

"For a couple of weeks. I thought I was putting on weight and kept meaning to up my exercise routine, but now..."

"Okay. Why don't you hop up on the bed and I'll have a feel. Unbutton your jeans if you would, please."

Beth climbed onto the examination bed, lying down and undoing the fastenings of her jeans. Dr Malik began to feel around Beth's abdomen, pressing down and examining the shape of the lump.

"Does this hurt at all?" she asked Beth.

"No."

"And no other symptoms? Nausea, anything at all?"

"I've been lightheaded on occasion, and tired too."

"Have you been working longer hours?"

"No. Life's been pretty much normal."

Dr Malik dug her fingers in a little deeper into Beth's abdomen. "When was your last period, Beth?"

"Ages ago, but that's normal for me. I only get them three or four times a year."

"Hmm," Dr Malik said, and broke off the examination to consult the file on the computer. "I see here your records show you have a uterine malformation and scarred fallopian tubes. When was that diagnosed?"

"When I was a teenager. My mother had me checked out when my periods were so irregular."

"Right."

Beth didn't think she could take the suspense much longer. She wanted to hear the truth. "Do I have cancer?"

Dr Malik smiled. "I don't think so. I want to check something."

Beth let out a long sigh at the doctor's words. Not cancer, but then what was it? A hernia or a cyst? But there was no pain. Could it be some sort of different fat she didn't know about? Beth watched as Dr Malik opened a drawer beside the bed and pulled out a box with a curling cable, connected to something resembling a microphone.

"What's that?"

"It's a Doppler monitor."

Dr Malik pressed a button on the box and held the other end against the swelling. She swirled the handle around in an arc, her eyes fixed on the display on the box. As Beth watched, the muscles around Dr Malik's eyes relaxed, and a smile appeared. She turned the display to Beth and reaching around the device with her thumb, pressed another button.

"Listen," she said.

A faint whumping noise, regular and unfamiliar, came from the speaker.

"What is that?" Beth asked, natural curiosity drowning her worries.

"That's the sound of your baby's heart."

"My WHAT?" Beth sprang upright, staring at the doctor. "I'm not pregnant. I can't be."

"You are pregnant, though I'd like to confirm it with a test."

"But I can't be," Beth repeated. "I can't have children. The doctors told me that." Tears filled her eyes. This was cruel torment. She wanted so much to believe the doctor, but it could not be true.

"Beth, I see nothing in your file that says you cannot have children. Unlikely, yes, but not impossible."

Tears misted Beth's eyes, blurring her focus. She grasped the tissue Dr Malik pressed into her hand and wiped them. "I'm pregnant? Honestly?" The tears were in full flow, the joy of the diagnosis joining the elation of hearing her child's heartbeat. She wiped her eyes again. "But my uterus…? Will the baby survive?"

"You only have half a uterus—unicornuate, so it's shaped a bit like a banana—but it will stretch enough to accommodate your baby. There is a chance you may deliver early, but we'll keep a close eye on how things progress. If you're as far along as I think, then you're almost through the most likely time for miscarriage."

"I can't believe it."

Dr Malik grinned at her. "I want to do a quick test to confirm it, but I'm confident you're about three months pregnant. Congratulations." She moved to a storage cupboard and extracted a plastic cup. "Now, if you could please oblige me with a urine sample, I can then do a simple pregnancy test to confirm things."

Beth caught her lip with her teeth and glanced at the Doppler, then back at Dr Malik. "Before we do that…can I listen to the heartbeat again?"

"Of course."

Beth lowered herself back down and folded the zipper of her jeans open. Her eyes opened wide as the Doppler resumed its whumping. "Oh…" she whispered. Her hand moved to cradle her baby as soon as the doctor removed the Doppler.

Dr Malik picked up a plastic cup and waved it at Beth. "Sample please."

Beth zipped up her jeans and swung her legs down over the side of the bed. The world reeled and she grasped the edge of the bed.

"Head spin?"

"Yes." The world righted itself and stood still again.

"Not unusual," Dr Malik said. "Take it easy. I'll wait here for you."

Beth accepted the cup and headed for the clinic bathroom. Her hands were shaking again, this time with the adrenalin rush of excitement. She collected a sample and managed to return it to Dr Malik without spilling anything.

Dr Malik placed drops of the urine in a hole in a pregnancy test, and within a minute, a positive result was already showing. "That confirms it. You're pregnant."

Beth stared at the pink cross confirming the existence of her baby. Tears welled again, and Dr Malik passed Beth a box of tissues.

"I'm sorry, Doctor," Beth said. "I never thought I would be so lucky as to have a child."

"It's okay, cry all you like. Now, you'll need to arrange for an ultrasound, preferably in the next week or two." Dr Malik consulted her computer. "You're thirty-four, right?"

Beth nodded. "Is my age going to cause problems?"

Dr Malik smiled. "There is an increased risk of some conditions in older mothers, but you're only just reaching that group. The scan will look for potential problems and will also give us a better picture as to how far along you are. At the moment, I would estimate your baby is due early October, but the scan will enable us to narrow that down. I also want you to have these blood tests." Beth watched as Dr Malik wrote on a request form. "I want to test your iron levels and also do the first trimester screening test. The screening test will show what the risk is for chromosomal abnormalities in your baby." Dr Malik passed Beth a couple of pieces of paper. "Right, now to check your blood pressure." Beth rested her arm on the desk and Dr Malik wrapped a cuff around it. "Your blood pressure is normally low, and it might explain the giddiness." Dr Malik fell silent as she waited for the automated machine to complete the test. "Yes, it's a bit lower than normal."

Beth felt overwhelmed by the bombardment of information being thrown at her. "Is that a problem?"

Dr Malik frowned. "Not at the moment. Blood pressure can drop during the second trimester, which I think you are now close to, so it's not uncommon. You will have to take care not to move suddenly, and be aware that you may feel dizzy now and then. I want you to keep exercising as that can help raise your blood pressure. What exercise do you do?"

"Yoga, and I swim."

Dr Malik shook her head. "Yoga is fine—tell your instructor you're pregnant. With your dizziness it would be better if you swapped swimming for something else, perhaps walking? Feeling faint in a pool is not a good idea, even if you're with someone else. So, no swimming for the time being."

Beth nodded.

"You'll also need to consider your antenatal care. I'm happy to provide that, or you can go to an obstetrician."

Beth nodded again. Forget the low blood pressure; her head was spinning just listening to Dr Malik.

"Get the blood tests done first. Book the ultrasound for a week's time and get your results before you go." She smiled at Beth. "Do you have any questions?"

"Yes, but I can't think of what they are right now."

Dr Malik laughed. "Get the blood tests sorted, then go home and tell your husband he's going to be a daddy, and celebrate."

"Thank you."

By the time Warren arrived home, Beth had worked herself into a knot of nerves. How would he react to the news? Until today, Beth had believed she'd never be a mother. And Warren had told her he wasn't too keen on having a family, so his response could be anything from elation to anger. Beth couldn't begin to guess how he'd take it.

The sound of his key in the lock reached her, and she went to greet him as she always did.

"Hello Beth," he said, drawing her into his arms. "How was your day, and how are you feeling?"

"My day was…unexpected, and I feel wonderful," she replied.

"What do you mean by unexpected?" Trust Warren to pick up on that and pursue it.

She pulled back out of his arms. "I'll tell you in a minute. Get changed out of your suit and I'll make you a drink."

His eyes narrowed as he looked at her, but she smiled at him and the muscles in his face relaxed.

"All right. I'll be back down shortly."

Beth watched as his hand went under his coat and reappeared with his gun. She turned away, hearing the clunk as he placed it in a drawer, then the click as the key turned in the lock. His footsteps disappeared up the stairs. She took a shaky breath, letting it out before moving to the drinks cabinet to pour Warren his usual whiskey. She sat on the sofa, waiting for him to return.

Warren dropped into his favourite corner and pulled Beth close. She waited for him to take a mouthful of his drink before talking.

"How was your day?" she asked him.

"Much like any other," he replied. "I want to hear about your unexpected day."

Excitement fluttered in her stomach as she thought of her news, sitting oddly with her worry about Warren's reaction.

Just tell him!

"I went to see Dr Malik today." Beth felt Warren tense at her side.

"You didn't tell me you were going to do that."

"I didn't want to worry you over something that might have turned out to be nothing."

"What something?"

She forgot sometimes that he was an investigator by trade. "I found a swelling in my belly."

"Beth!" He was facing her now, his face tight, and his eyes fearful.

"It's nothing bad, I promise."

"You're not reassuring me. What's wrong?"

"Nothing's wrong. Nothing at all." Beth gripped his hand and smiled at him. "Warren, I'm pregnant."

There was silence as he registered what she'd said. Emotions flashed through his eyes, too fast for her to read and understand. Her heart pounded as she waited for his reaction.

"You're pregnant?" he said, finally.

Her smile died as he stared at her.

"Yes, I'm pregnant. We're having a baby," she said. "It's good news." Her heart ached at the dismay she read in his face.

"Good news?"

"Yes, dammit." The switch flicked, the ache turning into burning anger. "It's fantastic news."

Warren stood and stalked across the room before turning to look back at her. He wiped his mouth, his other hand resting on his hip.

"You told me you couldn't have kids."

"That's what I'd been told. I didn't expect this to happen, but I'm happy it has."

"You don't sound happy."

"That's because you're acting as though you're horrified. Any other man would be thrilled."

She'd stood up now, facing him and throwing his negativity back.

"I'm not thrilled," he said.

"No kidding? Really? I hadn't picked up on that!"

"Beth!"

"Don't 'Beth' me." Her chest heaved with the pain of her anger, the fire dying leaving only heartbreak. "Just don't," she whispered, sinking onto the sofa again as tears welled. This was supposed to be a happy time, but he couldn't see it. Warren continued to stand on the far side of the room, staring at her.

"Are you sure?" he said eventually.

"Yes, I'm sure."

Another silence. The anger rose in Beth's chest again.

"So that's all you've got to say?" she said, challenging him.

"What do you expect?"

"I thought you might be thrown by the news, but I didn't expect such negativity."

"Beth, you knew I didn't want kids."

"Too bad. You're going to have one."

His hot gaze hit her from under scowling brows, his face hard. "Did you have treatment to solve your infertility and not tell me?"

"Did I what?" Her anger whipped into fury at his accusation, control almost gone.

"Did you? Did you plan this?"

Control vanished as her brain burned. "You honestly think I would do something like that, do you?" she yelled. "You think I would sneak around behind your back and trick you into having a baby when I knew your opinion?" Her chest heaved as she struggled to drag breath into her tight chest. "Yeah, absolutely. I'm a lying, deceitful, conniving bitch who has no regard for anything other than what I want! I sucked you in good, and now you have to lump it! You bastard!"

"Beth!"

"Go to hell, Warren."

"Stop it."

"No."

He was in front of her now, reaching for her. Her arms circled in the air, evading his grasp.

"Don't touch me."

"Beth. I'm sorry."

"I don't give a damn."

Warren stepped back, his arms dropped to his side. "Fine."

He turned and walked away, disappearing into the kitchen and leaving her fuming in the lounge room. How could he think she would do that?

The red heat faded from her head, replaced by dragging sadness in her chest. She needed space, somewhere she could breathe, away from the tension. She stood and headed for the doors onto the balcony. The cool night air eased the burn of her eyes when she stepped out. She closed the door, and headed to the far end of the balcony, sinking to the floor, her back against the rough render of the building. The lights of DC were coming on as the sun slid below the horizon. Her hand covered the bump in her belly.

"It's okay, little one. It'll be okay, I promise," she whispered.

A movement in her peripheral vision attracted her attention. Warren stood at the door watching her, the muscles around his eyes tight, his mouth open, as if he wanted to say something, but couldn't. She looked back out over the city, the hurt too much to make the first move to reconciliation.

The doors opened, and she heard Warren approach.

"Come inside Beth. It's cold out here."

"I'm angry."

"I know, but please come inside."

Beth looked at the hand he held down to her for a moment.

"No." She turned back to the lights.

The hand stayed, hovering in her peripheral vision. "Beth?"

"Go away, Warren." The hand dropped. "I need space to calm down."

"I see."

His footsteps retreated into the apartment as hot tears welled in her eyes. Her hands covered her baby as tears rolled down her cheeks to drop from her jaw and onto her chest.

The footsteps returned. A soft blanket appeared in her blurred vision and gently wrapped around her, cutting the chill of the evening air.

"I'm going to make dinner," Warren said. Beth couldn't work out his tone; it was flat, with no emotion. His footsteps retreated into the apartment again.

Beth's eyes dried, and she stared at the increasing lights of the surrounding city. She had been a fool to hope Warren would be happy about the baby. He'd always said he didn't want children, that he didn't want to bring a child into the world he'd seen through his job as an FBI agent. What he didn't understand was life didn't have to be that way. Their child would be like them; good, decent people. Why couldn't he see?

It wasn't long before the footsteps returned.

"Dinner's ready."

The hand appeared again, offering help. She looked at it, but didn't take hold.

"You need to come and eat, Beth."

She did. There was the baby to think about. She took his hand and his strong fingers grasped hers as he pulled her to his feet. The world swayed around her at the movement and she fell against him.

"Sorry," she said. "It's all a part of it, apparently."

She felt his arms tighten around her, the warmth of his body seeping through her shirt.

"I've got you." His deep voice almost brought her to tears again. She pushed away, and he loosened his grasp.

"I think I'm okay now."

He said nothing, stooping to pick up the blanket and followed her into the apartment.

They ate dinner in silence. Warren's frowning preoccupation relieved Beth of having to start a conversation. She picked at her food, knowing she needed to eat, but the constraint between them made her throat so tight she could barely swallow. She saw him glance at her glass of water, then at his glass of red wine, and his frown deepened. Beth sighed.

When they finished their meal, Warren sat back in his chair, his fingers toying with the stem of his wine glass. Beth waited for him to speak, not wanting to hear what he wanted to say, but knowing she had to listen.

"I don't want to tell anyone yet."

Beth couldn't help herself. "You're not ashamed, are you?" She watched his cheeks redden. "Great," she said, and picked up his plate, stacking it on hers.

He grasped her wrist, preventing her from clearing more of the table. "I'm not ashamed, but I'm not prepared for the comments." His colour deepened.

"Since when have you cared about other people's opinions?"

"Since they might look at me as a randy old goat."

"And I'm a trophy wife, right?"

His face had shut tight, locking her out.

"You're not a trophy wife."

"Too right I'm not."

"I'm not asking for much. You've dumped a lot on me and I need time."

"You've had a lot dumped on you? I'm the one who is carrying a baby and who has to think about everything she does and whether it will affect it."

"I didn't say that. But let's be honest— you wanted this child, not me."

"You had enough fun conceiving it with me. Now it's all too much to deal with and you need time? Well, take all the bloody time you need!"

Beth leapt to her feet, intending to head to her laptop and immerse herself in work. Her head had other ideas. The room spun and pitched. She reached for the table as she staggered, her hand meeting Warren's arm as he grabbed her and prevented her from falling. She struggled, trying to push away, but his hold was too firm.

"Beth, please, don't," his said as he fought against her. "We're not going to solve anything by fighting."

Her anger died as she leaned against his chest. Her arms crept around him and he held her close.

"Please understand I need time. I need to work though it; what it all means. Is that okay?"

She sighed. It was all she could fairly expect. "Yeah. Just don't take too long; I will start showing soon."

"I'll do my best."

Beth listened to the solid thumping of his heart under her ear, the sound reassuring and calming her as she ran her hands across his back. "I may have to tell someone at the lab, especially if the giddiness continues."

She felt his muscles flex as his arms tightened, as if warding off any loss of balance.

"Maybe. What did the doctor say about that? Is it going to continue all the way through?"

"It's not uncommon. My blood pressure is naturally low and it has dropped further. It's normal, but it means I may experience giddiness for a while."

"Hmm."

She didn't want to give him another reason to dislike the pregnancy, but honesty was a given between them. "I'll be careful."

"Should you be at work?"

Deep breaths, keep the temper under control. "I'm clear to work, and I will."

He'd sensed her tension. "I don't intend to stop you, but I want to know you'll be okay."

"I'll be okay, I promise."

Beth woke. She could hear no sound in the room and knew before she reached out that Warren wasn't beside her in the bed. His place was cold; he'd been gone a while.

She rose, slowly as not to wake the giddiness, and went out to the top of the stairs. A faint light showed from one side of the lounge room; the side where Warren had his desk. Beth paused, debating whether to go down or return to bed, then shrugged and headed for the lounge room.

Warren sat at his desk, chin resting in his cupped hands, absorbed by something on his laptop. He turned as she approached, acknowledged her presence, and looked back at the screen.

"I couldn't sleep," he said.

Beth stood behind him and laid her hands on his broad shoulders. She felt the tension in his muscles and began to massage them.

"Work?" she asked.

"No. I'm reading how my age could affect our baby's mental health," he replied.

"Is that what it says?" She wanted to make light of it, but Warren's concerns were genuine and being flippant wouldn't help.

"Studies show that an older father could mean an increased likelihood of depression and other mental illnesses."

His shoulders slumped under her hands. She wrapped her arms around his and leaned forward to kiss his cheek. "We'll keep a watch out for signs as our child grows older." She took a deep breath. "There's something else I should mention." He tensed in her arms. "Because of the shape of my uterus, the baby may come early."

She waited for her words to sink in as he stayed rigid in her arms. After a minute he sighed and lifted a hand to grasp one of her arms.

"There's so much…" He broke off and sighed again.

"Write down your questions and we will make an appointment to see someone to get answers," Beth said.

"What about Down's Syndrome?"

"I had blood tests this afternoon—First Trimester Screening it's called. That, with the ultrasound I've booked, should tell us if there's a problem."

"And if there's a problem?"

"Then we'll be prepared." She kissed his cheek again. "I wish I could tell you everything will be fine, that our baby will be born with no issues, but I can't. All we can do is find out what we can and love our baby when it arrives."

The shoulders wrapped in her arms tensed again as he continued reading.

"Are you coming up to bed?" she said, making her voice low and husky. For the first time she could remember, he ignored the invitation in it.

"Not yet," he said. "You go back to bed. I'll be there in a little while."

"Okay," she said, releasing him and standing up. "I guess I'll see you later."

"Yeah," he muttered, absorbed in his reading.

Annoyance narrowed her eyes, but she held back her words. He'd asked for time and she'd have to give it. Without another word she turned and climbed the stairs to the bedroom.

Chapter Twelve

"I will do my best for you, Mr Cole, but you will be looking at a long jail term."

Jerry went from white to grey, swaying in his chair. George wanted to grab the front of his prison overalls and give him a good shake, but that wouldn't help things at all. The boy needed all the support he could get. He'd brought this on himself and he didn't need his father to remind him.

"What is the evidence they have?" George asked. He'd done some reading on evidence that could be used these days. It was amazing what could be found now.

"Security surveillance, fingerprints from the door of the bank, the remains from the fire, and the bag. That is one of the main pieces of evidence connecting Jerry to the robbery and shooting. The thing that clinched it is two of the bank customers identifying Jerry from a line up as the man with the gun."

"They don't have the gun?"

"They don't need the gun, not with the rest of the evidence they have."

George scowled and the lawyer. "What's the bit you said about the fire?"

The lawyer sighed. "They found the place where Jerry burned his clothes after the robbery. A piece of leather, matching the type of boot Jerry owned right before the robbery, was found in the ashes of a fire. One of the FBI's scientists, who happened to be walking in the area at the time came across it. She thought it unusual and reported it." The lawyer shrugged. "Plain unlucky. They found tyre tracks that match the truck, and Jerry's footprints." The lawyer looked at Jerry, who kept his gaze on the ground. "Your only hope for a lighter sentence is a full confession and the names of the others involved in the robbery. It would give me something to bargain with."

Jerry didn't lift his head or acknowledge the lawyer's comment in any way. George feared for his son, feared for him to a level he didn't think possible. He'd always thought there was nothing he couldn't help Jerry through, but this was beyond anything he'd ever imagined. The fear sat deep in his gut, in his soul; primal and dark. George feared for his son's life.

"Why did you do it? Why did you rob the bank?" he asked. "Can you at least tell me that?"

Jerry lifted his eyes to meet his father's. He said nothing. His blank, pale face gave no clue to the thoughts in his head.

"I'm sorry, Pa."

The blank eyes filled with pain for an instant, and then they were directed at the floor once more.

George knew a moment of complete frustration. The longing to belt the answers out of his son grew almost too much to contain.

"I think we're finished here," the lawyer said as he stacked his papers into the file. "Mr Cole, we need to leave now."

George reached over and grasped his son's arm. "Stay strong, Jerry," he muttered.

"Bye Pa."

Jerry hadn't raised his eyes and didn't watch as George and the lawyer rose from their seats. The lawyer banged on the door, and moments later, George was on the outside while his son was on the inside.

"I gotta do something," he muttered.

"Then find out who his accomplices are," the lawyer responded. "That's his only hope."

Then he had no hope. The threats had been clear, and Jerry would go to jail regardless of what happened, so there was no way he could avoid any reprisal. George could have wept there and then as the frustration took him to breaking point.

"Are you all right, Mr Cole?" the lawyer asked.

"My son's shot someone and is going to jail for a long time. What do you think?" he spat back.

"I'll do my best."

George let out a long breath. "I'm sorry, it's not your fault."

"Take it easy, Mr Cole. One day at a time."

They had reached the outside of the building now.

"I'll be in touch," the lawyer said, and he left George and walked towards his car.

George watched as the man got in his car and drove away. There had to be something he could do. Jerry had done wrong, and had to pay for his crimes, but he was just a kid. What had he done wrong to make Jerry do something like this? Jerry had always been good. George couldn't fathom what reason Jerry would have had to rob a bank. He earned money working for the family business, he wasn't into drugs— there were no signs of it, anyway. Then why? Why? The question revolved in George's mind as he made his way to his car. He pulled his keys out of his pocket and aimed the car key for the lock. Then he stopped. Someone had left him a message, written in the dust on the side of the car.

Say nothing.

George spun around, scanning the parking lot for any sign of someone watching him. There was no one. He couldn't see anyone nearby.

No movement in the bushes, no movement in the other cars. He turned back to his car, rereading the words. Then he ran a hand over the writing, smudging it, and unlocked his car with trembling hands.

There was no hope for Jerry. There was nothing he could do.

Chapter Thirteen

"You wanted to see me, sir?"

Angus Toovey, the Deputy Director of the FBI, looked up from the papers on his desk.

"Warren, come in and sit down. Yes, I have a few things I want to discuss with you."

Warren cast a swift glance at Angus as he walked over to the visitors' chairs by the desk and sat down. Angus hadn't met his look, and there was nothing to read in his face. Warren hoped it wasn't anything too taxing. Three days on and he was still trying to grasp the news of Beth's pregnancy and all it meant. The weekend had been strained—not something he'd experienced with Beth before. Each of them had tried to act normally, but the tension was evident all the same. Warren hated it. He wanted life to go back to normal, but normal had changed, and so had his relationship with his wife. Now was not the time to be dwelling on it. He had a job to do and the rest would have to wait. Warren sat back in the chair, relaxed his muscles, and focused his mind on his work.

"I read your report on the response to the recent increase in hoax bomb threats." Angus rocked back in his chair, his hands clasped over his stomach. "The measures that have been put in place all seem logical and reasonable." Warren waited in silence, not sure where this was going. Angus didn't seem to know where it was going either. He was searching for words. "The threat against the FBI labs was resolved quickly, and I hear the perpetrator was found within hours."

"Yes sir. He left his caller ID on. It was a simple matter to track him down."

"He wasn't arrested though. Was that wise?"

Warren's body tensed, an instinctive hostility to the implied criticism of his agent's work, and a decision Warren agreed with.

"The caller's son had been arrested earlier in the day on serious charges and the man's house searched. I understand his wife was considerably shaken by the events, and the man reacted. The agent who interviewed him concluded the man was genuinely remorseful and believed he wouldn't be of any further trouble."

"I believe your wife was also considerably shaken by the bomb threat."

Warren forced himself to sit silently for a moment until the first heat of his anger had passed. "My wife was not shaken by the threat. Her condition was unrelated to the incident." Her *condition*? How could something so utterly life-changing be described as a condition? The implication too, that Beth was in some way a fragile and easily frightened person, annoyed the heck out of him. "I stand by my agent's decision to issue a warning and take the matter no further."

"Very well. That brings me onto another matter." Angus leaned forward and picked up a pen, his forearms resting on his desk. "This time you are spending at the Washington Field Office has raised eyebrows." Warren clenched his teeth to stop any words emerging. "Your job doesn't require you to participate in investigations. Your skills are required in headquarters, managing a large division within the FBI."

"Are you instructing me to cease these activities?" Warren challenged Angus. He'd unlocked his teeth, but still held a tight rein on his temper.

"Are they necessary?"

"I believe so."

"Because you feel you need to keep your hand in, so to speak?"

"No. I believe the best way for me to keep in touch with those in the field, to understand how decisions we make affect them, is to work amongst them. By gaining their trust and respect." Warren took in Angus' sceptical look. "And I want to make the agents in the field look at us as not just the empty suits they call us, but as fellow agents."

"Noble ideas, but it's not your job to do that. The agents in charge of the field offices are responsible for solving morale issues."

"It's more than morale. It's letting them know we're all on the same team and that they aren't forgotten in the bureaucracy we deal with every day."

"You're beating your head against a brick wall."

I sure am, right here in this office. "I plan to keep participating with investigations when time permits," Warren stated. He watched with interest as Angus fiddled with his pen, buying time before he responded to the challenge.

"When time permits. So long as it doesn't impact on your other responsibilities."

Responsibilities. Warren's mind flew back to Beth at that word. His responsibilities were about to increase tenfold. His throat tightened at the thought.

"Of course, sir," he answered.

Angus held his gaze for another moment and then nodded. "Excellent. I'll let you get back to your office."

Warren stood up, his irritation at Angus' comments still burning. He nodded and left the office without another word. He was chosen for his position because of his skills, including personnel management. Throughout his management career, from Special Agent in Charge onwards, he'd worked to get the best from his staff and build trust and understanding. Angus should leave him to do his job, should trust him to do it in the best way Warren knew how.

"Pearce! How are you?"

Warren looked at the colleague who'd greeted him. "I'm well, Lefroy. Yourself?"

"Great thanks. How's that wife of yours?"

Pregnant. "Beth's well, thanks." That familiar knot of tension took up residence in his gut. *We're having a baby.* "I must keep going, catch you later."

The anger may have disappeared, but Warren's thoughts kept returning to the ramifications of the pregnancy. His world had been turned upside down. No more peace and quiet at home, no more comfortable affluence—the cost of raising a child would eat all their savings. His wife would put the child first, as she should, and he would have to wait his turn. Selfish, sure, but he was used to having Beth to himself. He didn't even know how to hold a baby, let alone change one. The thought of being left alone with a screaming infant when Beth went out left him cold. And who would look after the child when Beth went back to work? Did she plan to return to work, or did she want to stay at home? He couldn't imagine her being content giving up her career. Would he have to cut back his hours? He couldn't, not that simple in a position like his. Warren walked back into his office reception area, his mind spinning with his thoughts.

"Excuse me sir, the latest budget reports have been delivered by Finance. They're on your desk for your review," Lisa said as he passed her desk.

"Thanks." He paused at the door to his office. "Lisa, can you please hold all calls for the next half hour?"

"Yes sir."

Warren closed the door and headed for his desk. The budget reports waited for him in a neat pile. He changed course away from the desk and came to a stop by the window. Warren stared out for a moment before turning to survey his office. The large space contained not only his desk, but a meeting table and a group of comfortable chairs for more relaxed discussion. A mahogany bookcase, filled with his reference books, stood against the wall closest to his desk. He'd worked hard to achieve this, to rise to the high position he now held. For the first time though, he was honest with himself. Did he really want this? Was this what he'd worked for—a large office and an endless round of meetings and briefings? He didn't want to answer that question. It had to be answered, or did it? Did he want the truth, especially now he needed to provide for a child? Was that where the turmoil lay—the temptation of Sam's offer against the needs of his wife and child? His child. Warren's chest tightened. That was the real truth. He was unprepared to be a father; the thought terrified him.

"Get a grip, man," he chided himself. "You can do this. If you can run a section of the FBI, you can change a diaper." He sucked in a deep breath and then released it in a long gush of air. There was one person who could give him the answers he needed.

Warren picked up his cell phone, looked up a number, and dialled.

Warren was the first to arrive at the café, and he'd only just taken his seat when the man with the answers arrived.

"How are you Warren?"

"I'm...actually, I have no idea how I am." He stood up to shake the man's hand. "Thanks for agreeing to meet me so quickly Aden."

"It's not a problem. I was in the area, anyway."

Warren watched Aden as he ordered coffee. He'd first met Aden when he'd been an FBI agent and defence tactics instructor. Aden, and his wife Sarah, had both left the FBI soon after, to join Sam in his private investigation agency. More importantly right now, Aden was the father of baby Logan.

"How's things going, Aden?" Warren wasn't ready to leap into the deep end of his planned conversation yet.

"Things are busy at the agency." Aden's startling green eyes flicked up at Warren. "We could use your help…"

Warren couldn't think of an easy answer. He was trying to deal with the sudden knowledge that he wanted to help; wanted it more than his job at the FBI. He stomped on it—he had other things to think about first.

"How's the family?"

"They're great!" Aden's eyes lit up. "Logan has started walking and he's getting into everything." The broad smile that accompanied the statement took any suggestion of complaint away.

"How old is he now?"

"Eleven months. He's advanced for his age." The joy in Aden's face had turned to pure pride in his son's achievement.

Warren couldn't help smiling back at him. "I wouldn't expect anything else from a child of yours and Sarah's." The smile faded. What would his child be like? What would it excel at?

The waiter arrived with their coffees, placing them on the table before gliding away to attend to other customers.

"So," Aden said as he reached for the sugar. "What can I do for you, Warren?"

Warren took a deep, silent breath. This was harder than he'd expected.

"I need this conversation to stay confidential, Aden. I don't want you to mention to anyone what we discuss."

"Of course," Aden replied, stirring his sugar into his coffee. "You can count on me. Issues at work?"

"No." Warren took a sip of his coffee. *Just say it.* "Beth's pregnant."

The green eyes opened wide, a broad smile spreading across Aden's face. "That's fantastic news! Congratulations Warren!" The eyes crinkled with amusement. "Let me guess. You're worried? Scared, even?"

Warren scowled at the younger man's grin. "It's not funny." Maybe this had been a bad idea.

"No, you're right. It's not funny. What it is, is normal." Aden leaned forward as his smile died. "You weren't expecting this, were you?"

"Beth had been told she couldn't have children, and to be honest, I was relieved."

"You don't want this child?"

Warren searched Aden's face for condemnation, but saw only understanding. "I've seen so much during my career that bringing a child into this world seems cruel."

"That's why you're scared?"

"Among other things."

"Like two's company, three's a crowd?"

"It's selfish, I know."

"That saying is wrong, you know. Your child will add to your relationship with Beth, not take away from it. Sure, there will be nights when you don't get much sleep, and days when you won't get much time alone with her, but let me tell you…" Aden broke off, a tender smile lighting his face. "There's nothing compared to holding your child in your arms, to seeing them smile when you walk in the room, and to have them hold onto you like you're their whole life." Aden's broad grin spread again. "It's the most incredible feeling you'll ever have. I wouldn't trade it for anything."

Warren looked at Aden's glowing face. His words helped, mostly anyway.

"And I think you will be a great dad," Aden added.

That helped. Aden, in Warren's opinion, was a good dad himself. The comment gave him the confidence he hadn't realised was missing.

Warren relaxed back into his chair and smiled. "Thanks Aden. It's been a shock. I didn't know anything apart from how much things will change."

"They'll change, but it's all for the better." Aden took a mouthful of his coffee. "When's the baby due?"

"October, they think. Beth's having a scan or something soon to get a better idea on when."

"Ultrasound. Make sure you go along too, it's wonderful to see the baby."

"Can you see it?"

"Yeah. It's not like a photo, but you can."

"There's so much to learn."

"I'm around if you need to talk."

Warren smiled. "Thanks."

Chapter Fourteen

"I told Aden about the baby today."

"You did? I thought you didn't want to tell anyone yet?" Beth hoped it was a good sign, but the look on Warren's face didn't encourage the belief. "When did you bump into him?"

"We met for coffee."

"He called you?"

"No. I called him. I wanted to ask his advice."

"About?"

"The baby."

"Because you had concerns?"

"Yes."

Beth tossed her book on the sofa. "Great. You had concerns, so you called Aden. Any of these concerns something I should know about?" Her throat had tightened, making her voice more high-pitched than normal.

"I wanted to ask him about being a dad."

Okay, so not something he could ask her. Beth swallowed her annoyance and attempted a smile. "Not something I can help you with."

Warren moved to sit beside her. "Try to understand. It's a lot to take on board. I just need time to get my head around the enormity of it."

"A lot for you to take on board? What about me? I'm the one carrying our child, and I'll be the one giving birth, and then feeding it."

"But you wanted this."

"And you don't."

"I didn't say that!"

"You haven't said too much about wanting it, either."

"Give me a chance!" He was yelling at her now, responding to her own loud accusations. "No, I didn't ask to have children. Yes, it's a huge shock…" he stopped, his chest rising and falling rapidly, "and I don't want to fight about this."

Beth wrapped her arms around him and held him tight. "I'm sorry."

"Me too." Beth felt his hand run through her hair. "I keep thinking about all the things we need to get and organise. Is your car big enough? Should we look at a larger apartment?"

She sat up. "Slow down Warren. My car is fine, and no, we don't need a larger apartment. These are all things we can work through together." She took his face between her palms and kissed him. "Stop worrying, it will be okay."

"How can you be sure?"

"Because this is you and me. Together we can do anything."

The crease between his brows eased. "Just promise me one thing."

"Sure."

"Don't climb any trees until after the baby is born."

She narrowed her eyes, but there was no hint of a smile on his face. After a moment, a gleam escaped his eyes and his mouth curved.

"Warren! I thought you were being serious."

"I am. No falling out of trees."

"That's easy enough."

"Not for you, it's not." His smile faded as he stared at her. "Please promise me you won't climb any trees, or do anything else risky. I don't want either of you hurt." His hand rested over their baby.

Beth's heart lifted, but she said nothing, not wanting to make a big deal over Warren's action.

Beth laid her hand over his. "I promise. Now, can I make you a coffee?"

"That would be great, thanks."

She lifted his hand, kissed it and dropped it in his lap, before standing up and walking to the kitchen. These discussions were hard, but at least Warren was communicating with her, not hiding his feelings.

She topped up the kettle and set it to boil, then bent to collect two mugs from the cupboard. As she stood up again, the room moved violently, swaying and spinning. Beth dropped the mugs as she reached for the bench to steady herself, but before she could grab hold, the room blurred and went black.

Warren's voice calling her name was the first thing Beth noticed. The second was a sharp sting in her left arm, somewhere near her wrist. Someone touched near the smarting pain and she groaned.

"Beth, it's okay. I'm here and Heather's on her way."

That made sense. She hurt, and Heather, her best friend and an ER doctor, was coming to the rescue. Beth opened her eyes. Warren hovered above her, his hand was stroking the side of her face.

"What happened?"

"You fainted and you've hurt your arm. Does it hurt anywhere else?"

Beth mentally felt over her body. "No. Just my arm." She glanced down at the offending limb. "Oh geez," she exclaimed.

"It's not bleeding badly," Warren reassured her, though his face was pale and tense enough for both of them.

Beth closed her eyes, but the image of the piece of broken crockery embedded in her flesh swam through her mind. "Ow."

The sound of the front door of the apartment opening and bouncing of its stopper was followed by the arrival of Heather, with Sam close on her heels.

"Hey sweetie," Heather greeted her. To Warren, she said, "You can let go now."

Warren released his hold on her arm as Heather took over. He crouched on Beth's other side and held her other hand as Heather inspected the injury.

"Most people would gracefully slump onto the floor, but no, you have to land on something sharp." Sam's grinning face swum above Beth.

"Shut your pie-hole," Beth returned, earning a chuckle from Sam. Heather ministrations were sending burning pain through her arm and she squeezed Warren's hand.

"Ooo, I love it when you talk Aussie at me!"

"Beth," Heather interrupted. "We're going to take you to hospital so they can remove the piece of china from your arm and stitch the wound. I need to make it stable first, so stay still. I'll try not to hurt you too much."

"Did you hear that Beth," Sam piped up. "You've got a piece of a country in your arm."

Beth tried not to chuckle as Warren groaned beside her. "You're a drongo, Sam," she said.

"Sam," Heather interrupted again. "I need you to hold this still while I fix it in place."

Sam's face disappeared, replaced by Warren's. His free hand smoothed her hair away from her forehead as she clung to the other. Heather was doing her best, but it hurt like crazy.

"Okay," Heather said after a few minutes. "Beth, I will support your arm, so I want you to leave it relaxed okay?"

"Okay."

Heather looked at Warren. "Warren, I want you and Sam to lift Beth onto her feet, and you," Heather looked back at Beth, "let us do most of the work."

"Okay."

Between them they lifted her off the floor and onto her feet.

"Are you feeling okay?" Heather asked, peering into Beth's face.

"Yeah, I'm okay." Her arm hurt and she was a little light-headed, but otherwise fine.

Their strange procession made its way down the elevator and to the parking lot under the building. They eased her into Sam's car, taking such care of her arm she almost laughed at the bizarre picture they formed. Almost. The sharp burning in the arm Heather still supported from beside her stopped her.

Warren turned from the front seat to look at her once they'd left the parking lot. "We need to tell them."

She ignored the reluctance she read in his face. "I agree. I don't want them finding out when I get questioned at the hospital."

"That's what I was thinking. You or me?"

"I think preparation is necessary, considering Heather is holding my arm."

"What on earth are you two talking about?" Sam asked.

Beth looked at Heather. "Hold it steady, okay?"

"Tell me what you were talking about, or I'll twist it," Heather threatened. "Are you sick? Is that why you fainted?" Beth heard fear in Heather's voice.

"No. I'm pregnant."

"What!" the Daltons yelled in chorus.

"That's fantastic news," Sam shouted, slapping Warren on the arm. "You old dog."

113

Beth winced. At least it wasn't 'randy old goat'.

"That's wonderful, Beth," Heather said, smiling. "How long have you known?"

"Only a couple of days. We needed to get used to the idea before we told anyone."

"How far along are you?"

"Not sure, about three months my doctor thinks."

"And you said you couldn't have kids." Heather shook her head. "I told you to get another opinion."

"Don't need it now," Sam said. "Outstanding news."

Beth looked at Warren. He looked smug, pleased with himself. The male pride at fathering offspring had woken in him. He was coming around to the idea of becoming a father, of having a child.

"Thanks for letting us know," Heather said, cradling Beth's arm. "I'm so pleased for you both."

Before long they were at the hospital and Beth was being examined by the duty doctor. Warren stayed by her side, but Heather and Sam had disappeared.

"Okay," the doctor said after finishing his examination. "I'm confident no arterial veins have been hit. I'll numb the arm, remove the shard of china, clean and stitch the wound, and you'll be out of here before you know it." He grinned. "Well, maybe not quite that fast."

He swabbed her skin and injected the site with local anaesthetic. "I'll give that a chance to work, and then we'll get you fixed up."

He disappeared behind the curtain of the cubicle which was flung back moments later by Heather and Sam. Heather's face was flushed, and she and Sam both grinned like a pair of naughty school kids.

"We brought you something," Sam announced.

"I wrangled the use of this for ten minutes," Heather said, pulling forward a machine on a trolley.

"What is it?" Warren asked.

Beth knew. "An ultrasound machine?"

"Not only that," Heather said, "but I also persuaded Tina here to come and operate it for us." Heather drew forward a petite blonde, dressed in hospital uniform.

Tears welled in Beth's eyes. She blinked them away as Warren grasped hold of her hand.

"Thank you so much."

"Don't cry, sweetie. I want to see your baby as much as you do. And we can make sure little bean is okay."

"We'll see the baby?" Warren's voice broke in.

"You will," Tina confirmed. "Mrs Pearce, can you please unbutton your jeans?"

Warren took care of the buttons as Tina turned on the ultrasound machine and positioned it so they could see the screen. Warren's hand had taken a death grip on her free one, his eyes wide, somewhere between fearful and excited.

Tina squirted cold gel on Beth's stomach and applied the probe to her belly. It vibrated on her skin, but she barely noticed as images appeared on the screen. Tina moved the probe around in silence, then holding it still, pointed to the screen.

"There you go, Mr and Mrs Pearce, your baby." Warren's hand loosened on Beth's as Tina traced shapes on the screen. "There's the head, and the spine, and you can see the heart beating."

The vision on the screen blurred as tears filled Beth's eyes.

"That's incredible," Warren whispered.

Beth looked to him. He stared at the screen, a smile spread across his face. His eyes glistened as he turned to Beth.

"Our baby," he croaked. He lifted his free hand to wipe the moisture away from his eyes. His kissed her hand and then turned back to the screen. "Is it okay?"

"I can't do a full assessment, Mr Pearce, but the heartbeat is nice and regular, and from a quick glance, it looks healthy." She gave him a serious look. "That's a brief assessment. You'll need a full scan done to check your baby thoroughly."

"I've booked a scan for late next week," Beth said, staring at the screen.

"Can you tell how far along the pregnancy is?" Heather asked. "Beth's been told about three months, but she's not sure."

"I can do a quick measure," Tina confirmed and turned to the screen. Lines appeared over the image as Tina clicked buttons and twirled the probe against Beth's abdomen. "From the measurements, I'd say the pregnancy is twelve weeks along. That makes the due date around…" she consulted a chart, "the first week of October." Tina glanced at the clock. "I'd better get this back now. Sorry I can't stay longer."

"Hang on," Warren said, plunging his hand into his pocket. He pulled out his phone and within seconds had taken a photo of the screen. "Thank you."

"Yes, thank you, Tina," Beth echoed as she wiped the gel from her tummy with paper towel. The image of their baby floated in her mind, precious and wonderful. Warren took the paper from her and dropped a kiss on her forehead.

"I love you," he whispered.

She smiled. "I love you too."

Tina wheeled the cart away as the doctor returned.

"Right," he said. "The fun's over. Now for the rest."

"Is that comfortable?" Warren asked as Beth laid her arm on the pillow he had arranged.

"Much better." She sighed. Her pale face worried him. Anxiety for the health and safety of his wife and child twisted his guts into a knot.

"Can I get you a cup of tea?"

"I'd rather you sat down beside me," she said, holding her hand out to him. Her fingers trembled as he grasped her hand. He sank down beside her and slid an arm around her so she could rest her head on his shoulder. They sat in silence. Warren stroked her arm, caressing her skin as she relaxed against him.

"It was wonderful of Heather to organise the quick scan," she said into the quiet.

A rush of tenderness almost brought tears to his eyes again as he thought of the image of his child, the baby that grew inside the woman at his side. "It was incredible." He paused, trying to find the words to express how he felt. "I want to hold our child," he managed.

"You do?"

"I want to hold my family." He stopped again, searching for words. "I want to be a father. I want to see our child grow up."

He cradled Beth as best he could, careful not to disturb her injured arm. She lifted her smiling face to receive his kiss.

"I was so reluctant to accept the change in our life, but seeing our baby…" he broke off, laying a hand over his child.

"I know, but I was pretty confident you'd come around to the idea of fatherhood."

Warren smiled at her. "You were right."

"I'm always right."

Her shining blue eyes and soft lips were too tempting, and he kissed her again, a long and tender kiss. When he broke the kiss, he eased Beth's head down onto his shoulder once more. He wanted to discuss an idea he'd had after seeing the ultrasound image.

"Have you thought about names yet?" he asked.

"It's wandered through my mind once or twice, but there's plenty of time yet. Do you have something in mind, a family name?"

"The only family name on my side is Joseph, and I'm not keen on it. What about your side?"

She shook her head. "No, none I'm aware of."

Warren didn't reply immediately, wondering if it was too soon to nominate the name that had sprung into his mind. Beth stirred against his shoulder.

"Warren, you have a name in mind, don't you? I can hear your brain whirring away."

"Remind me to oil it before bed."

She chuckled. "It doesn't need oiling. Go on, spit it out."

He kissed her hair, her gentle scent mixing with the sharpness of the medical smell from her dressing. "I do have a name in mind," he admitted. "Matilda."

"Matilda?"

"Yes, Matilda."

Beth twisted her neck to look up at him. "That's not a name I expected you to like."

"Don't you like it?"

"I do, actually, and not only because of the link with Australia. It's a lovely name."

"It came to mind when I saw our baby earlier."

"Do you think it's a girl?"

"I don't know." He thought, and then added, "I would like a daughter."

"What if it's a boy?"

"I would like a boy just as much."

"Really?"

Warren pictured their future, his family. A son or a daughter.

"I don't mind which we have," he lied.

"I hope for your sake it's a girl then," Beth's reply came, stunning him. How did she pick up on that? "Though I think you would love a son just as much—you just don't realise it right now." She squinted up at him. "You can't hide things from me, Warren. I can feel your soul." Beth sucked in a sharp breath. "There's something else I'm beginning to feel, too."

"Is your arm hurting?" He'd hoped the local anaesthetic would last longer.

"It's starting to," she said, shifting it on the pillow, trying to ease the discomfort.

"I'll get the paracetamol," Warren said, easing himself from her side, trying not to jar her.

"Thanks."

She looked so tired, so worn. Warren stooped and released the footrest mechanism, and Beth's feet rose.

"I'll get your tablets and then make you some tea," he said. "Don't move, beautiful Beth."

Her thankful smile reassured him. He doubted the paracetamol would help much with the pain, but Beth had to be careful what medication she took. There was so much to think about with the baby. Their baby. Warren could feel his smile widen across his face. His baby.

"I think we should tell a few people about the pregnancy," Beth's voice floated in to him in the kitchen. "I need to let Kamal know, and probably the people I work with, too."

Warren carried a glass of water and the tablets back to her. "They do need to know what's happening, especially if you will have problems with giddiness. I need to let Toovey know. He'll probably hear about it from Kamal and it would be better coming from me." The anxiety came back to rest in his gut. "What if you faint again?"

Beth swallowed the tablets before replying. "I won't. I'll just make sure I move slowly until things get better."

"Perhaps you should get a lift to work for the next little while. You won't be able to drive for a few days with your arm, anyway."

She nodded. "I'll ask Elliot. He's been happy to give me a ride in the past."

"Or you could take a few days off."

"I'm quite capable of working."

He stood, hands on hips, considering her from under his brows. As much as he wanted to protect her from any possible harm, Beth would resist any effort on his part to do that. There wasn't much he could do, but hope for the best. The sound of the boiling kettle distracted him, and he headed for the kitchen.

Warren sat at his desk, staring at the pages spread open before him. His brain didn't take in any of the words or figures on the paper; he was busy sorting out who needed to know about Beth's pregnancy. He wasn't keen to tell anyone. Not because he didn't want the child, but because it was none of their business. The child. His child. He reached for his phone and brought up the ultrasound image of his baby. His eyes scanned the picture, taking in every minute detail it revealed as a smile grew on his face. Was it a girl or a boy? He couldn't tell, and he wasn't sure he wanted to know right now.

Warren reached for the phone on his desk and hit the button for his PA.

"Yes sir?"

"Can you please contact Deputy Director Toovey's office and see if he can spare me a few minutes?"

Lisa was back on the phone in a few short moments.

"Sir, Deputy Director Toovey can see you now."

"Thank you, Lisa."

He looked at the image once more before putting his cell away. He would tell the Deputy Director the news and sound him out about some leave for the period after the birth. When Beth told Kamal, it wouldn't be long until the grapevine spread the news, and some people needed to hear it from him. With this in mind, he stopped by Lisa's desk on the way out.

"Yes sir?"

He tapped her desk with a finger. "I wanted to let you know before word gets out—Beth and I are having a baby." He liked the way the words sounded, but it still felt strange. He braced for possible negative feedback, but he didn't need to.

"That's wonderful news!" Lisa exclaimed, jumping to her feet and skirting the desk. Warren prayed she wouldn't try to kiss his cheek, but Lisa knew him better than that. She beamed at him. "I'm pleased for you both."

"Thank you, Lisa."

Lisa hesitated, and Warren braced himself again. "I don't want to embarrass you sir, but I think you will be a wonderful father."

Warren smiled. "I hope so."

"Am I able to tell others the news?"

What did he want? "If they ask, sure." He sighed. "It's not a secret, but…"

"Don't worry sir, I know what you mean."

Warren nodded. "Thanks."

"Come in Pearce. What can I do for you?" Toovey asked.

At least the Deputy Director was in a good mood. "Sir, this is a courtesy visit to let you know I intend to apply for an extended period of leave to begin in October."

Toovey frowned. "For how long?"

"At least a month."

"Not the best time to be taking the leave, Pearce."

"The timing is unavoidable, sir. Beth is due to give birth then and I would like time at home with her and our baby."

Toovey's open mouth and staring eyes was all Warren had expected. Now for the comments.

"A baby? Your first?"

"Yes." He waited for it. *At your age?*

"Most men would be looking at becoming grandparents at our age."

There it was.

"Most men are not me, sir." *And I can give you a few years.*

"Very true, Pearce. Well, congratulations, and I'll make a note of your request."

"Thank you, sir."

Warren turned and left the office before he became angrier. He had been right. Randy old goat. He thought of his child's image and smiled. He wasn't going to care what others thought of his pending fatherhood. It was none of their business. It still stung though. He doubted Beth was being subject to the same sort of comment.

"Leaving it a bit late, aren't you? I mean you're not young, and as for Warren…"

"What do you mean, *as for Warren*?" Beth snapped back. "He's fitter and healthier than your Desmond, by a mile! And I'm not old! Warren and I will be running around long after you and Desmond have slowed down."

"Yeah, because you'll have a little kid to run around after."

"At least we'll be fit enough to keep up with it."

"What are you saying?"

"I'm defending myself and Warren from your snide remarks, that's what I'm saying. You want to have a go at us? Don't expect me to take it and not give it back!"

Beth glared at one of the fellow scientists she shared her news with, waiting for her to reply, but another voice broke in first.

"Beth's got a point."

"I don't want your opinion."

"Too bad. Warren Pearce is one fit and healthy specimen of a man. He could father my kids any day."

"Excuse me?" Beth exclaimed, caught between indignation and laughter as the first scientist stalked off.

"Hey Beth, I say it as I see it."

"He's spoken for."

"Don't I know it! I wish a man would look at me the way he looks at you. Mmm, mmm. You are one lucky girl."

Beth laughed. "I sure am."

"Well, congratulations. I'm thrilled for you guys."

"Thanks."

"Don't let old sour puss get you down, either. She's jealous."

"Maybe. I shouldn't have snapped at her."

"Oh yes you should have. Do you know what your problem is? You're too nice."

"Now you're making me blush."

"Get outta here, girl. Go find some work to do."

Beth tapped on Kamal's door and waited for his invitation to enter. "Good morning, Kamal."

"Hello Beth." He smiled and then frowned at her arm. "What have you done?"

"I fainted last night and landed on a broken coffee mug. A few stitches, and it's sore, but I'm fine."

"You fainted? Is everything all right?"

Beth smiled, a reaction she couldn't suppress when she thought of the baby. "That's what I'm here to see you about. My blood pressure is low at the moment, and I'm having a few dizzy spells. It'll pass soon though, I'm told."

"Is that what happened the other day with the evacuation?"

"Yes."

"What's caused it?"

Beth's smile broadened across her face. "Warren and I are having a baby."

Kamal stood and walked around the desk, beaming. "That's fantastic news! Congratulations to you both."

"Thanks. I'll do the formal notice and what-not later, but I didn't think it right not to tell you, and Warren wanted me to let you know about the dizziness. I'll be careful in the lab so it doesn't affect me."

"Warren's right. It's better to let me know, just in case. I think you should let the First Aid officer in your area know of your pregnancy, too. Let them know about the dizzy spells, too please. When's the baby due?"

"October sometime. I don't know exactly yet."

He smiled. "Keep me posted."

"I will."

"On another subject, we will need the pollen samples from the robbery case sooner rather than later. The Coles are now telling the lawyer they're not sure if the bag left behind is theirs, or just looks like it. The wife is being vague—saying she's not sure—so I want to see if we can link it to the farm beyond any doubt. With the collection of plants she has, the pollen should tell us one way or the other."

"No problems. The samples are prepared, so I'll get onto it first thing."

"Thanks Beth." Kamal smiled. "And take it easy. If your arm hurts, I want you to head home."

"I will, don't you worry."

Chapter Fifteen

Jerry woke from a fitful doze as the door of his cell clanged open. A bright light, a torch, shone in his eyes. He raised a hand to shield them, but his night vision was ruined and he could make out nothing.

"Is this the one?" a voice rasped, deep and husky.

"Yeah, that's him."

Shit. Jerry's heart pounded as he scrambled to free his legs from the rough blanket and sit up. A fist grabbed a handful of his shirt and assisted him to rise, his skull cracking on the bunk above. Stars spun in his eyes for a moment and he was thrust against the cold concrete wall of the cell.

"Get out," another voice growled, and one of the group pushed the man on the top bunk out of the room.

The bright light still shining in Jerry's eyes stopped him seeing more than the shadowy outlines of the surrounding men. His heart hammered in his chest as he tried to think, but nothing came. He was powerless, frozen.

"Where is it? Where's the money? My boss wants answers, and I'm here to get them," the voice rasped.

"I don't…I don't…" Jerry managed. The hands pulled him off the wall and then slammed him back into it. His head bounced off the hard concrete and the bright light became riddled with spots.

"Where is it?" the voice demanded again.

Jerry couldn't understand. The world was full of darkness and movement beyond the light. His limbs were heavy, his voice gone.

"He's not going to tell us."

The raspy voice swore as a hand pulled him forward. The world tilted, his head colliding with the concrete once more and it all went dark.

Jerry heard the voices first.

"You stupid bastard. He's out cold. Fat lot of use that was."

"Just softening him up for the next time."

Jerry's gut cramped, bile rising in his throat. *Next time.*

"We gotta get him to talk."

"How do you know it's worth it?"

"I just do. It's worth it all right. I got word from outside that he was on that bank job in DC. If we find out where the money is, my boss says we'll get a cut."

"How much time do we have?"

"He wants an answer by next week. We'll do him as soon as he's back on the floor."

Jerry found his voice. "No."

The bright light returned, burning his eyes through the slits of his eyelids.

"He's awake."

"Get him up."

"Screw you," Jerry whispered.

"What did you say?"

Jerry no longer cared. They weren't going to stop, so he might as well talk while he could. "Screw you."

The men laughed. The light dropped and Jerry saw the toe of a boot swing at him, ploughing into his face with an agonising crunch, then nothing.

George replaced the telephone receiver, his shaking hand making the hard plastic rattle into position. Nausea rose into his throat as cold anger turned his blood to ice. He stood looking at the telephone, the messenger of bad news.

"George?"

Daisy's voice quivered from the kitchen doorway.

"What is it, George?"

He unfroze his shocked body and shuffled towards his wife. "Come into the kitchen, love."

Daisy grabbed his arm, her nails digging into his skin, but she followed him and didn't resist when he pushed her into a chair. George lowered himself down until he felt the solid seat of the chair take his weight. Everything seemed different, unreal. He thought of the news they'd given him and cleared his throat.

"Our boy got into a fight. Apparently, he provoked another prisoner." He stopped, fighting the anger once more. His Jerry wouldn't do that. Someone had set him up, and they would pay.

"Go on," Daisy whispered.

"He's not good, Daisy. He's in the prison hospital. They say he's got bad head and face injuries." George reached out a hand to Daisy as she crumpled in her seat. She made no sound, just shrivelled before his eyes. "They're doing what they can."

"I want to see my boy." Her voice, barely more than a breath, tore at his broken heart.

He swallowed again. "They said we can go tomorrow. The prison is in lockdown right now. They're trying to find out who he fought with."

George caught Daisy as she slumped to the ground from her chair, sobs shaking her body as her grief overtook her control. George held her tight, his anger rising cold and hard, as he planned his revenge on those who'd hurt his son.

"Good morning sir, how can I help you?"

George swallowed his nerves and puffed out his chest. "I want to see the man who runs the investigations area." He stared at the lady behind the counter at the FBI. She smiled; her lips curved anyway. George saw no warmth in her face.

"Do you have an appointment, sir?" She was cold behind the polite mask. George wasn't going to be deterred.

"Yes."

She knew he was lying. He saw the way her eyes narrowed and her lips compressed. "Who is it you have the appointment with?"

She thought she had him there. Her smirk was sliding into place as he responded.

"Pearce, his name is."

Her face froze for an instant and then she smiled again. "Your name, sir?"

"George Cole."

"Just one moment Mr Cole."

George watched her pick up a phone and press some numbers.

"Good morning. I have a Mr Cole here who says he has an appointment with EAD Pearce."

The lady blinked a few times as she listened to the person she'd called. "Thank you," she said and replaced the receiver. "There is no appointment for you with EAD Pearce."

"There must be a mistake," George said with as much authority as he could muster. "I had a call confirming my appointment late yesterday."

"I'm sorry Mr Cole. EAD Pearce's assistant was clear that there is no appointment arranged for you."

"But I must see him!" he pleaded, his voice loud.

"Mr Cole, sir, please calm down."

George glanced around. People were staring at him, particularly those manning the security checkpoints. He turned back to the lady. "Please, can you call them again and check again? I only want a couple of minutes."

"Mr Cole, I think it would be a good idea if you left now."

George reached out to her, but his wrist was grabbed from behind and his arm twisted up his back.

"Sir, please calm down," a deep voice said in George's ear. His shoulders slumped, his back bent. It had been a stupid idea to come here, and stupid to think they would let him in.

The force pulling his arm back eased and George turned to the man who'd restrained him. "I just want to see Pearce," he whispered. The tears filling his eyes made the tall man before him, still holding his wrist, blur. The strong grip remained, but George had no fight left and his arm fell limp.

"Why do you want to see him?" the tall man asked, staring down at him.

George sniffed and wiped his eyes with his free hand. The man cleared. Not a guard, as George had thought, but a muscular man in a suit. An agent, perhaps. "I want him to help my son."

"Who is your son?" the man asked, his eyes narrowing.

"Jerry, Jerry Cole."

The man's eyes lifted as he repeated the name silently, as if trying to bring to mind an elusive memory. The lips closed firmly as the man's intense gaze fixed on George once more. "There's nothing you can achieve by trying to force your way into the FBI headquarters. I suggest you go home."

The tall man released George's wrist and stood back to allow a guard to escort George out of the building. The humiliation of failure was nothing compared to the knowledge he'd failed his son. All fight gone, George stepped obediently out of the door and walked away from the building.

The tall man watched him go and turned to the lady at the counter who'd stared open mouthed at him.

"What was that man's name?"

"George Cole, sir."

The tall man nodded as if confirming a previous conclusion. "And he claimed to have an appointment?"

"Yes, sir."

He turned to the guard who'd returned. "Make sure he stays away."

"Yes sir."

The tall man stood staring at the door for a moment, his hands on his hips as he chewed his bottom lip in thought. Finally, he sighed, his hands dropping to his side. He turned back to the lady at the counter. "Call my assistant and let her know I'm going out for a while."

"Yes sir."

Warren turned to the door and followed George.

George shuffled up the sidewalk, barely noticing which direction he took. He waited at the pedestrian crossing for the light, only realising it had changed when the people either side of him moved off. He hadn't gone to the FBI with any real plan—he just wanted someone to do something, and the man in charge was the obvious choice. A search of the FBI website had revealed the man's name, but it hadn't helped him at all. He'd been refused entry, refused everything.

A bench beckoned to him and he slumped down on it. He had no idea what he would do now. And Jerry lay in the hospital, hurt and alone.

"Mr Cole."

The deep voice was back. To add insult to injury, the man had followed him. George didn't bother to look up at him. He just wanted the man to go away and leave him alone.

"I left. I wasn't going to hurt anyone." George tried to sound angry, but it came out as tired. Probably because that's what he was. Bone tired.

"I followed you to hear the rest of your story."

"Why?" George felt the bench move under him as the tall man sat down beside him.

"Because that's why you were at headquarters just now. To tell me something."

"Huh?" George lifted his head. The man beside him rested his arms on his thighs, his head turned towards George.

"I'm Warren Pearce. I believe you wanted to see me."

"You? You didn't say before!"

"I didn't think I wanted to hear what you had to say. I was heading out when I heard you say my name, so I hung around to see what you wanted. When you became...agitated...I had to step in." Pearce frowned at him. "I recognised your son's name. So I followed you and ask what it was you wanted to tell me."

"After you had me kicked out."

"I wanted to see how much trouble you were prepared to cause. If you'd fought, I would have left the guards to deal with you, but you didn't. You looked defeated. That's what got me curious."

Warren leaned back on the bench as George stared out at the passing traffic. He didn't push him to talk. The older man's hands trembled as they rested on his thighs. Warren reflected on what he knew about the case involving George's son. It wasn't something he would normally be involved with, the task of investigating the bank robbery left to those in the field office. The news of the assault on George's son had rated a line in the daily brief Warren had had emailed that morning. Not uncommon, until George had turned up at the counter. Maybe he wanted to share information.

"I want to know why bad things happen."

George's statement wasn't what Warren had expected. "I want to know too," he replied.

"Why was my son attacked?"

"I don't know, but it could be for any number of reasons. The prison will investigate it, and perhaps your son will be able to shed light on what happened."

The older man fell silent again. His fingers clenched on his legs now and Warren heard the hiss of his breath through gritted teeth. If the man wanted to tell him something, Warren would have to prise it from him.

"Your wife grows orchids, doesn't she?" Warren asked. "My wife loves plants too; she's a botanist. I used to find plants growing in all sorts of strange places in our home, from the basement to inside the bathroom cabinet." Warren chuckled. "All part of her experiments, she says."

"Daisy has her greenhouses," the old man muttered. "Don't let her bring plants into the house if I can help it."

"We don't have a garden, but at least my wife has eased up on the number of plants these days." Warren glanced down at the man's hands. The tension had gone, and they lay relaxed on his thighs. "She likes to go out into the forests whenever she can. Loves trees. A little too much if you ask me. She loves climbing them."

"I used to do that as a kid."

"And fall out of them? My wife does that too."

The old man wheezed a chuckle. "You'd think she'd learn."

"Not when it comes to the trees."

Warren allowed a silence to grow, hoping George would break it this time, continue the flow of voices.

"Jerry used to like climbing trees," George said finally. "He and his friends." The old man's fingers tightened once more. "At least his friends back then wouldn't leave him if he got stuck, or...."

"Or what?" Warren asked quietly.

George cleared his throat. "Don't remember what I was going to say."

Warren released a silent sigh. Close, but no luck. George clenched his hands into tight balls. Maybe it wasn't over yet.

"Does your wife have good friends?" George asked.

"She does."

"I bet with a husband like you her friends wouldn't threaten her or her family if she let them down."

Warren stayed relaxed on the bench, denying the fierce urge to act on the information George was relaying.

"No one threatens my wife and gets away with it, friend or not."

George's legs were jiggling now, the tension in the older man's body demanding release.

Warren leaned forward so his head was closer to George's. "Did they threaten you, George?"

The jiggling grew more violent.

"Who was it? Jerry's friends?"

"I'm not saying anything."

"If you tell me who they are, we can lock them up and the threats will stop."

George shook his head. "No. The threats won't stop. I've said all I can say." He stood and walked away without another word.

Warren watched him go, pondering his next move. If George had been threatened, then he'd taken a huge risk being seen talking to an FBI agent in public. The last thing Warren wanted to do was endanger the old man and his wife, so he stayed sitting on the bench for a few minutes before getting to his feet to head back to HQ. As soon as he was inside the building, he pulled out his cell and dialled.

"Burns."

"Pearce here."

"Yes sir."

"I just had a visit from George Cole."

"Jeez sir, I'm sorry. I didn't think he would bother you."

"It wasn't a bother. He wanted to tell me something."

"Sir?"

"Nothing direct, but he's being threatened by his son's friends. I think he believes they're tied up in the robbery."

"We're already onto it, sir."

"I thought you would be, but from the sounds of it the friends Mr Cole senior is referring to aren't his son's close friends. I'd look further away than that. Cole senior also believes they are responsible for the fight in the holding section of the prison last night. He thinks it was an attack."

"As do we, and how those prisoners got into the holding cells is another mystery we're working on. We need the identity of the son's attackers. See where the links are."

"Let me know."

Warren continued up to his office, shedding his jacket upon arrival, dropping into his chair and swinging it around to stare out of the window. The emotional pain in the old man's body lingered in Warren's thoughts. The grief caused by the son's actions, topped with the grief of the hurt done to his son. It was nothing new to Warren. He'd witnessed similar grief more times than he cared to remember. The worst of humanity had been paraded past him time and time again. And did it still affect him as it had as a junior agent? Yes, and now even worse. The ultrasound image of his child danced in his mind. What kind of person would his child be? Who would befriend them? Would they be safe from the worst the world could show, or would they feel the force of evil that wound its way through society? The temptation to lock his child away from the world and keep them safe was almost overwhelming. But what did Beth always say? You can't live forever, so you might as well live for now. It was true enough, but he wanted to live forever. He had so much to live for.

He swung the chair back around and surveyed his office. It had seemed like a kingdom not that long ago, but now it was more like a prison. Comfortable and luxurious, but a prison nonetheless. As much as the grief old man Cole had felt, Warren had felt alive while they'd talked. He had been doing something, investigating, finding out, using his skills for something other than meetings and high-level decision making, and it had felt good. It had felt right. It was time to make a decision. He picked up his cell phone and dialled.

"Sam. Any chance you can come down to my apartment tonight? I think it's time to have a serious conversation…"

Chapter Sixteen

Peter stared at the door as it moved, the sliver of light on the wooden floor increasing to a broad beam. A silhouetted figure appeared, and Peter recognised the outline.

"Reuben," he said.

The light reduced back down to a sliver once more and the dark figure shuffled forward. "Peter."

Peter sighed. "Good, all here."

"Except the boy and Mac," Matty said, from Peter's right.

"Except them," Peter confirmed.

"Where's Jerry?" Reuben asked as he lowered his large frame onto an old milk crate.

"Feds came and got him last week," Matty said. "Searched the farm, they did. Cuffed him and took him away."

"How the hell did they find him?"

"Idiot left a bag at the bank. His mother identified it."

"Damn. Now what do we do?"

"He won't talk," Peter interrupted. "No way will he dump us in it."

"You sound awful sure of that," Matty growled.

"I am." Peter crushed the fury that had simmered in his brain all morning. "What I want to know is who ordered his bashing in jail?"

"I didn't even know he was there," Reuben said. "Don't look at me."

"And I sure as hell didn't. I'm not the ones with friends on the inside," Matty added. "So don't blame us. Did you?"

"No, no way. Not to Jerry."

"What about Mac?"

"Doubt it. Mac's well out of it. He scarpered the first sign of the feds being around. Rang me and told me he was heading for Canada and wasn't coming back. Said he didn't want nothin' to do with it any more, not even the money."

"Can we trust him?"

"I don't see that we have a choice right now. Besides, he knows we won't hesitate to take him down if he talks."

Peter watched the other two, but they didn't even try to hide their expressions. Reuben chewed his nails as he frowned at Peter, and Matty stared at him as if waiting for further instruction.

"If none of us called the bashing, then who did?"

"Maybe they found out what he was there for."

"After his money? That was fast work." Peter shook his head. "I don't believe it."

"They may not have had any reason," Reuben offered. "One of those things."

Peter sucked in a long breath as he thought of Jerry, hurt and helpless in jail, releasing it slowly through his nose. "His old man is going to see him later today."

"You know a lot," Matty said, his narrowed eyes directed at Peter.

"I've been hanging around. I heard George talk about it this morning."

Matty sat up straight. "They haven't seen you, have they?"

"What do you think I am, stupid?"

"Settle down." Reuben shoved an arm between Matty and Peter. "It won't help if we fall out now."

"You're right," Peter agreed. "We need to keep things chilled."

Silence filled the old barn as the three men sat thinking. The distant sound of sheep in the field was the only interruption. Peter sighed, his thoughts taken up with Jerry's plight. The young man wouldn't talk, but he would be in for more beatings. Peter wouldn't be able to contact the men he knew on the inside for days, so he had no way of finding out who was responsible. He would need to arrange for protection if his guys weren't the ones who'd set up the attack. Jerry wouldn't survive too long if he didn't.

"So what happens now?" Matty asked.

"We keep our heads down and our mouths shut," Peter replied. "And we stay clear of each other from now on, too."

"And the money?"

"Stay with the original plan and keep it hidden for now."

"Until when?"

"Until we all agree it's safe."

"Then when do we meet to decide that?" Reuben asked.

Peter sighed again. He was regretting starting up the group to do the robberies. "Meet back here in a month and we'll decide then. We should know what's going on with Jerry by that time." Poor Jerry. It really wasn't worth it.

"Okay," Matty said, levering himself to his feet. "In a month, then."

Reuben waited until the barn door had closed behind Matty before speaking. "Is Jerry going to be all right?"

"I don't know," Peter answered. He stared up at the gap between the top of a side wall and the roof where he could glimpse blue sky. "I really don't know."

"Hang in there, buddy," Reuben said, and clapped him on the shoulder before standing and stretching. "Maybe the evidence will go missing, or the place they keep it will burn down and they'll have to let him go."

"Yeah, right."

"You never know. Stranger things have happened."

Peter watched Reuben saunter to the door and disappear. He made no move to leave, embracing the dark silence of the old barn. The tiny patch of blue sky disappeared behind a cloud, breaking Peter's reverie. He sighed again and reached for his pocket, pulling out a small photo. He stared at the image for a moment, then caressed it with a gentle finger.

"I'm sorry Jerry, so sorry."

He wiped his misted eyes with the back of his hand and returned the photo to its hidden place. The energy to stand and leave had deserted him. His gaze found the gap in the wall again, and he sat staring out to the sky.

Chapter Seventeen

Sam leaned back in the chair and watched as Warren set up the chess pieces on the board. A familiar scene, one Sam wouldn't want to hazard a guess on how many times it had played out. Chess games with Warren were one of the constants in Sam's life. They'd had many discussions over the board, and tonight would be no exception. Warren had something on his mind and Sam was sure he knew what it was. His long friendship with him had also taught him to wait for Warren to bring up the subject. If there was one man who wouldn't talk when he didn't want to, it was the one sitting opposite him.

"Your move," Warren announced.

Sam studied the board, debating which move would lead to a game long enough for Warren to have time to say what he wanted to say. He glanced up, catching Warren staring at him from under his brows, then reached out and pushed a pawn forward. Game on.

Warren sat back and rested his chin on his long fingers, his face immobile as he stared at the board. A long silence, then a hand reached out to move a piece forward.

The game continued in silence for a while before Sam decided it was time to surprise his friend. He picked up a bishop and placed it where it could be taken by one of Warren's pawns.

Warren's brows rose. "That's a bold move."

Sam smiled. "It's an opportunity you shouldn't miss. Are you going to take it?"

Warren's eyes narrowed. "I'll have to assess the risks first."

Sam shrugged. "The risks are minimal. Do they outweigh the benefits?" He watched Warren's mouth curl.

"I'm beginning to think the benefits are too great to be ignored."

Sam chuckled. "I thought they might be. Do you want to hear what's on offer?"

"The truth?" Sam nodded. "I almost don't care what you're offering." Warren held up a hand. "Almost." The faint smile died, replaced with a slight frown. "I have a family to think of now."

Sam watched as his friend's face softened. He would give almost anything to be in Warren's shoes, but it wasn't to be. He and Heather were content now. They'd learned to live knowing there wouldn't be any kids. Sam would live fatherhood through Warren's experience.

"First, I want you to know I have spoken with Aden and Sarah, and they are in full agreement with what I am about to propose to you."

Warren nodded.

"We're offering a major role in the new contract providing investigative services for a large legal firm, and we're interested in you also assisting in other areas. We'd like you to work a minimum of seven days a fortnight, but if you want to be full time, that is fine too." Sam grinned. "I thought you might want to spend more time with Beth and the baby, you see." Warren's wide eyes told Sam he'd been right in that thought. "We each draw a salary from the business. It's not the rate you're on now, but it's still a decent amount." He named a figure. "If you want to buy into the Agency and be a partner, we're more than happy to discuss that too. Are you interested?"

Warren's eyes flicked up at him, full of amusement. "I am. You're offering me a chance to get back out doing investigations and being…useful, I guess is the word I want." He sighed. "I need to do some sums and talk to Beth about what she wants to do before I decide."

"Absolutely," Sam replied. "You'll have to do the necessary training and exam to get your PI license, but we can fast track it with your FBI experience taken into account. I'll get the paperwork underway while you do that, shall I?" Sam grinned at Warren's smile. "I thought so."

"I have to talk to Beth first."

"I know."

"And I'd have to give my notice in at the Bureau."

"Of course."

"And the baby…"

"If you join before the baby arrives, we'll work around any time you want to take off."

"So what's the negative? There has to be one."

"You'll still have to write reports."

Warren chuckled. "I can manage that."

"Good. Now are you going to make a move, or are you conceding the game?"

Warren packed away the chess board once Sam had lost to him—again—and left. Beth had gone to visit Sarah and Aden, and would be back soon. Warren looked at the clock on the kitchen wall. He wanted to take Sam's offer, but he wanted Beth's opinion first. He'd once asked her if he should have left the FBI when Sam did, and she'd unhesitatingly said he wasn't ready. And he hadn't been. Now he was. Did she know that? How would she feel about him being hands-on with investigations again, now they were starting a family?

The sound of Beth's key in the lock snapped him from his thoughts as he instinctively moved towards the door to greet her. She stepped into his arms and he drew her close. He kissed and released her.

"Do you want a cup of tea?" he asked. He wanted to start the discussion, but plunging in right here and now was not tactically wise.

"Yes please." Beth's blue eyes held his, and he leaned down to kiss her upturned mouth once more. Her soft lips on his wiped his mind of Sam's offer as he ignored everything but the woman he held.

"Mmm," she murmured when they broke the kiss. "My man."

"My Beth," he replied, kissing the tip of her nose. She laid her head on his shoulder once more, her face tucking into his neck and her warm breath fanning his skin. Contentment filled every corner of his soul.

"Were you going to make me a cuppa?" Beth asked, her question warming his skin with the breath it rode.

"I am," he said, loosening his hold on her. She slipped out of his arms and followed him as he headed for the kitchen. "How are the Youngs?"

"They're all well. Logan is growing so fast." Beth leaned against the kitchen counter, watching him as he filled the kettle. "I offered for us to babysit him when they go out in a couple of weeks for their anniversary."

Something very like fear took up residence in Warren's gut. He'd never had much to do with baby Logan before. "What if I drop him?"

"I think the question should be, what if I drop him?" Beth's amused look made him smile. "With my arm the way it is." She waved her bandaged wrist in the air.

The kettle boiled and Warren poured the steaming water over the tea bag in Beth's mug. "You've looked after him before. I haven't," he said.

"Warren, if I can do it, you can do it."

He reached for the fridge, extracting the milk and adding some to the mug. "I guess so, and I need the practice."

"It won't hurt."

He carried her mug back into the sitting room, putting it down on the coffee table. Beth waited for him to settle into his usual spot and then curled up at his side. It was a familiar routine, one they carried out almost every evening, and one he loved.

Warren leaned forward to pick up Beth's mug and passed it to her.

"How was your chess game?" she asked him after taking a sip of her drink.

"I won."

"I'd guessed that."

Warren smiled. "He wins sometimes."

"Even I've won on the odd occasion."

"Usually by distracting me."

"That's about the only way I can win," she said. "But I've never heard you complain about it."

He smiled. "No complaints here."

They lapsed into silence, Beth sipping her drink while Warren waited for the right time to bring up Sam's offer. When Beth rested her mug on her leg and tilted her head back to rest on the cushions of the sofa, Warren took the plunge.

"I had an interesting talk with Sam this evening."

"Oh?"

"He offered me a position in the agency."

"Again? He won't give up—you do know that, don't you?"

"I know. If I take an offer he might."

"Oh?"

Warren took a deep breath. Beth's reaction so far hadn't given him any sign of what she was thinking. "The offer he made is very good."

"And you want to take it?"

He still couldn't work out what she was thinking. "I'm considering it, but it's not a decision I want to make without hearing what you think."

"You want to know what I think?"

"Yes." His heart pounded in his chest as his muscles tensed. She wasn't giving anything away.

Then she smiled. "I once told you that you are a man of action and it's not in your nature to sit back and let others do everything." She turned her blue gaze on him. "I know the FBI is an important part of your life, or has been, but I don't think you enjoy it the way you used to. Your role is an important one and you're good at it, but as I said, you're a man of action, and sitting in meetings is slowly driving you mad." She sighed. "This move was inevitable and I think it's time. There is a part of me that wants you stay in the FBI." She shrugged. "You're not the only one who feels protective. If you become a PI you'll be back to taking risks, or more risks. I want you to be safe, but on the other hand I know you can look after yourself. If this means you enjoy your work again, then do it. But it has to be your decision, and your decision only." Her eyes crinkled as she smiled. "You will have my full support, whatever you decide."

"It will mean I won't be earning as much."

"But you'll be happy and that's what counts. I'm sure whatever you earn will be more than enough for us."

"And the baby."

"Yes, and the baby."

He hesitated before continuing. The last thing he wanted to do was to pressure Beth, but there was one question he needed answered before he accepted Sam's offer.

"What are your plans regarding work?" he asked.

"After the baby's born, you mean?"

"I don't want you to feel you have to return to work. If you'd rather stay at home and look after the baby, I'll support you."

Beth relaxed back into his side. "I will want to go back to work. I think I'd miss it too much if I don't, but I wouldn't want to return too quickly. Maybe take up to twelve months off." She glanced up at him, her forehead creased. "Is that okay? I don't want to put financial pressure on you to stay at the Bureau if you are ready to leave."

He reached out to smooth the puckered skin between her eyebrows. "We have enough money with our savings to cover any possible shortfall."

"Even with the cost of raising our child?"

"I think so."

The tension in his muscles drained away as Beth sighed and snuggled back against him. "That's settled then. When will you resign?"

"I need to settle things with Sam and the Youngs first, and I must give a month's notice."

"At least you won't be my senior anymore."

"Thank goodness."

"Too right."

He chuckled. Damn he loved this woman.

"So does that mean Sam will be your boss?"

"No. I want to go in as a partner. They're offering me the option to buy into the agency. And before you ask, yes, I'll have the money for that. With my payout of entitlements from the Bureau, I should have enough to cover it without touching our savings."

"Damn. I was looking forward to seeing Sam trying to tell you what to do." Beth chuckled, her body shaking against his. "I would buy tickets for that."

"Sorry to disappoint you." He was grinning himself as he imagined the scene. "Speaking of entitlements, Sam said I could take whatever time I needed when the baby arrives, and also said I could drop my hours back if I wanted to."

"Do you?" Beth's voice rose with surprise.

"I'd thought about it," he admitted.

"Well, I think you should, if you want to."

He slid his hand down to cover the child growing in her belly.

"Maybe I could look after the baby one day a week while you're at work." Did he just say that? Warren's gut tightened at the thought. He could do it. He'd have time to get the hang of it.

Beth's hand come to rest on his. "Sounds perfect."

Chapter Eighteen

It was as though someone had flicked the switch and the course of George's life changed.

The call came at daybreak as the sun peered over the horizon and crept across the land. The fresh morning air held a hint of damp earth as if the ground had been turned over and watered during the night. It enticed George out into it, but before he could step across the threshold, the sharp sound of the phone bell stopped him.

"Who the heck?" he muttered as he retreated into the depths of the house. A sudden chill ran through his skin, a premonition of bad news.

"Cole household," he announced into the receiver.

"Mr Cole?"

"Yes. Who is this?"

"Mr Cole, my name is Murphy. I'm the Warden at your son's prison."

The chill of premonition intensified, spreading through George's veins. The breath disappeared from his lungs, making speech impossible.

"Mr Cole, I'm very sorry to have to tell you that your son was attacked again last night. The guards responded immediately, but there was nothing they could do."

The tremors started deep in George's body, spreading out through his limbs. His weakened grip struggled to retain hold of the telephone.

"What?" His voice shook along with his body.

"I'm very sorry Mr Cole," Murphy said. "We did all we could, but he died."

He couldn't feel. Ice had taken over the fibre of his being.

"Mr Cole?"

George gathered his strength. "My boy's dead?" he whispered.

"I'm very sorry, Mr Cole. We've begun an investigation and his attackers will be brought to justice."

"My boy's dead," he whispered again, his brain stuck in an unending cycle of disbelief.

"Please pass on my condolences to your wife. We'll be in touch later for your instructions regarding funeral arrangements. Goodbye."

The phone went dead. George stared at it for a long minute before replacing the receiver in its cradle.

Daisy sat staring at the surface of the kitchen table, trying to understand. Why hadn't Jerry been kept safe? There had already been one attack, and closely following that, a second attack. Where had the guards been? Why hadn't anyone helped him?

The more she thought about it, the more the injustice carved a hole in her very core. It ate at her, a vast empty space now filling with anger; anger directed at the ones responsible for this tragedy. The prison guards and the ones who had caught Jerry and left him in the prison—the FBI. Something had to be done. The rest of the robbers were still uncaught, still free. But not Jerry. It wasn't right.

A maelstrom of emotion swirled like a tornado. An intense grief for what she'd lost twisted with fury at the impotence of those whose jobs it was to protect the vulnerable. She would find out their names. She would watch them to see if they took appropriate action, see if the other robbers were caught, and see what justice would be brought. Delays wouldn't be accepted. She wanted answers, and she wanted them fast.

First thing she needed was a list. Who was involved, and who was responsible. The attackers, the guards, the FBI. She paused and thought. The FBI was a large organisation. It would be difficult to find out exactly who was responsible for each area, like those who dealt with bank robberies, but surely the names of those higher up the list would be available, at least on the internet. She fumed again at the lack of results chasing the other robbers. If they found one, surely, they would find the others? Maybe she would have to help with that in her own way.

George watched her. She could feel his eyes boring into her, assessing her. How could she reach out to him? She was numb on the outside, and burning within. Yet he didn't see it, his own grief for his son clouding his mind. They were two people living in their own separate worlds, but in the same house. Jerry's death had come between them, changing their roles in their relationship. Daisy watched her husband as he shuffled around the kitchen making yet another cup of coffee. The strength and solidity she'd always felt him provide her was crumbling before her eyes. She felt it leave him and enter her, fuelling her anger and resolving her desire for revenge. Now she was the strong one, the defender of the family. Her heart now cold and hard as steel, the death of her beloved son robbing her of warmth and life. There was only one purpose left— to repay the debt of Jerry's death in full.

She needed a plan. She needed space to think, to allow ideas to come to her. George stood still, watching the kettle on the hob. Daisy's gaze wandered down his back, then to his hands resting on the counter. No, he wouldn't be of help to her. He wouldn't want to be a part of it. Her mouth tightened. Why hadn't she realised it before? She was the leader in their marriage, George the follower. She ran a successful business, he helped. He had taken the figurehead role, but she was the controlling brain. She had to keep him ignorant, or he would stop her.

"I'm going outside," she announced, pushing herself up from her chair.

George turned and frowned at her. "Shouldn't you rest?"

Daisy bit back an impatient response, answering quietly. "I want some time on my own, in peace."

She watched his face to see if he suspected anything. His eyes were dull with pain. "Okay then."

As she suspected, he had lost his strength. It was up to her.

Daisy let the front door slam shut behind her and made her way to the first of the sheds behind the hothouses. The door was chained and padlocked against intruders. Daisy wrestled with the stiff lock, wriggling and tugging until the bar came free. The rusty hinges groaned, echoing the pain in Daisy's heart as she opened the door and stepped through into the dim light.

She stopped and looked around the small space. The air was damp and musty, cobwebs linking the shelves to their contents. Dust danced in the feeble light penetrating the cold air; a crisscross of beams looked as though a haphazard motion sensor guarded the contents of the shed. Daisy moved through the beams, breaking their path, heading for a metal cabinet at the back. It wasn't locked, but the handle had rusted with disuse and opened reluctantly.

"Ah," she sighed as her eyes found what they sought.

"Don't even think about it." Peter's arm reached across Daisy's shoulder, pushing the door closed again.

She shut her eyes, her heart pounding loud in her chest as her fists clenched. "You scared me, Peter."

"And you're scaring me, Daisy. That dynamite is so old it's become unstable. You should get someone to dispose of it."

The hard grip of his fingers hurt as he hauled her around to face him. The shock of hearing his voice was nothing compared to the shock of his appearance. His grey skin stretched over the bones of his face, his once-bright eyes dulled and red rimmed. She reached up and touched his cheek.

"Oh Peter," she whispered. His eyes filled with tears as he grasped her hand in his. "You know?"

He nodded, his eyes misting with tears.

"We miss him, don't we? You and I, the two who knew him best."

He didn't answer her, his head lowered, her hand held in his. Daisy patted his shoulder and slipping her hand from his, turned back to the cupboard. "I'll make them pay."

The claw-like hands grabbed her shoulders again, pulling her back.

"Don't be foolish, Daisy," Peter said. "He wouldn't want you doing that. You'll only end up getting hurt yourself. And what about George?"

"George has no fight left."

"Then he needs you more than ever."

Daisy stared up into Peter's eyes. "Why did you do it? Why did you rob the bank?"

Peter shook his head. "I wish to God we hadn't." A tear ran down his cheek. "One of the others suggested it. They'd got away with another robbery years ago and said it was a good way to get money, and lots of it. We thought we had it worked out…" Peter's fingers dug into Daisy's arm. "Stupid, stupid, stupid. That's why we did it. We were the worst kind of idiots." Tears coursed down Peter's cheeks. "I'm so sorry."

A great agony rose through Daisy's body, tearing through her veins in violent, shaking waves. They broke against Peter's chest as he held her fast in his arms, hot tears soaking his shirt. She became aware of Peter's body shaking, sobs rising from his chest as they shared their grief; one for a son, and one for a lover.

Daisy wasn't sure why she had come up with the plan she had settled on, but it would give great satisfaction to fulfil it. Those who had led Jerry to his death would pay the price. A life for a life—wasn't that what the bible said?

It hadn't been hard to work out who else had been involved with the bank robbery. Jerry had several friends, but there were now noticeable absentees. Peter was one, but somehow Daisy didn't see him as the cause. Peter had loved Jerry and still did. If he had to be punished, then the grief he suffered punished him enough. He had lost the one thing he treasured, and now it was the turn of the others to lose something too.

Daisy wriggled the key in the filing cabinet lock. Another stiff lock. What was with locks these days?

"Just can't get quality anymore," she grumbled. Her old boot slammed into the bottom drawer, a multitude of black scuff marks showing the tale of many a swift kick dealt to the cream metal. "Finally." The key turned and Daisy pulled open the middle drawer, her fingers moving through the files hanging in green rows. A pause, then her hand dived in and extracted a buff folder. "Reuben."

"Are you all right in here? I heard a bang."

George's head appeared around the door, startling Daisy.

"I'm fine. Just looking up some records for the business," she replied.

"Don't overdo it."

His sad smile strengthened her resolve. "I won't, but I need to keep busy." Her own grief rose into her throat; a great lump swelling and aching. She tried to swallow it, but it refused to budge. George saw her distress and reached out, taking her hand in his. She gripped it hard, their gaze meeting for a long, message-filled moment.

"Would you like a cup of coffee?" George asked.

"That would be wonderful, thank you."

He flicked her a smile. "I'll bring it in for you."

Daisy closed the door behind him and turned back to the file. She shuffled to her desk and laid it down before lowering herself into her office chair. The file was slender, not containing more than the essentials, but the essentials were what Daisy was after. Address, and next of kin. If novels were anything to go by, he would have headed to home territory—somewhere he felt safe, somewhere he knew well. Daisy knew Reuben well enough to know he wasn't the brightest of men. She was confident he would have headed home, wherever that was.

Her finger traced down the sheet of paper in the front of the file. Reuben had lived nearby, but odds were, he wasn't there anymore. He hadn't turned up for work since Jerry had been arrested and she hadn't heard from him.

"Leesburg," she muttered. "Not far away, but how to contact him?"

The sound of George's nails clacking on the door handle warned her this time. She flipped the folder closed and turned the seat around.

"Coffee," he said, leaning forward to place the mug on her desk. Daisy noticed the tremble of the liquid as the mug moved past her. Reuben would pay for what he'd done to her men.

"Thank you, love."

George's mouth curved, a smile of pleasure. After all these years of marriage he still loved to do things for her. The smile warmed her frozen heart, but only for a moment.

"I'm going to feed the hens now," he said, giving her another quick smile before leaving the office.

Daisy stared at the door after he'd closed it. She had time to go to the nearby farm supplier and get what she needed.

"Fool," she muttered, shaking her head. She couldn't go to the local supplier to get everything. If they worked out what had happened, then she didn't need the cashier to remember what she'd bought. She'd have to go somewhere else, and use cash. If you used your card, they could trace it. A smile crept across her lips. Watching all those crime shows on TV was paying off. What else would she need? Some of those throw-away gloves? Wouldn't hurt. She would have to make sure she wore none of her work clothes when she carried out the plan. No clues to leave behind. The smile faded as the storm gathered on her brow. That damn woman in the FBI had led them straight to Jerry using the plants. Daisy debated adding her to the list. Was it worth the risk? How would she be able to find her, or even get close? All things that needed to be considered, but for now, Reuben was the man she wanted.

Daisy read the address on the file once more, then closed it. One thing at a time. She'd do a trial run, and she needed to contact Reuben. After that she'd set her plan in motion.

Chapter Nineteen

It made a satisfying whump; the ground trembled and dirt rained down around the area. A moment taken to wait, listening for a shout of surprise or for someone to call out, but there was nothing bar the rustle of wind through the trees.

"A few more minutes, just to be safe."

The seconds ticked by, but no one came. No sound of human movement at all. The test was undiscovered. Rising from the protected spot and scanning the forest showed it was clear—there was no one else around. The detonation site wasn't far away and was reached quickly. Soil that had been piled on top of the explosive had been scattered around, but that was to be expected. The hole it had rested in was larger; that too, expected. It was the size of the hole that caused satisfaction. Just right. Large enough to cause chaos, but not so large as to cause widespread damage. Anyone standing too close might not fare well, but with careful planning, the area would be clear when the next explosion erupted.

To be sure of requirements, the impact area was paced and noted, and an assessment of the amount of damage caused by the explosive completed. It was perfect. The broad smile dawned again. A successful test; now for the real deal.

The bag used to carry the components to the site now collected, it was time to head back. A few minutes dodging trees and the path came in sight. There was still no sign of other people in the area. It was all clear. It was an easy matter to step out of the trees, onto the track, and head down towards the car.

The scenery passed went unnoticed. All thoughts were on the campaign planned and now ready to execute. It hadn't taken long for the idea to grow or the plans to be made. The initial target had to be rejected and an alternative decided upon. Security around the original target could have been overcome, but not in the timeframe that was necessary. The alternative would be more enjoyable to execute and the resulting chaos would exact all the revenge desired. Almost. The spark of happiness dimmed in the mind, leaving sadness and grief. Life was unfair, and someone would pay. The pain would be eased knowing others shared it.

Voices drifted up the track, breaking into thoughts. A group of people by the sound of loud conversation and laughter. There was no alarm in the noise, so it was unlikely they had heard the explosion. They would not remember one solitary walker.

The voices grew louder and flashes of colour showed through the greens and browns of the forest. A group of brightness, moving through the undergrowth. The colours took form as the path led closer. A glance in their direction was enough to identify them. A group of students, out on a field trip. The age put them in college, the older people probably tutors or professors. Another furtive glance; the male tutor was looking and then looked away. No eye contact. That was good. The path emerged abruptly in a small clearing. A right turn, and it was a short stroll to the parked car. Success for part one.

Mick stared after the figure disappearing down the track.
"What's the matter?" Rennie asked him.
"Don't know. Something about..." he shrugged. "It's nothing."

Rennie followed Mick's gaze. "They're gone now, so you can stop squinting down the road. It's time to move on to the next location or we won't finish in time."

Mick pursed his lips for a moment, then as his face relaxed, he shrugged again and turned back to the students.

"Okay everyone, grab your things, we're moving on."

Chapter Twenty

The ground shuddered underfoot and Daisy landed on the damp ground, tasting wet leaves and earth as her face buried itself in the landscape. Soil pattered around her, then silence. Time passed. Her right eye took in the limpness of the leaf filling her vision as her brain ticked over, making sense of the world. A sudden fear swamped her. Her brain, suddenly switched on, screamed at her to move, but her body refused. The world looked normal, but something wasn't right, and her brain knew it. Her body refused to budge, so she gave up the fight and closed her eyes, surrendering to whatever danger was around.

A drop landed on her cheek and slid down to the corner of her nose. She twitched as it tickled its way along the valley, to her eye. Its torment made her move her hand to relieve her skin. Daisy opened her eyes. The leaf remained in front of her right eye, blocking her vision. She brushed it away and stared up at the darkening sky. The surrounding trees waved their branches in the breeze, the sound of rustling leaves soothing her. Daisy stretched out her legs and arms before rising to sit up. A feeling of unease settled in her stomach, reminding her that all was not as it should be. She could remember the thump under her feet and looked around to see if danger was obvious.

"Nothing. You foolish old woman," she muttered. "Get up before you stain your clothes."

The dampness of the leaves seeped through the knees of her jeans as she rolled onto them to get off the ground. Once on her feet, she smoothed her hair and pulled her sweater down over her hips. It was then she noticed the loose earth lying on the ground before her.

"What on earth…?"

Daisy crept forward, her eyes fixed on the soil scattered around. She continued forward, curiosity quenching any fear. She topped a small rise in the ground and found the source. Daisy stared, her mind trying to process the images her eyes sent it. A body, torn apart from the centre. Shredded skin, blobs of red and white spread over the surrounding ground. Daisy spun and staggered away as fast as she could, her eyes seeing only the image her mind replayed. Time and time again she collided with trees and bushes as she fled the mangled remains in the woods. She recognised the eyes that had stared up at her from the bloodied remains. Reuben. What had she done?

Beth stepped back and surveyed her work. A welling sense of achievement filled her, and she sighed with pleasure.

The dark polished wood of the dining table glowed from under the crisp navy-blue napkins arranged on the white side plates. Silver cutlery gleamed under candles in elegant silver holders, and wine glasses, polished free of fingerprints, reflected the surrounding arrangement. She sighed, leaning forward to nudge a fork into line.

"Table done, tick," she said, and turned to the kitchen. Beef roasted in the oven, the smell causing a rumble of anticipation from Beth's stomach. "Not yet," she muttered, patting her tummy. "Potatoes, vegetables, ready to go on," she continued. "Apple pie ready to go in the oven. Right," she said, sweeping her gaze around the kitchen, "time to get changed."

Beth walked up to their bedroom and opened her closet door.

"Hmmm."

Her hands flicked through the garments hanging up, lingering on a black cocktail dress, then moving onto a navy-blue dress with a full skirt and sleeveless top.

"Perfect."

Beth undressed, then slid the dress over her head, allowing it to settle around her. The colour brought out the vivid blue of her eyes. It was not too dressy, but not casual either. She swung her hips, and the skirt swayed around her legs. Navy blue pumps to match, then into the bathroom.

"A touch of mascara." She wielded the tiny brush, deft movements enhancing her lashes. "A touch of gloss." Her lips shone, full and inviting. "Hair." Beth ran her fingers through her long, dark curls. "As is, I think." She gave her reflection an approving nod and headed back down to the kitchen.

After donning an apron to protect her dress, Beth took the beef out of the oven and basted it, added the potatoes, and returned it to the oven.

The sound of a key in the apartment door had Beth flinging off the apron and walking out to meet Warren. He took her in his arms and kissed her.

"There is nothing better than coming home to you," he said. "Is that roast beef I smell?"

"It sure is," Beth answered, squeezing his waist.

His strong fingers lifted her chin, and he kissed her again, this time a long and tender kiss that left her floating. He released her, and went over to his desk, dropping his briefcase by its side. His firearm was placed into the lockable drawer and secured.

"Can I get you a drink?"

"I'll have a juice, thanks," he replied.

"A juice?"

He chuckled. "A juice."

"Are you okay?"

This time he laughed. "I'm fine." His smile softened. "We're pregnant, so no alcohol."

"You can still have it!"

"I don't want to. I want to go through this pregnancy with you." He shrugged. "Besides, I don't like drinking wine when you are only drinking water or juice."

Beth stood on tiptoes to kiss him. "Juice it is."

Beth followed Warren as he carried the apple pie to the table. She waited for him to set it down before putting the jug of cream beside it.

"How big a piece would you like?" she asked, hovering the knife over the dish.

"Not a small one." He inhaled as she pierced the crust, slicing though the pastry. "That smells so good."

Beth lifted the slice out of the pan and dropped it neatly onto a plate. As she passed it to him, she knocked his glass, making it wobble.

"Oops." She thrust out her hand to steady it, but only made matters worse as she hit the glass, making it tilt and topple over. Warren reached out with a napkin to stem the flow of water as Beth tried to do the same. Their hands clashed, Beth trying to snatch hers out of the way, but connecting this time with a candle. The water mopping turned into a minor firefighting exercise before they ended up standing beside a wet and smoking table.

Beth stared at the mess she'd made of her beautiful setting, then raised her eyes to meet Warren's. Instead of the annoyance she expected, his eyes danced with amusement. Her own smile started, and then she giggled. An answering chuckle from Warren, and they launched into roars of laughter.

"My pie has gone cold," Warren managed eventually, starting Beth into more gusts of laughter. She mopped her eyes, circling the table to step into his arms.

"I'll warm it up for you, my brave firefighter," she said, still trying to catch her breath.

His chuckle vibrated in his chest. "It's been a night to remember."

Beth pulled out of his arms to survey the mess again. "At least it was only the napkin that burned, not the table."

"I guess we should be thankful for that."

She slid back against his chest, savouring the warmth of him. "We have a lot to be thankful for."

She felt his muscles shift as his arms tightened. "We sure do," he said. He kissed her nose. "Why don't you go into the sitting room while I make hot drinks."

"Do you want a hand?"

His expression as he glanced at the dining table had her chuckling.

"I think you should sit down and leave me to the dangerous tasks," he replied.

"Maybe you're right." The amusement she felt kept her grinning as she headed into the lounge room and sank onto the sofa. She had planned a perfect evening, but despite the drama, it was working out. The happy bubble of contentment Warren gave her swelled and blossomed in her heart. She couldn't ask for more from life.

The love of her life walked into the room bearing two mugs.

"Here you go, Beth," he said, placing a mug on the coffee table. "Be careful."

"Yeah, yeah."

Warren lowered himself into his corner of the sofa and raised his arm for her to curl into his side. Beth leaned against him, enjoying the solidity of his strong frame and the protective arm wrapped around her. After a few minutes, she noticed his fingers strumming on the arm of the sofa.

"Something on your mind?"

She felt rather than heard his sigh.

"Something doesn't feel right."

"With what?"

His fingers tapped faster. She waited for him to answer.

"I don't know."

"Gut feeling?"

"Yes."

"Work or home related?"

His arm tightened, holding her fast. "Not home, thank God. That would drive me crazy if I thought you were in danger." His hand came up to cup the side of her head and draw it to his chest. Warren's heart pounded under her ear. She slid her arm across his belly, holding onto him.

"Then it's work related."

"I think so." The hesitation in his voice surprised her. When it came to his gut feelings, he could usually nominate a cause.

"Is it something else then?" His body shifted under her hand.

"I don't know."

The small movements under her hand told her of his frustration without any need to look at his face. And he hated not knowing. His chest rose and fell with another sigh.

"It'll come to me. I only know it's not about you."

"That's something then." She slid her hand back across his belly, feeling his abs contract under her touch. A fire lit deep down inside her, her breath shortening as her heartbeat picked up in response.

She slid her hand higher, quickly undoing a button of his shirt and moving her hand onto his skin. She heard the intake of breath as he responded to her touch, his own arm tightening around her.

"Beth," he whispered as his fingers lifted her chin.

She looked into his brown eyes, now glowing as if reflecting the fire burning in her body. A moment of stillness, then his head lowered and their lips met. A strong hand found her thigh and lifted it so her leg lay across his lap. She broke the kiss, her heart pounding with desire, and pushing herself up, she slid onto his lap.

His hands cupped her butt, pulling her firmly against him as his mouth found hers once more, and they became lost in their desire for each other.

Chapter Twenty-One

Warren received the report of the bombing from Jones at the Critical Incident Response Group as he arrived at his office after a meeting mid-afternoon. His gut went into overdrive, sending signals that had him cancelling his plans. Within minutes he was heading to Quantico and the Bomb Disposal Squad. He strode unannounced into Special Agent in Charge Loman's office, catching the man off guard.

"Sir," Loman said, springing to his feet. "I wasn't expecting you."

"Relax Loman. I'm interested in this so I came down. Tell me what you know."

Warren dropped into the chair opposite Loman's desk and watched him gather his thoughts. Loman never rushed into anything—a good quality for someone who dealt with explosives.

"A single explosive detonated late yesterday afternoon in a forested area known as Red Rocks Park, just outside Rockville. The explosion was reported by a couple walking in the park at the time. The local sheriff's department attended to locate the scene and make it safe while they waited for our guys to turn up."

Warren nodded. He knew this bit from the report that had been sent to him.

Loman continued. "A deceased male was located at the scene. Preliminary cause of death was an explosion near his abdomen. It took out his torso, leaving the extremities."

Warren's eyes narrowed, watching Loman, whose face had turned to stone. A natural reaction in someone who would have seen death many times before—a defensive mechanism so many of them had. "Go on."

Loman sighed. "At first we thought it may have been self-inflicted. There were no signs of a struggle in the area, and no signs he'd been dragged there. But forensics found at least two sets of footprints and the remains of rope on the deceased. They think he may have been holding the device and his arms tied to his body." Loman grimaced, no doubt imagining the scene as Warren was. "We haven't been able to identify the deceased yet, but I anticipate that will happen soon."

"Other forensics?"

"Being analysed. One set of footprints belonged to a woman we think; small and shallow. Maybe he walked out there with her."

"And she tied him up? A woman against a man?"

Loman shrugged. "It's possible. She could have knocked him out first."

Warren grunted. "Explosive?"

"Dynamite. From the impact of the blast we think one stick."

Warren leaned forward. "Thank you, Loman. Keep me informed."

"Yes sir."

Warren stood up and left the office, heading out to the afternoon sun. The itch to be more involved in investigations sent him striding along the path between the tactical response building and the labs. He loved the FBI, and it had given him so much, but he no longer felt he contributed meaningfully.

He stepped into shadow and pushed open the door of the labs. As he was already here, he might as well drive his wife home.

"Afternoon sir," the receptionist greeted him.

"Afternoon."

Warren turned away from the elevators and headed for the stairs. He took them two at a time, emerging on the floor containing Beth's lab. The only concern he had about leaving was he could no longer keep an eye on Beth. He wasn't directly in charge of her Division, but any incident that occurred involving his wife was reported to him instantly. It was more a matter of respect than fear, but it certainly sped up the lines of communication.

The door of her lab was closed and Warren slowed as he approached. No caution sign hung on the door, but he stopped and looked through the window before attempting to enter. His wife sat on a stool at her bench, a younger woman beside her. The other woman peered into the microscope as Beth spoke, then broke to look up at Beth who was explaining something with drawings she traced in the air. The woman nodded as Beth finished and looked into the microscope once more.

Warren's frown smoothed as he watched his wife at work. Her reputation as a skilled scientist was a constant source of pride for him. She worked hard to be the best she could, and it paid off.

Warren's cell phone rang in his pocket.

"Sir, we have an identity for the explosion victim. His name is Reuben Leach."

"Isn't he...?"

"Yes sir, he's wanted for questioning over the bank robbery."

"Right. Share the information you have with the investigating team. I'm heading over there shortly."

Warren looked up at Beth, who was helping the other woman pack away the materials they had been working on. He couldn't wait so he stepped up to the door and knocked before entering.

"Sorry to interrupt," he said.

"That's okay. We had finished," Beth replied, smiling at him. The smile in her eyes died as she stared into his, reading the urgency in them. She turned to her companion. "I'll put them back in the evidence locker, Josie. Let me know if you have any questions."

"Thank you, Dr Pearce," the other woman said and gave Warren a tiny smile as she left the lab.

"What's up?" Beth asked, as soon as the door closed behind Josie. "I wasn't expecting you here today."

"I had a change of plans and I thought I might drive you home."

The smile she gave him warmed him all over. "Great idea."

"Are you right to leave now?"

"I need to put this away," she said, waving at the box on the bench. "It'll only take a couple of minutes, but I can still get a ride with Elliot if you're in a hurry."

"I can wait." The truth was he'd rather drive her home any chance he could. Always protective, his instinct to look after her was in overdrive now she was pregnant with their child. He watched as she finished packing the evidence away, locking it in a cabinet. There was no sign of the dizziness, her neat movements unaffected. She pulled out her cell phone and sent a message.

"Just let Elliot know you're taking me home, and I'm ready," she said as she picked her bag up from her desk.

Warren held the door open for her and they left the lab. He forced his pace to match hers, the temptation to stride faster under strict control.

"I'm holding you up, aren't I?"

She hadn't missed a step as she made her comment.

"No. Well, not really."

She smiled at him as they arrived at the elevator. "You're almost humming with the need to get moving. You should have let me get a ride with Elliot."

"I need to head to the Field Office, but I want to take you home first."

The elevator pinged, and the doors slid open.

"Okay," she replied as they joined the others already in the carriage. They didn't speak again until they were clear of the building and out of earshot of others. "I appreciate you looking after me."

He knew that, but hearing her say it made him proud. Feminists wouldn't be happy about it, but it worked for him and Beth. She was still independent and strong, but she allowed him to take care of her, and he loved doing just that. Just as she took care of him. A marriage, a partnership they both agreed on.

"I would do anything for you." He spoke quietly, but sincerely.

She smiled and her hand sought his. "And I for you," she replied.

Once they had driven away from Quantico and joined the stream of traffic heading into DC, Warren spoke again. "Has Kamal asked you about full time work again?"

"No, he hasn't."

"What do you want to do?" Warren risked a glance at Beth as she stared out through the windscreen.

"I don't want to work full time. I want to spend time looking after our child."

"Then don't do it."

"What if they can't find someone to take on the few extra days and fill John's role?"

"They will have to."

"But what if they can't?"

"Maybe they can outsource."

"I'd have to do the call-outs."

He glanced at her again and smiled as their eyes caught. "We can work around that when necessary."

Beth shrugged. "I guess the forensic teams will step up when they can." She shifted in her seat. "When are you planning on handing in your resignation to the FBI?"

"I need to discuss that with Sam and the others."

"Are you excited about it?"

"About being self-employed and getting back to the basics of investigative work?"

"Yes, about that."

"I am."

"Good." Beth paused, her hand moving to rest on his thigh, warming his skin through the fabric of his trousers. "That's why you're impatient now, isn't it? You're getting involved in an investigation."

He sighed. He wished. "Only a small bit. I still have my job to do, and I need to leave the agents to do their work or they'll think I don't trust them."

"It's better than nothing. I'd rather you did something you enjoyed."

A sudden uneasy feeling hit. "You don't mind me leaving you alone for a while this evening while I go to the Field Office?"

"Of course not. I have things to do at home, and I'll do them faster if you're not under my feet. And I think I'll start driving myself again tomorrow."

"Are you sure?"

"Yes. The dizziness seems to be better, and while my arm twinges every now and then, it's not enough to stop me driving."

Warren rested a hand over the one lying on his thigh. "So long as you're sure. You can always get a lift at any time."

"I know."

They drove for a few minutes in silence.

"What about Isaac?" Beth asked.

"Who's Isaac?" Warren had no idea what she was talking about.

"As a boy's name. Isaac."

"Hmm, no."

"Andreas?"

"No."

"Matthias?"

Warren slid her a look from the corner of his eyes. She looked serious, but he wasn't sure.

"No."

"Habakkuk?"

Now he knew she was joking. "Not bad, but he might get teased, don't you think?"

"Maybe you're right."

Warren chuckled. "Got any more unusual names you want to try on me?"

Out of the corner of his eye he saw her smile spread. *Here she goes.*

"Gunther?"

"No."

"Hulbert?"

"No."

"Narcissus?"

"No." He was enjoying this.

"Probus?"

He laughed. "No."

"Skelly?"

"No."

"No?"

"No to all the above." He chuckled. "Got anything a little more traditional?"

"Traditional?"

"Yes. Traditional. I don't want to be adventurous with our child's name."

"Let me think. I've always liked Dominic."

"Dominic. Not bad."

"You like it?"

He glanced at her again, catching her look of surprise. "Were you joking again?"

"Actually no, I wasn't. I just didn't expect you to like it."

"I do. Dominic. Dominic Pearce. I like it."

"Matilda or Dominic." He heard her sigh of contentment, his smile uncontainable in response.

"Matilda or Dominic," he repeated. His child had a name.

Chapter Twenty-Two

Warren strode into the DC Field Office after dropping Beth at home and was met by SAC Burns.

"We have the information from the bomb unit, thank you, sir. The agents are going through it now." Burns opened the door of the investigation room, allowing Warren to pass through first. "At least we know where one of the robbers is."

"What about the others? Do you know who they are?"

"We do." Burns pointed at an image from the bank taken during the robbery by a security camera. "This one, working the tellers, is our dead friend." He pointed. "And the other man covering the customers is Peter Hill. The man working the tellers is Matthew Atkins. Hill has priors for shoplifting and MVT and was a close friend of Jerry Cole. Atkins has no recorded convictions, but has been arrested a few times and his prints are on file." Burns drew a deep breath. "Atkins worked at the orchid nursery and hasn't been seen since Cole was arrested. Nor has their truck driver, a Joshua Macintosh. We believe he drove the getaway car to where the swap vehicle was hidden. The truck at the nursery was searched, but as it is cleaned after every use, we don't have great hopes for any evidence."

"Blood?"

"Nothing yet. We've been back out to the farm and interviewed Mr and Mrs Cole, but they seem bewildered and were of little help."

"Genuine or faked?"

"I think they had their suspicions. They cooperated, but I don't think they will be able to help us further."

Warren, remembering his meeting with George Cole, was inclined to agree. "How's their business going?"

"Everything was quiet at the nursery. Both the Coles were inside when we arrived. I think the loss of their son has knocked the stuffing out of them."

Warren stood staring at the board. Photos, timelines, and snippets of information; all laid out before him for analysis. "Do they have any dynamite at the nursery?"

"We've checked the search report. There was a couple of ancient sticks in a locker. Mr Cole was advised to get an expert to remove them as they would be unstable."

Warren felt his blood go cold. George and the bomb threat. "Did you check if they were still there?"

"Yes sir. They were still there. We arranged for someone to collect them while we were there, so they have been disposed of now."

"Did they say why it was there in the first place?"

"They had some old stumps blasted when they set up the new greenhouses several years back. An old friend did it for them and left the unused dynamite at the nursery as the Coles had paid for it. Mr Cole had forgotten it was there."

"Verified?"

"The old friend is dead, but his wife remembered enough to verify the story."

Warren watched Burns as the SAC ran his eye over his working agents. He showed no resentment at being questioned about the investigation by senior management. Unusual. Most SACs would take offense, believing he doubted their abilities.

"We're closing in on the remaining robbers and the driver. We need to get to them before another explosive goes off."

"You saw the footprint information?"

"Yes sir. The only female currently in the investigation is Daisy Cole, but we need to wait on further forensic results. It may be a small man."

Burns was right. They needed more information, but it was too early to expect that yet. Time to go home to Beth.

"Thank you, Burns. Keep me informed."

"Of course, sir."

Warren's mind whirred as he made his way back to his car. So many possibilities, and until they had more information, they couldn't even speculate as to a motive. But damn it felt good to be involved again. He would have liked to have stayed longer, but a few noses would be put out of joint by his visit tonight—his replacement in his old position as Assistant Director one of them. He shrugged. It would not be his problem much longer. He unlocked his car and climbed in. Before he started it, he pulled out his cell phone and dialled.

"Sam. You home tonight? Mind if I drop up to see you? I want to do business."

Chapter Twenty-Three

George peered into the bedroom.

"Daisy love, do you want a cup of coffee?"

The stillness greeting his query confused him. "Daisy?" His shaking fingers found the light switch and flicked in on. Nothing. The emptiness of the room swamped him with relief. He would rather she wasn't there than she was and deadly still.

The relief lasted only moments, replaced by worry.

"Where are you, Daisy?"

The silent room returned no answer as George stared at the bed, thoughts churning. Had she not gone to bed for a nap as she'd said she would? He shook his head; no, he could remember hearing her go up the stairs. She had been in bed when he'd left the house, but where was she now?

George headed for the greenhouses. "That's where she'll be," he muttered as he crossed the grass to the nearest greenhouse. He stuck his head through the opening. The neat rows of orchid plants stretched out before him. The blooms stood still in the calm air, seeming to be frozen in place. Their beauty was lost on him now. It meant nothing.

"Daisy?" His voice quivered on a high note. "Daisy?"

There was no response. George scanned the beds and peered under the trestles supporting them. No sign of her. He staggered out and across to the second greenhouse. The same frozen scene met his eyes, but again no sign of Daisy.

George stood staring, his mind refusing to focus. Where was Daisy?

"Daisy? Daisy?"

George called again and again, circling the greenhouses and around to the sheds and old barn.

"Daisy? Where are you?"

Daisy leaned back on the park bench as watched the people pass her by. None of them looked at her, none of them seemed to notice she was there. They strode on, eyes fixed on phones, the sidewalk; anything but another human. Suited her fine. Her thoughts drifted back to Jerry's funeral the day before. They'd laid him to rest near her parents' graves. His coffin was covered by all the flowers she could find in the beds of the nursery. Every single bloom. Her vision misted as tears gathered and rolled down her cheeks. The pain was almost too much to bear, but she had to be strong. There were things that needed to be done yet.

She had to wait awhile before he came, but it paid off. A beat-up old pickup truck rounded a corner and drew to a stop on the opposite curb. The driver twisted his head, searching the people walking along the sidewalk, his gaze coming to rest on her.

Daisy waited for him to move, her heartbeat racing. Would he approach her, or would he drive away? As she watched, he pulled a cap on, low over his eyes, and opened the door, sliding out to the road. Daisy's heart picked up another notch as she watched him cross the road to her bench. He nodded, then sat down beside her. She could feel the tension in his body radiate out as his eyes shifted back and forth; watching, following.

"I have what you need, Matty," she whispered.

His eyes stopped their restless seeking and came to rest on her face. "Thank you, Daisy. I appreciate you doing this for me after everything that's happened."

"I'm not doing it for you, I'm doing it for Jerry. He wouldn't have wanted me to leave you to suffer." She pushed the carrier bag full of food she'd been nursing into his arms.

"Have you heard from any of the others?" he asked.

"I saw Peter once, but that's it. Do you know where they are?" Daisy held her breath. Her attempts to find Mac had been fruitless, and she was praying Matty knew where he was.

"No. Haven't seen them." He swallowed. "I sure am sorry about Jerry."

Daisy clenched her fists, her nails digging into her skin. "I know."

Matty patted her arm. "I have to go."

Daisy nodded. "Goodbye."

Warren listened to the information being relayed through the phone. Rigid muscles in his jaw and a gathering frown didn't ease when he hung up the call. Another bomb. This one had happened on the outskirts of a small town just outside DC. A pickup truck was torn apart as it drove along a quiet road. The verbal report had been brief, the investigators on their way at the request of local law enforcement.

His eyes rested on a file to one side of his desk. It couldn't be a coincidence, not this close to the last detonation. Was the victim one of the names on the list in the file? Were there any witnesses? If it was linked to the robbery, who had the motive and knowledge to carry out the bombings? The rapid tattoo of his fingers drummed on his desk as his brain spun.

"Sir?"

Lisa's voice came from the doorway, startling him out of his thoughts.

"Sir, you have a meeting starting in five minutes."

His brow cleared. "Thank you, Lisa."

She smiled and then withdrew, leaving Warren to prepare for his meeting with the Director. He'd been lucky to get time with him so soon, and he had no intention of wasting it.

Warren unhooked his jacket from the back on his chair and slid his arms into it, shrugging his shoulders to settle it correctly. A smile curved his lips as he opened his top drawer and reached for an envelope. His hand stilled, hovering over it.

"Are you sure? There's no going back," he whispered to himself.

The smile grew and his hand closed on the envelope, lifting it out of the drawer.

"So, John is definitely not returning?"

Kamal shook his head. "No."

"I'm not surprised. He went through a lot."

Kamal's eyes narrowed as he looked at her. "You've been through a lot too in your time."

Beth's tummy tightened at the reminder of past events. "That's true, but I've only been in real danger once, and even then, I knew rescue was on the way." She looked down at her wedding band and twisted it on her finger, remembering. After a moment she looked up at Kamal. "I'm not willing to work full time."

"I can't say I'm surprised, but I am disappointed."

Beth watched Kamal for signs of annoyance, but there weren't any.

"You could always outsource some of the work the technicians can't do."

"We could. Call-outs are a different thing."

"The other forensic team members and any agent with some training can do the basic evidence gathering." Beth saw a gleam of amusement emerge in Kamal's eye. "You knew I would say all of this, didn't you?"

The gleam turned into a grin. "I was clinging to a tiny hope you would increase your days, but yes, I was sure this conversation would run as it is." The smile faded, and he drew a long breath, letting it out with a sigh. "I would like you to be available for the more complicated call-out cases. Is that possible? Barring your maternity leave period, that is." Kamal flicked open a folder on his desk. "The Arboretum have indicated they are willing to assist with supplying a botanist while you're away, but it's only a short-term solution."

Beth nodded. "The call-outs shouldn't be a problem."

"Thank you, Beth. I appreciate it.

George heard the car's tyres scrunching on the gravel and turned to watch Daisy's arrival. She parked on the far side of George's truck, blocking her from his sight. He couldn't make out what she was doing in the car, but she didn't immediately emerge. He craned his neck, trying to see through his truck. Daisy's head bobbed, then rose as she swung open the door and stepped out. He watched her head move along his truck to the back of her car, and then the lid of the trunk swung into sight. Daisy's head disappeared, then reappeared. An extended arm pulled the lid down and she turned to walk away from the house and behind a greenhouse.

George stared after her for a moment. A quick nod of decision, and he left the room to follow her. He reached the car; Daisy was out of sight. A quick press and the trunk lid rose again, but there was nothing there. The lid closed with a thunk, and he headed down the side of the greenhouse.

"Daisy?" He couldn't see her when he reached the far end, and there was no response to his call. The doubt sitting in his mind became a twist of unease in his gut. "Daisy?"

The clang on metal on metal reached him and he headed towards its source. "Daisy?" He rounded the corner of the barn and saw her at the door of the old shed. "Daisy!"

Daisy spun around, the lock hitting the ground with a thud.

"There you are, George."

"I've been home for a while. I thought you were asleep, but you'd gone when I came home." He watched her face, seeking her thoughts.

She didn't answer him right away, picking up the lock and concentrating on fastening it on the shed door. Her face showed nothing.

"What were you doing in the shed, and where have you been?" His unease grew at the set look of her face. No emotion showed; even her eyes were lifeless. "Daisy? Are you all right?"

Something moved across her face; some deep thought or feeling, gone before he could understand it.

"I'm fine, George. I was putting something away."

She didn't meet his gaze and moved back towards the house.

"Where have you been?" George's heart pounded, both wanting and not wanting to know the answer.

She finally met his gaze. "I went for a drive. I needed some time to think over things." Her look dared him to doubt.

George took a breath and then released it without speaking. Sometimes it was better not to know. He hadn't seen her while he'd been out himself, so she wouldn't know where he'd been. The unease became worry. "Come inside and I'll make you a cup of coffee," he said.

Daisy smiled, and they walked back to the house together.

Chapter Twenty-Four

Warren wrestled with his conscience for all of ten minutes before he stood and left his office.

"I'll be out for a while," he said as he passed Lisa's desk.

"Sir, will you return for the meeting scheduled after lunch?"

Warren's teeth clamped shut on a hasty response. Even though he'd now handed in his resignation, the Director was yet to formally accept it, and he still had a job to do. "I'll be back in time for that."

"Thank you, sir."

He hesitated, debating whether to tell Lisa of his decision. She'd been his assistant for many years and should hear of his resignation from him, not the office grapevine.

"Lisa, this morning I gave the Director my resignation from the FBI. He hasn't yet given a formal acceptance, but I'll be leaving in a month."

Lisa's mouth dropped open, her eyes wide. "Sir?" She blinked, collecting herself. "Do you mean it?"

"Yes."

She blinked again, several times, and swallowed. "I'm sorry to hear that, sir. I'll miss you."

Warren watched in horror as tears welled in Lisa's eyes and rolled down her cheeks. His instinct to leave, fast, was stopped by compassion for his assistant. He glanced around, found a box of tissues and picked them up to offer to Lisa.

She took one and gulped as she dried her tears. "I'm sorry, sir. It's a shock. I never expected you to leave until you had to." Her lips trembled, and she grabbed another tissue as the tears flowed again. "What am I going to do when you leave?" Her shoulders shook as she sobbed into the tissue in her hand.

Warren glanced around, seeking someone who could help, but there was no one in sight. Lisa's head was bowed over her desk as she continued to stem the flow of tears.

"Er," he said, and placed the tissue box on the desk in front of Lisa. "I'm sorry, but I need to get going." He turned and strode out of the suite and down the hall to the stairs. Once in the cool concrete stairwell, he took a couple of deep breaths. He'd not seen that reaction coming. Abandoning her probably wasn't the best way to deal with it, but he had no idea what to do and he figured if he left her alone she would have time to compose herself. He'd dealt with many other women in tears, but it was different when it was a part of an investigation and he could distance himself; offer comfort without it being personal. The only woman he would comfort on a personal level was his wife. Warren smiled to himself as he ran down the stairs. He would leave the FBI, he would do what he wanted, and he would spend more time with Beth. Life was looking up.

"You're back, sir."

Warren assessed Burns' mood, searching for resentment, and decided to get straight to the issue. "Is that a problem Burns?" He watched the resulting struggle of thoughts pass across Burns' face. Interesting that the man didn't hide his thoughts from him as he knew a good SAC could. He waited for the answer.

"That depends on why you're here."

Warren kept the smile at bay. "I'm not here to check up on you or your agents."

Burns allowed his smile to escape. "In that case sir, you're welcome. Come through to the investigations room."

Warren didn't move to follow Burns immediately. Burns stopped after a few steps and turned back to him, his brows raised.

"Sir?"

"You accept my presence, even welcome it. Most SACs would resent someone like me wanting to take part in an investigation under their control. Why?"

"Why?" Burns chuckled and shook his head. "Sir, you really don't know why?"

The uncertainty Burns' words caused was something Warren wasn't used to. What did he mean? Did Burns want to make use of his connections?

"Why don't you explain it, Burns?"

The smile died from Burns' face. "Because you're the best," he replied, and then turned and walked to the investigations room.

Warren stared after him, his mind working to accept the compliment. A rosy glow he identified as a mixture of pride and humble gratitude welled in him, strengthening his determination to help Burns and his agents to the full. This was his motive for being an agent in the first place, and the realisation that his skills were appreciated gave him a sense of purpose he hadn't felt for a long time.

Shaking himself from his stunned immobility, Warren hastened to join Burns.

"We've received the preliminary information from the bomb squad," Burns said as Warren joined him at the long table. Burn slid a piece of paper across so Warren could read it.

"Single victim, male. Explosion occurred while the vehicle was moving and it subsequently crashed into a tree. Cause of death was the explosive, not the crash." Warren felt his face assume its familiar impassiveness as he read the description of the scene. "Definitely aimed at the victim personally, not a general destruction of the vehicle."

"And your hunch was right, sir. The vehicle is registered to Matthew Atkins, one of the suspects in the robbery case."

"Too much of a coincidence for it to be anything else." He looked up at Burns. "Two bombs killing two people in a matter of days."

An agent sitting nearby gave a slight cough and looked at Burns, who nodded at the unspoken question.

"Sir," the agent began. "Our list of suspects has expanded to include the family of the man shot during the robbery."

Warren nodded; that was logical.

"The brother of the shooting victim is a builder. We're finding out if he has explosives training and a license."

"He has motive."

"There are two agents heading out to interview him now."

Warren nodded.

"And the Coles," Burns added. "We need to keep track of their movements too."

"George Cole came to see me right at the beginning," Warren said into the silent pause. "Fronted the HQ reception desk demanding to be allowed in."

"So he has determination. They stopped him, I assume?"

"They tried to. He was causing a fuss, and I was passing through at the time and caught what was going on." Warren frowned, remembering. "I followed him out afterwards and spoke to him."

"You did?"

Warren glanced at the astonished agent. "He was so determined to see me, and I wanted to know why. What was so important that he would risk the consequences of causing trouble at HQ?"

"What was it about, sir?" Burns asked.

"He told me in roundabout terms that threats had been made to keep quiet about the investigation."

"Ah," Burns sighed. "That's where that came from. Zonardi filled us in. We did ask the Coles about it, but they denied it and stated they hadn't seen any of young Cole's friends since."

"Do you believe them?"

"I don't believe anything without evidence," said the agent.

The two older men looked at him, then at each other. Warren raised his brow and Burns flicked his eyes to the ceiling.

"Evidence is always handy, but so is instinct," Burns said. "Especially when evidence is unobtainable."

"Yes sir," the agent mumbled, his cheeks glowing.

"So, as there is no evidence at the moment, do you believe them?" Burns asked.

"No sir." There was no hesitation in delivering the answer.

"Why?" Warren prompted.

The agent paused and then shrugged his shoulders. "They looked uncomfortable."

"Both of them?"

Warren's eyes narrowed as he studied the agent. The young man was processing his thoughts to come up with the answer he needed.

"It's funny," the agent said, finally. "I can't decide. She was calm and quiet, and he seemed worried." His cheeks glowed. "I think her attitude said more. She wasn't concerned at all."

"Not a frightened silence?" Burns asked. Warren glanced at him. His encouragement was good—better than the sarcasm he'd received from his SAC early in his career. No doubt Burns would have been through the same.

The agent shook his head. "No. She was calm, not frightened, but didn't want to answer questions. That's why she was uncomfortable."

Warren didn't have time to see Burns' reaction. The SAC was already on his feet, heading across the room to talk to an agent. The agent sprang to his feet, listened to Burns, then headed towards the table, Burns behind him.

"Modin, with me," the agent said as he passed.

The agent sitting with Warren rose and followed the other agent out. Two more agents entered the room and strode up to Burns.

"CCTV footage, sir," one of them said, holding a fist of USB sticks up.

"Good," Burns responded. "Footage from the town Atkins was driving away from. With luck we'll see something."

"I'll help go through them," Warren offered, then added, seeing Burns' surprise, "It's not boring when you haven't done it for a while."

A glimmer of understanding sparked in Burns' eyes, and he smiled. Before he could reply, Warren's cell phone buzzed.

"Excuse me," he said to Burns, then answered it. "Pearce...thank you, Lisa. Please let him know I'm on my way." Warren pocketed the phone, biting down the disappointment Lisa's message had caused. "Sorry Burns, I have to go."

"That's okay sir, I understand."

Warren looked at him and made a snap decision. "Here's some advice, Burns. Consider long and hard before you accept promotion. Ask yourself what you really want."

Burns stared, then blinked. "Thank you, sir, I'll remember that."

"I hope you do." Warren nodded, and with a sigh and a look around at the activity, turned and left the room.

Modin and the senior agent he accompanied, Agent Lind, arrived at the Coles property and were met by silence. Modin climbed out of the sedan and stared around him. No cars were visible, and the greenhouses stood still as birds flew overhead.

"House first," Lind said as he strode past Modin.

Modin hurried to follow him, arriving on the porch as Lind knocked on the wooden door. No sound answered the knock, and Lind glanced at Modin.

"Go round the back."

Modin ran down the steps and jogged around the house to the rear. No one appeared, either from the home or any of the other buildings he could see, and all was quiet. Three quick steps had him on the back porch and knocking on the back door.

"Mr Cole? Mrs Cole?"

No response. He moved to the window nearest the door and peered in to the kitchen. All was still, and no one in sight. He turned around as Lind appeared around the side of the house.

"No sign of anyone," Modin reported.

"We'll check the outbuildings," Lind said, then stopped, raising his hand as the sound of tyres on gravel reached them.

The two agents hurried down the stairs and strode around to the front of the house. A pickup truck had parked beside their car and George Cole was standing by the driver's door.

"Mr Cole," Lind said. "I'm—"

"The FBI," Cole interrupted. "What do you want now?"

"Sir, I'm Special Agent Lind, and this is Special Agent Modin," Lind waved a hand in Modin's direction. "We want to have a chat about how things are going with the investigation."

"The one into who killed my boy?"

"No sir. I am sorry, but that investigation is being completed by the Justice Department and it's out of our jurisdiction. We're trying to locate the others involved in the robbery."

Cole's shoulders sagged. "You'd better come in."

"Is Mrs Cole about?" Lind asked.

"No."

"Will she be long, do you know, sir?"

Modin watched Cole's face with interest. His eyes widened, and then all expression vanished. *He doesn't know where she is.*

"I don't keep tabs on my wife. She is free to come and go as she pleases."

Lind nodded and waited for Cole to lead them into the house. Cole made to move in through the door, then stopped and turned to the agents behind him.

"On second thoughts, we might sit out here and talk."

"Wherever you are comfortable," Lind responded with a smile, and waited for Cole to seat himself on a wooden chair. Lind perched on the porch railing, and Modin made do standing by the top of the steps. There was a pause of silence. Modin kept his mouth shut; he understood the tactics Lind used and waited.

Their patience was rewarded when Cole spoke. "What do you want to know?"

"Are you aware that Matthew Atkins died this morning?" Lind said.

Cole's back straightened as his eyes widened again. It was a momentary pose before his shoulders dropped again. "I didn't know."

"That's the second to die."

"The third," George spat. His hands gripped the arms of his chair as he pushed himself forward. "He's the third to die!"

"Atkins worked for you, didn't he?"

"He worked for my wife, the treacherous bastard."

"So you're not sad he's dead?"

"Serves him right if you want to know. He got what he deserved."

Lind allowed the following silence to sit for a moment before continuing. "Can you please tell me where you were this morning?"

"Are you accusing me of killing Matty?" George remained tense, sitting upright in his chair.

"I'm not accusing you of anything," Lind replied.

Cole didn't relax, but the tension had nothing to do with anger, Modin realised. The old man was scared. But of what?

The silence drew out again as the agents waited for Cole to answer.

"I went to the hardware store to buy a new handle for my spade."

"The hardware store back down the road?" Lind asked.

"Yes." Cole had relaxed back into his chair, but his fingers still gripped hard onto the arms. "That's the one."

"And you can't help us with your wife's whereabouts?" Lind asked, his eyes drifting towards the greenhouses. Modin had enough experience with Lind's peripheral vision to know he still watched Cole.

Cole's gaze shifted to his car. "I'm not her secretary."

"Does she have one?" Lind asked, his face still turned away from Cole.

Modin watched as Cole glanced up at Lind, then turned away from the greenhouses to look in the opposite direction. "No. Did all that stuff herself."

Lind levered himself from his perch. "Thank you, Mr Cole. We'll be leaving now. Please pass our regards on to Mrs Cole."

Cole nodded, but didn't rise from his chair. Modin descended first from the porch and waited for Lind to step alongside before heading to the car.

"So," Lind said as they pulled out of the driveway and onto the road. "What struck you as the most interesting part of that interview?"

"Cole's assumption that Atkins' death wasn't an accident."

"Was it an assumption, or did he know?"

"Was that a rhetorical question?"

Lind laughed. "Unless you know the answer, I guess it is." He steered the car into the parking lot of the hardware store. "We might get a clue as to the answer here. I want you to have a look around at what this place sells while I talk to the staff." Lind leaned forward to stare out of the windscreen. "It looks more like a farmer supply depot than the kind of hardware store you and I might be familiar with." The senior agent's face grew serious. "I want to know if they sell explosives for ground clearing, and whether they've sold any recently."

Modin nodded and opened the door to climb out.

"Don't mention names," Lind cautioned. "We don't want gossip getting around. If Cole thinks we suspect him of blowing people up, all hell could break loose."

"I'll be discreet," Modin assured him.

Lind watched the young agent branch away to case the store. He wasn't sure of his abilities, but everyone had to start somewhere. Lind shrugged and turned towards the man standing at the counter.

"Special Agent Lind," he announced, pulling his credentials out to show him. "I would like to ask you a few questions."

The young man's eyes popped at the sight of Lind's credentials, and then flicked down to his waist, searching for his gun. It was something Lind had seen more times than he could count, and he waited for the man to return his attention to Lind's face.

The wide eyes finally looked up. "I'd better get the manager." Before Lind could speak, the young man turned and disappeared into an office behind the counter. He sighed and allowed his gaze to wander around the store as he waited for the manager to appear. There was no sign of Modin and Lind hoped he wasn't causing a stir. The last thing they needed was the locals spreading the news of FBI Agents asking questions about explosives.

Modin had found what he'd been looking for. A small counter near the rear of the store sported a short list of items available for purchase, including dynamite and detonators. The list was accompanied by a list of requirements before the items could be purchased or ordered. There was no obvious signs of storage of the items and Modin concluded they were stored in a separate secure storage area.

Absorbed in his task, Modin didn't notice someone approach.

"Can I help you?"

The list of items Modin had been studying flew across the counter, disappearing behind it as he spun around to front the speaker.

"I'm sorry. I didn't mean to startle you."

Modin took a steadying breath to calm his pounding heart. The woman in front of him slowly looked him up and down, a smile growing on her lips.

"I don't remember seeing you here before," she said, "and I don't think I would forget you."

The smile on her face grew as Modin felt his face grow hot. "I'm just passing through," he managed.

The smile stayed on the woman's face as she lowered her lashes, looking up at him though their blackened lengths.

"Well, I'm glad you stopped by," she said. "Can I help you?" Her gaze slid from his face to the counter, her brows rising as she realised what he'd been looking at. "You after something special?"

"Er, no," Modin replied. "I saw the list and was surprised to see what was on it. I've never seen anything like that before," he added quickly as she lifted her eyebrows further.

"We supply the farmers around these parts." The smile had dropped from her face and her eyes had narrowed. "Are you here checking up on us?" she demanded.

"No, no. Nothing to do with me," Modin stammered. "I was just curious."

The suspicion faded from her face as the smile returned. "Well then, Mr Just Passing Though, how can I help you?"

Modin's heart was racing again at the inviting look she cast at him. He needed to think of something, quickly.

"Um, my girlfriend asked me to pick up something for her," he said, pleased at his quick thinking. He breathed a silent sigh of relief as the flirtatious look disappeared.

"What is it you're after?" she asked.

His smugness vanished in an instant. *Damn*. His eyes lit on the display behind the woman.

"She wants some new wellington boots," he said, pointing.

The woman turned and moved towards the display. "What size is she?"

Modin's heart rate ramped up a few more notches. "Nine?" He held his breath. His sister wore size nine. Or was it size seven? He released his breath as the woman accepted his answer and returned to the display.

"Here you go," she announced, turning back to Modin, a pair of boots in hand.

He recoiled at the sight of her offering. These were no black wellington boots. Roses of all colours covered the surface, the sheer riot of colour hurting his eyes and making him blink rapidly.

"Your girlfriend will love them; they're very popular," the woman said, thrusting them into his arms.

"I'm not sure..." Modin said.

"They're perfect," the woman said firmly. "Come with me and I'll put them through the till for you. Credit?"

Modin followed helplessly. If he dumped the boots and left without them, the woman would suspect he was lying and no doubt she'd tell all her friends within hours. He had no choice. Maybe he could give them to his mom.

The woman rang up the sale and took his card with a smile. "Come back if ever you're passing again," she said, and gave him a wink.

Modin grabbed the boots and hastened out of the store, hoping to put the boots in the car before Lind saw his purchase.

No luck.

Lind was leaning against the door of the car, waiting for him. The senior agent's brows rose as he spotted the boots, and then a broad grin spread across his face.

"Found a bargain, did you?"

Modin's face burned as Lind roared with laughter. He thrust the boots into the trunk. "Long story," he muttered.

"I look forward to hearing it," Lind gasped, his arms holding his stomach. "But it can keep until we get back to the investigation room. This is something everyone will enjoy."

Modin ignored him and slid into the car. "It could have been worse," he said when Lind had sat behind the steering wheel. "It was either the boots or continue being hit on."

Lind burst out laughing again. "I look forward to hearing about it."

"What did you find out?" Modin asked, wanting to turn the conversation away from the horror now resting in the trunk.

Lind's grin disappeared. "Cole was there earlier and bought the handle as he said, but that was early this morning—over four hours ago."

"Do we go back to the Coles'?"

"No. We report to the SAC and let him decide what happens next. Did you find out anything—other than what kinds of boots they sell?"

Modin glanced at Lind, but he wasn't laughing. "They sell explosives; mainly dynamite. They also sell detonators and other relevant items. There was a list of requirements to be met before anyone can purchase them, so they seem to be following the rules. If Cole has purchased any of it, it would be recorded."

Lind shook his head. "The manager said Cole doesn't have the registration or license to purchase explosives from them. We'll need to check the store's record with the appropriate authorities before we judge the truth of the manager's assertion. Legit sellers don't mess around with that kind of thing—the consequences are too big." He shook his head. "We'll head back to DC and fill in SAC Burns, and see what the next move is." Lind's body shook with chuckles. "And you can tell us all about your purchase."

Chapter Twenty-Five

Daisy had a new target, a new person to track down. Reuben was gone and so too was Matty. Peter was still around, but he suffered enough, in Daisy's mind. Leave Peter. He understood her grief and her desire for justice.

The new target would provide a challenge. Daisy knew where the person could be found at times, but getting close would be hard.

Daisy sat in her old Ford, a slip of paper resting on her thigh as she scanned the cars emerging from the entrance road and turning onto the main access road. She had to be careful; sitting in a car near the entrance to the Quantico Marine Base was asking for attention and that was the last thing she needed.

Her hand smoothed the piece of paper around the curve of her thigh, running over the name written across the lines— Dr Elizabeth Pearce. Her mind played a memory: a woman striding across from one of her greenhouses and an agent calling her name. The information had been confirmed by poor Jerry's lawyer. The scientist who had led the FBI to their door, and to Jerry. Now she waited, hoping for a glimpse of the face she vaguely remembered, hoping to follow her and find a way to talk to her. Daisy wasn't sure what would happen, but it had worked so far. Both Reuben and Matty were dead. She wasn't sure how the scientist fitted into the plan, but Daisy felt compelled to find her, to connect with her.

Cars drove by, none of them bearing a familiar face. Daisy glanced at the clock on the dashboard. Time was passing; too much time. Heads had turned toward her as cars passed. Each passing minute increased the risk of questions being asked.

Another car, another turned head. It was too much. Daisy's heart pounded as she turned the ignition key, moved off and joined the flow of traffic leaving the Quantico base. She hadn't seen the woman. There were too many cars; it wasn't going to work.

A glow of red on the dash grabbed Daisy's attention.

"Damn it," she muttered. She'd been too preoccupied with her mission to notice she was low on gas. On cue, a large sign for a gas station appeared and Daisy pulled over and drew up at the pumps. It took a moment for her to raise the energy to open the door and climb out. George would wonder why she was using so much gas, too. He would notice; he always did.

Daisy opened the cap and pumped gas into the car. A white sedan pulled up behind her and a brown-haired woman climbed out. Daisy almost dropped the hose she held when she realised the woman she'd been seeking was right here in front of her.

Think fast.

She came up with a plan.

Daisy returned the pump to the station and began searching for her purse. She checked the front of the car and then the back seat. As her search continued, she became more distressed, alarmed at not being able to find it. Next was the trunk. Still no purse. She turned around, tears starting in her eyes, searching for help. The woman was watching her, her brow creased and her face tense.

Daisy turned back to the car and went through the pretence of searching for her bag again, and then stood staring at the pump, tears now trickling down her cheeks.

It worked.

"Ma'am? Is something wrong?"

Daisy turned toward the warm, gentle voice. The woman had approached her and was watching her with concern.

Daisy spread her hands in a gesture of helplessness. "I seem to have left my purse at home." She allowed her voice to wobble. "I don't know what to do."

"Let me help you look for it," the woman said, and peered into the car. Daisy held her breath, hoping she wouldn't notice the small wallet she'd stuffed into a gap under the dashboard.

The two women searched the car, but to Daisy's relief, the wallet wasn't found.

The woman glanced at the pump. "How about I pay for your gas," she said.

Bingo.

"Oh, I couldn't let you," Daisy said, throwing in a sniff and dabbing at her eyes.

"It's only twenty dollars. Please let me pay."

Daisy squeezed out a few more tears. "That's so kind of you, dear, but you must let me repay you."

"No, no. It's okay," the woman assured her. "You don't need to."

"I insist," Daisy said. "If you give me your address, I can pop it in your letter box."

Daisy noticed the immediate gesture of withdrawal and held her breath.

"You don't need to repay it," the woman repeated.

"I must," Daisy repeated, lifting her chin but managing a lip tremble. She could see the woman hesitate, then relent.

"Okay," the woman said. "How about we meet somewhere and you can return the money? Maybe at a park?"

Daisy stomped on the flash of annoyance. A quick thought, and she smiled at the woman and mentally crossed her fingers.

"I'd like that, but I don't want to inconvenience you. You've already gone out of your way."

The woman smiled at her. "In that case we can meet at a park in my neighbourhood." She stepped back to her car and leaned in, picking up her bag. The woman scribbled a few words on a scrap of paper and handed it to Daisy, along with twenty dollars. "Place and time," she said. "Does that suit you?"

Daisy read what the woman had written and then smiled up at her. "Yes, and thank you so much for coming to my aid. I'll never forget your kindness."

"My pleasure," the woman said, smiling.

Daisy watched for a moment as the woman returned to finish pumping gas into her car, the piece of paper clutched in her hand. It would be easy to follow her home from the park, and then…

Chapter Twenty-Six

The apartment door flew open and Beth dropped her cookie on the floor. Warren erupted into the room, and before she could retrieve the cookie she was scooped into his arms and swung around.

"Hello to you too," she giggled as Warren eased her feet back to the floor. Her answer was a firm and thorough kiss, and then she was pulled against Warren's chest.

"Hello, my amazing, wonderful, and incredible wife," he said, his voice rumbling under her ear. Beth pushed away from Warren, enough to look up to his beaming face. His exuberance infected her, and bubbles of joy filled her, but she wasn't sure what had caused his good mood.

"You're in a good mood this evening."

His smile broadened, if that were possible. "I handed in my resignation this morning and spent some time at the Field Office."

"So, you quit the FBI, an organization you've been a part of and loved for twenty-five years, and then dived right back into FBI work, and it's left you with this huge buzz?"

"Got it in one."

"Who are you, and what have you done with my husband?" Beth grinned up at him. "Where is the cool, calm, and collected man who left home this morning?"

Beth felt Warren's hand cup her head and draw it back down to rest on his chest. "He took the step to take control of his life again," he said.

"I've enjoyed my years with the FBI, but it doesn't fulfil me anymore. I feel like my life is about to begin again."

"It is a time for change," Beth responded as sadness crept through the joy. She couldn't account for it and pushed it down for analysis another time. This was Warren's moment.

"Incredible changes," Warren said, his voice suddenly low and gentle. He released her and placed a hand over the swelling in Beth's abdomen. "How is my family today?" Beth heard his breath catch and the arm circling her waist tightened. "My family," he repeated tenderly.

Tears pricked at Beth's eyes and she blinked to banish them. "Your family is well."

"Good, because without my family I have nothing."

Beth pulled out of his arms. "Are you happy?"

"I am."

"Really?"

He frowned down at her. "What do you mean?"

"I mean, are you really happy or are you telling yourself you're happy?" She swallowed. "Not that long ago that your opinion was different…"

"Beth. I'm happy. I'm more than happy, and I mean every word of it. The idea of being a dad still scares me, but I can't wait for it to start. I want our child." He kissed her forehead. "The future is looking wonderful."

George didn't say a word when Daisy walked into the kitchen. He watched as she filled the kettle and set it to boil and then sat down at the table opposite him.

"I had visitors waiting for me when I got home this afternoon," he said, his gaze on her face.

"Who?"

Was it his imagination, or did a spark of fear light her eyes? "The FBI."

"Oh, them," she said.

George tried to read her expression, but came up with nothing. He had no idea what she was thinking or how much she already knew. "Matty's dead."

Daisy's lips curved into a smile. "Serves him right."

George's throat went dry. Daisy didn't seem either surprised or upset. What did she know about all of this? "You think so?"

Her smile grew. "Yep. Karma has come and got them both. The question is, who's next?" Daisy's eyes met his, and he was surprised to see a question in them as if he knew the answer.

"What do you mean, who's next?"

"First Jerry, then Reuben, and now Matty. Who is next on the list?"

George could hear his heart pounding in his ears. "I don't understand."

Daisy seemed disappointed. Her mouth drooped and her shoulders sagged. "They have to pay—all of them."

"Daisy, you're scaring me. Who has to pay?"

Her eyes stared at him, clouded and confused. "They all do. And it's happening. You know that?"

George hadn't felt fear like this for a long time. What did Daisy know?

"Where were you this afternoon?"

She stared blankly at him and then shook her head. "I went for a drive."

"Where?"

"I...I don't remember."

George lunged forward and grabbed her wrists. "Don't lie to me, Daisy!" The fear overrode everything, taking control. "Where were you, and what do you know?"

Tears flowed from Daisy's shocked eyes. "I don't remember everywhere I went. I drove, then parked and thought for a while, and then drove some more." She drew a trembling breath. "You're hurting me, George."

He released her wrists, but stayed leaning across the table. "We have to stick together Daisy. We have to look out for each other."

She nodded, her eyes downcast. "I'm sorry I worried you."

He slumped back into his chair. "I'm sorry too."

Daisy shifted in her chair. "I'm not the only one who's been spending time away from the house." George lifted his head to meet her narrowed eyes. "Where did you go?"

He dropped his gaze from hers. "I can't tell you."

"Why? Were you doing something you shouldn't? Is that the real reason for the FBI's visit?" Daisy leaned forward, her eyes suddenly wide and sharp. "Did you do in Matty?"

The kettle whistled, startling them both. George's chair scraped on the floorboards as he pushed it back.

"Answer my question!" Daisy's brows lifted and her mouth curved up in a widening smile. "Did you kill him?"

"Of course I didn't." He struggled to comprehend Daisy's excited anticipation and her belief he might have been responsible. "I'd never do something like that." His confusion grew as Daisy's mouth drooped. "Did you want him dead?"

"Jerry's dead, so why not the others?"

"Daisy!"

"I'm just being honest."

George stared at his wife, suddenly a stranger to him. Gentle Daisy wanting people to die. He felt goose-bumps raise on his skin.

"Did you kill him?" he whispered. His chest tightened as he watched Daisy consider his question. She opened her mouth, then shut it with a snap. Her eyes closed for a moment, then opened wide.

"I didn't kill him. There's a difference between wanting revenge and carrying it out."

The tight squeeze on his chest eased. He nodded.

"I understand, and I'm sorry I thought you had."

"That's okay," she replied. "We're both under a lot of stress." Daisy stood and moved over to the kettle. "Do you want a coffee, George?"

"Yes thanks." He watched Daisy turn to the kettle. Her back to him, he didn't see the satisfied smile curving her lips.

Chapter Twenty-Seven

Burns finished reading the report and laid it on the desk with a sigh.

"The brother of the victim has a license to handle explosives, but he's been out of the country for the past week."

"Verified, sir."

"And the rest of the family have no history of explosive training or licensing of any kind."

"None, sir."

Burns slid the report into a file and stood. "Thanks Lind." He watched as the agent left the office. His hand rested on the file as Burns thought about the case. Leads that circled around, not resulting in forward motion, were delaying the investigation. Two bombs in two days, and the public was starting to show signs of panic and paranoia. Media outlets had cooperated, to a degree, but they needed to solve this one fast.

The watch on Burns' wrist caught his eye and he started up from his chair. EAD Pearce had requested a briefing and Burns needed to get moving if he didn't want to be late. And he didn't. Working with Pearce, even in short grabs, was all Burns had thought it would be. Pearce's words of advice ran through his head again. He shook his head; it was hard to believe Pearce had regrets in accepting promotion, but that's what he'd said, or implied. As he gathered together the documents he needed, Burns tried to imagine himself in Pearce's role. Leading the Criminal Investigative Division was a huge responsibility, but what did it actually entail? They all joked about the 'empty suits', but endless meetings and the politics of upper management would drain most men of at least some vitality. Burns' mouth twitched as he walked out of his office door. EAD certainly didn't lack vitality; in fact he had difficulty picturing Pearce enduring long days of sitting around discussing policy. The humour faded as Burns remembered Pearce's words. He would do well to keep them in mind.

"Director Stanton wants to see you, sir," Lisa said as Warren walked through the door of his office suite. "He asked for you to go up as soon as you arrived."

Warren nodded, wary of setting Lisa off again if he mentioned his resignation. "Thank you, Lisa."

Warren walked past her desk, into the quiet of his own office and dropped his briefcase by his desk. A quick glance at the pile resting in his tray revealed a report from the Assistant Director of the Investigative branch regarding the bombings. It would have to wait though, the Director's summons more important right now. He smiled as he headed out of his office door, looking forward to having his resignation accepted.

"Director's office," he said to Lisa as he passed. "Shouldn't be long."

A quick run up the stairs and he was striding down the hallway towards the Director's door.

"Go straight in, Mr Peace. Director Stanton is expecting you," he was instructed as he arrived.

Warren knocked and then entered without waiting. "Good morning, sir."

Stanton looked up at him and waved him to a chair. "Have a seat, Warren."

Warren shot the Director a look from under his brows. First names, huh? He couldn't stop the smile that emerged once more.

Stanton sat back in his chair. "I hope you're going to tell me you've reconsidered."

"No sir, I haven't. And I won't. This is the right thing for me to do."

"Even with a baby on the way? It's a secure job."

Annoyance damped down the contentment Warren had been feeling. This use of the baby and Warren's ability to provide for his family, only strengthened his resolve. "I wouldn't compromise the wellbeing of my family, and this move will not affect that."

Stanton seemed to realise he'd erred, making placating movements with his hands. "I didn't mean to imply that, Warren. I'm trying to find a way to get you to remain with the Bureau."

"Thank you for the compliment, but my decision stands, as does my resignation."

"I did the wrong thing in promoting you, didn't I? I should have left you in a position where you could still be involved, not condemned you to stand back and watch."

"I accepted the promotion of my own free will, sir." Warren shrugged. "I can't go back now, and I don't think I want to, either, even if it were possible."

Stanton rose to his feet. "Well, with reluctance, I accept your resignation." He held his hand out for Warren to shake. "We'll announce it later today."

Warren shook his hand. "Thank you, sir. If you'll excuse me, I have a briefing I need to attend."

"The robbery and bombings?"

"Yes."

Stanton smiled. "I suppose I should tell you to leave it to those in charge of the investigation, but in a way that is you." The smile broadened to a grin. "And I'd be wasting my breath." The grin died, replaced with a frown. "How do you do it? Get involved without annoying those leading the investigations?"

"I leave them to run it. I help out and give my opinion when asked."

Stanton smiled again. "So simple."

Loman was in Warren's office drinking coffee when Warren arrived, but sprang to his feet as Warren walked through the door.

"Morning, sir."

"Morning Loman."

Warren skirted his desk and removed his coat, hanging it on the back of his chair. He grabbed the reports off his desk and joined Loman at the meeting table as the man finished pouring him a coffee.

"Thanks," he said, accepting the steaming mug and sitting at the end of the table. "We're waiting on Burns, but he has a couple of minutes yet."

Loman nodded and resumed sipping his coffee as Warren flipped open the AD's report and scanned through it. There was a lot of detail in it, which Warren ignored, preferring to hear it from the men involved, and it concluded with a list of possible suspects and proposed further action. He closed the cover and pushed the file aside and reached for his coffee.

Loman placed his now empty cup on the table and turned his head to Warren. "How is Dr Pearce? I haven't seen her since the bomb threat."

Warren felt his whole body warm at the thought of his wife, and the baby she carried. An unstoppable smile spread. "She's well, thank you. And pregnant."

"Pregnant? That's great news, sir! Congratulations!" Loman looked as though he would pound Warren on the back, but thought better of it, beaming at Warren instead. "Kids are the best thing in the world. I have six, so I should know."

"Thanks Loman." *He has six kids?* Warren felt nothing but awe for Loman right now. Six? Impressive, and scary. He didn't know what to say. A knock on the door, followed by the entrance of Burns, rescued him.

"Good morning, sir. Sorry if I kept you waiting," Burns said as he walked across to the table.

"We haven't started yet. Coffee?" Warren said.

"No, thank you." Burns placed a file on the desk and took the seat opposite Loman. "I've just received the report on the interview with the initial victim's family."

"Good," Warren said. "We'll start with that then. Loman, are you up to date with the investigation Burns' team is conducting?"

"Yes sir. The field office has kept us informed."

Warren nodded. Communication was flowing between the sections as it should. "Okay, Burns."

Burns opened the file in front of him, but spoke without looking at it. "With the link between the bomb and the bank robbery established, my team looked into the background of all those connected with the case. The family of the initial robbery victim was interviewed yesterday, particularly the brother of the victim." He now glanced at the report before continuing. "The brother has an explosives licence as part of his work as a builder." Loman nodded, in agreement or understanding, Warren wasn't sure. "He hasn't had a lot of experience handling explosives, and has never purchased or stored them, only assisting when they were used on site. He states, and it has been confirmed, that he was out of the country during the past ten days at an international conference." Burns turned a page in the file. "No other members of the family have a record of explosive training or registration, and they could all account for their time since around the first bombing until now. We have names of people who should be able to verify this, but that is yet to happen."

"Conclusion?" Warren asked.

"The family all have motive— revenge. I think their anger is directed at Jerry Cole, not the other robbers. If they wanted revenge, I believe they would have targeted the Cole family first."

"I agree," Warren said as Loman nodded. "Loman, your turn."

Loman sat forward, resting his arms on the table. "The explosive used in both bombings was dynamite, with an electric match on a timer as the detonator. Homemade stuff; the kind of device that could be made after reading a few articles on the internet. The first bomb was a single stick of dynamite, the second used two. First victim seemed to be clutching the bomb to his chest. The second bomb appears to have been sitting on the bench seat of the pickup truck, next to the victim."

"Disguised as something innocuous?" Warren suggested.

"That's what we think," Loman confirmed. "The second victim was seen holding a carry bag of some sort when he climbed into his vehicle. We can't find a witness or any camera footage to show where he got the bag from. There are fibres matching the description of the bag around the detonation site, so we're assuming for now that's where the bomb was located. Again, the detonation was provided by an electric match on a homemade timer."

Burns spoke. "The identity of both victims has been confirmed. They both were friends of Jerry Cole, and match the descriptions of two of the bank robbers."

"The family of the victim have been ruled out, so who are the suspects? And what is the bomber's motive?"

"The bombs were made from materials easy to access by those who know how, and simple to construct," Loman said. "The old dynamite was removed from the Coles' property by my team, and there was no sign any of it had been touched. Neither of the Coles have known access or training in explosives."

"That's the sticking point, isn't it," Burns said. "Known. They could have learnt all they need to know from someone else."

"Access to dynamite isn't easy without a licence."

"Unless you know someone."

"Motive?" Warren asked into the atmosphere of tension, bringing the discussion back on track.

"Anger over the death of their son," Burns said.

"Who else?" Warren asked.

"Not a random act," Loman said. "Not even a vigilante. They would pass on the information to us, or beat them to a pulp. Blowing them up is personal."

"I agree. What about the remaining bank robber, Peter Hill? And there's the driver too, Joshua Macintosh."

"Motive?" Warren asked.

"Silence? Keeping all of the money?" Burns suggested.

"They had shotguns. Surely that would be an easier way to go about it? Does he have any record with explosives of any sort?"

"Nothing recorded, sir, but Peter Hill has worked on farms in the past, and has worked for the Coles for the last four years. Macintosh was their driver. We've had word that Macintosh crossed into Canada the day after young Jerry Cole was arrested. The authorities there are looking for him."

"When was the blasting done on their property for the greenhouses?" Warren asked.

Burns opened his file and flicked through the papers. "The greenhouses were established nearly five years ago. Just before Hill started at the nursery, according to our information. Macintosh has been there about a year. I'll check on Hill's start date, to confirm," he said, making a note.

"The shotgun would still be easier," Loman said. Warren had to agree with him about that. Why would Peter Hill change his weapon of choice?

"That brings us back to the Coles."

"In light of the explosion yesterday, I sent two agents out to interview the Coles," Burns said. "Neither of them was at home when the agents arrived, but George Cole arrived soon after. When he was informed of the death of Atkins, he showed no surprise, nor did he ask for any details of what happened."

Warren thought back to his impromptu meeting with George. He didn't seem like a killer, but like a tired and defeated man. But men who thought they had nothing to lose sometimes lost all restraint and could commit horrendous acts. His gut told him no, but that wasn't good enough.

"Where had he been?"

"To the local hardware store to buy a new handle for a shovel. The agents verified he'd been there." Burns' lips twitched, but he continued after a moment, "but the store claimed Mr Cole had purchased the handle some four hours earlier. The store also sells dynamite, on order, but state that Mr Cole never purchased any explosives from them."

Warren watched as Burns' eyes dropped to the page in front of him and his lips twitched once more. *What did the man find so amusing?* Only one way to find out.

"What's so funny?"

Burns allowed a broad grin to form. "The young agent who went out there couldn't think up a story fast enough to satisfy a saleswoman and ended up buying a pair of wellington boots." Burns chuckled. "Very fetching they are, sir, all covered in a flower print."

Warren smiled as the other two men laughed. He'd miss this part of the FBI. "So we have some missing hours to account for with Mr Cole. Did he say where Mrs Cole was?"

"Mr Cole said he wife was a free woman, and he didn't keep tabs on her."

"And?"

"The agents got the impression he had no idea where she was." Burns closed the file again and laid a hand over it. "I want to invite the Coles in for questioning. Whether they'll cooperate, if they're home, is an interesting question. There's not enough evidence to arrest them, so that's not an option at the moment."

"I might be able to help out with that. George Cole has sought me out before, and he might be willing to talk to me."

"I'd appreciate that, sir. I'm doubling efforts to locate Hill. All the leads we've had so far are going cold, but we're persisting. I have surveillance on the cemetery where young Cole is buried. If he and Hill were close friends, there's a good chance Hill would want to visit the grave. It's a long shot, but you never know."

"We have an alert out for Hill with registered sellers of explosives," Loman said. "None of them recognise his photo, but if he tries to buy or steal anything, we'll know immediately."

"And the Coles?"

"Nothing with them, either."

"Black market?"

"Who knows? The relevant undercover team has been alerted and they're checking what they can, but they can't ask too much without giving away their cover."

"Good," Warren said. He looked at Burns. "Let me know when you are heading out to the Coles and I'll come along."

"Will do, sir."

A knock on the door heralded Lisa. "Sir, I've just had a call from the front desk. There's a Mr Cole down there insisting on speaking to you, and only you. He said it's regarding information about the bombings."

Chapter Twenty-Eight

Warren asked Lisa for a fresh pot of coffee as Burns hastened down to sign George Cole in and escort him up to the office. She had just brought it into the room and placed it on the sideboard when Burns led George in.

"Welcome, Mr Cole," Warren said as he moved forward to meet George.

"I don't want to talk to anyone but you," George said, his eyes hooded by his puckered brow. "Only you."

"Can I get you a coffee?" Warren asked, ignoring George's statement.

"I don't know I'll be staying," George responded, crossing his arms across his chest and thrusting out his chin.

Warren didn't answer straight away. He poured a cup of coffee, added sugar and milk, and carried it to George. "How about I introduce these men to you while you drink this," he said, passing the coffee to George. "When I've finished, you can decide if you want to stay or leave."

George stared down at the steaming coffee, then at the three men watching him, his gaze coming to rest on Warren. "I guess there's no harm in that."

"Excellent," Warren said and led George over to the armchairs. George chose one and perched on the edge of it, Warren sat in the chair beside him. Loman and Burns settled into the other chairs in the group and waited for Warren to speak.

"Mr Cole," Warren said, "these two men are agents who work as part of the Criminal Investigative Division I oversee. The gentleman that escorted you up here is Mr Burns, Special Agent in Charge of the Washington DC field office. He is running the investigation into the robbery in which your son was involved. The other gentleman is Special Agent in Charge Loman. Mr Loman is in charge of the Bomb Squad and has been working with Mr Burns as they investigate the recent bomb attacks. They are both good agents, and I trust them. If you still want to talk to me alone, I will ask them to leave. I will, however, brief them on our conversation as any information you have is important in helping find the bomber." Warren waited a moment and then added, "I can also guarantee they will treat you with courtesy. You have nothing to fear in allowing them to be a part of the conversation."

Warren watched George as he thought over what he'd said. He kept his posture and face relaxed, but his heart raced as he waited for George's answer. This was their best chance of a lead on the bomber, and George could walk out of the door if he wanted to. The silence lengthened as they waited.

George tipped up his cup, draining the last of the coffee. He leaned over and placed the cup on the table beside him and then turned to Warren.

"You trust them?"

"I do."

George sighed. "Then I guess that's good enough for me. They can stay."

Warren felt the tension drain from his muscles and noticed Loman and Burns relax back into their chairs.

"What is it you want to tell me, George?" Warren asked.

"I did it."

Damn it! He needed the recorder going. Warren took a gamble. "George, can you please wait before you continue? I'd like to record this." The old man's eyes had teared up, and Warren could see the tremor shaking his hands. They needed to move fast.

Burns dumped a recorder on the table in front of George and pressed the button to set it going and nodded to Warren.

"The time is eleven twenty-one on Tuesday the fifteenth. Present is Executive Assistant Director Warren Pearce, Assistant Director Loman, Special Agent Burns, and Mr George Cole. George Cole, you have the right to remain silent…" Warren continued until George's rights had been read to him and his acknowledgement recorded. "Mr Cole, please repeat for me your earlier statement."

"I did it."

"What did you do?"

"I blew up Reuben and Matty."

"Are you referring to Reuben Dervish and Matthew Atkins?"

"Yes." George's voice broke and tears trickled down his face.

Warren watched the old man beside him. The tears and slumped posture told him all he needed. He wasn't crying with remorse, he was heartbroken. "Who are you trying to cover up for?"

George's head reared up, his eyes wide. "I did it!"

Warren shook his head. "I don't believe you."

"I swear I did it! I blew those bastards up because of what they did to my Jerry. They led him astray and then had their friends beat him to death in jail." George leaned forward, spitting words from between gritted teeth. "They deserved it."

"That's the first true thing you've said so far," Warren replied, still relaxed in his chair. The other two had tensed when George leaned forward, but Warren had no doubt of his ability to deal with George if he became violent.

"No! I did it!"

"Then prove it."

"I blew them up with dynamite."

One point to George, but an easy guess on his part. The FBI had come looking for his old dynamite after Reuben's death. Simple to put one and one together and come up with a right answer.

"You're not licenced for explosives handling. How did you get the dynamite?"

"It's easy when you know people. Ask the question in the right place and you get the right answer."

A vague answer. Warren could see the other two from the corner of his eyes. They sat still, but Warren sensed no tension in the air. They knew where Warren was leading George.

"How did you make the bomb?"

"I bundled the dynamite together with tape, then put a detonator in the middle stick, and set a timer."

Warren sighed and leaned forward to look George in the eye. "You made that up." His voice hardened. "You need to stop making things up, right now. Lying to the FBI is not a good idea, and can lead to a lot of trouble for you." George's eyes widened, the muscles around them tense. "And all of this delays the investigation, and the apprehension of the real perpetrator." Warren stopped, and allowed the silence to lengthen as George took in their meaning. The other two men remained still and watchful, content to let Warren handle the questioning.

Warren waited until George showed signs of relaxing. "Where's Mrs Cole this morning?"

"She's gone to visit friends in the city," George replied. Warren didn't miss the tremble return to George's hands, or the wide, frightened eyes in his pale face.

"Where about in the city?" Warren heard Burns pull out a notebook from his jacket pocket and the click of a pen being readied for action.

"I don't know."

"I warned you about lying. Where is she?"

"I don't know!"

"I don't believe you."

"She told me she was meeting a friend and dropped me off here first. She said she would pick me up when she had finished."

"The friend's name?" Warren demanded as Burns pulled out his cell phone and dialled.

George shook his head. "I didn't ask."

Warren wanted to yell at George, but refrained. It wouldn't help. "Car registration and description?"

"Got it here," Burns interrupted, waving the file he'd been holding. "Arranging a search now."

"No! Please leave her be."

Warren stood and moved in front of George, suddenly sympathetic with the old man. Wouldn't he do anything for Beth if he had to? George was only trying to protect the woman he loved. "We have to question her and find out if she is involved. You've made it plain you believe she is—why else would you fake a confession? We'll find her, bring her in and ask her a few questions. If we're satisfied she has no involvement, we'll release her again. At least you'll know, one way or another."

Chapter Twenty-Nine

Beth stopped and turned her face to the sun. The sidewalk outside their apartment block had exchanged the early morning commuters for the mid-morning moms with their young children, and the elderly walking along with shopping bags in hand. Her eyes followed a young mother with a small boy in tow. They walked hand in hand; the boy skipping and jumping over cracks in the concrete. A smile curved her lips as her hand reached down to touch the bump in her belly. Happiness bubbled inside her as she thought of the future. A child for her and Warren to love and nurture, and Warren happy in his new job. Life was as perfect as it could get.

A sudden cloud moved overhead, dimming the warmth of the sun's glow. She glanced at her watch and walked towards the park she had nominated to the lady at the gas station the previous day. There was no real expectation of the lady showing up to return the money, but as she wanted to go for a walk anyway, this was as good as any route to take.

Five minutes' brisk walk brought Beth to the park entrance. She strode in, making her way towards the centre, scanning the grounds for any sign of the lady. A circuit of the play equipment—she would bring their child here to play—revealed no sign of the lady in the park area. Beth paused, hands on hips, looking around. Another look at her watch showed she was on time. She hesitated, tempted to move on and forget about the meeting, but the memory of the lady's pleading eyes the previous afternoon had her heading for a park bench to wait. It wouldn't hurt to sit for five or ten minutes, in case the lady was running late.

Beth lowered herself onto the bench and looked up and down the path again. Still no sign of the lady. She pulled her phone out of her pocket to check for messages. Warren would hear from the Director this morning and he might try to call her if he had time. There was nothing there, so she pushed it back into the pocket it had come from and looked around once more. This time she spotted the lady approaching. She had just entered the park from the same direction Beth had and was making her way towards the bench.

Beth stood as the older lady approached. "Good morning."

The lady smiled at her and sat on the bench, placing the bag she carried on the seat beside her. "Good morning."

Beth looked down at her for a moment, and then resumed her seat. She could take the time to talk for a few minutes if the lady wanted. A small act of kindness never hurt. "How are you this morning?" she enquired.

"A little tired," the lady admitted. "Thank you for meeting me. It would have weighed heavy on my conscience if I couldn't repay you, both the money and for your kindness." She smiled at Beth. "My name is Daisy."

Beth answered her smile. "I'm Beth."

"Hello Beth," Daisy said, and then reached into her bag. "I have your money here." She passed Beth an envelope and then reached into the bag again. "I hope you don't mind, but I made you a fruit cake to say thank you." She passed Beth an old biscuit tin that had the lid taped down. "I didn't want the top to come off in the car," she explained, touching the tape.

"You didn't have to," Beth said as she accepted the offering. She wasn't fond of fruit cake, and Warren avoided cake of any kind if he could. Maybe she could give it to Sam and Heather.

"I wanted to," Daisy said, beaming at her. "I can't thank you enough for coming to my aid yesterday."

The older lady's lips trembled and Beth, touched, reached for her hand, squeezing it gently. "It was my pleasure."

Daisy returned the slight pressure of her fingers. "It's been a hard few weeks for me, so it's nice to know there are kind people still around."

Beth's ready compassion stirred, filling her with pity for the woman beside her. "Do you want to talk about it?" she asked, throwing away all thought of her walk.

Daisy raised tear-filled eyes to hers. "I couldn't. You didn't come here to listen to my worries." She sniffed, diving a hand into a pocket and pulling out a tissue. Daisy dabbed at her eyes and then managed a smile. "I'd rather hear about you. You look happy, and I'd like to hear about happiness."

Beth leaned back on the bench, keeping hold of Daisy's hand. Telling Daisy about the good things in her life would be easy, but she didn't want to make the woman feel worse about her own life. "Well, I'll tell you one thing that's happened in my life." Her cheeks glowed as her smile grew. "I found out that my husband and I are expecting a baby, one we never thought we could have."

Beth stopped at Daisy's reaction. The older lady's eyes had shot open, and her face had paled. The look only lasted a split second before her face resumed its previous expression.

"Did I upset you?" Beth asked, concerned.

"No, it's okay," Daisy said.

Beth noticed Daisy's eyes flick to the tin now sitting beside Beth on the bench. "Is something wrong?"

The older lady shook her head and swallowed. Her eyes flicked to the tin once more.

"Are you hungry? Would you like some of the cake?" Beth asked, puzzled.

"No, no," Daisy said. "It's just the memories." Daisy looked down at their joined hands. "It's not your fault. My son is dead."

"Oh Daisy, I'm so sorry! I didn't mean to upset you." She slid an arm around Daisy's shoulders. "Tell me all about him."

Burns' cell phone buzzed as he was preparing to leave Warren's office in search of food for them all.

"Burns…excellent!...yes…what?" He looked up at Warren. "Be careful, don't alarm her, but do it now!"

He hung up the phone and walked over to Warren. "That was one of my agents. By pure luck he found Daisy Cole's car as he was returning from another assignment. He and his partner searched the area and found Mrs Cole." He glanced at George, who had half risen from his chair, and then looked back at Warren. "She's in a park on Scott Street, but she's not alone." He swallowed. "She's with Dr Pearce, who seems to be hugging her."

"What?" Warren roared.

"My agents will apprehend her now and escort her in for questioning. They'll call me as soon as they have her safe."

Warren glared at Cole. He was struggling for breath, his chest squeezing tight in a horrible, but familiar feeling. Ice settled in his brain at the thought of Beth being in danger. It took a supreme effort, but he kept control.

Burns' phone buzzed again. Warren wanted to snatch it out of his hands, but the control remained intact.

"Yes…" he looked at Warren. "They have her, and Dr Pearce is safe."

Beth trotted beside the agent who held firmly onto her arm, leading her away from Daisy. She risked a turn of the head to look back; the other agent who had interrupted them had been joined by another two, and they were questioning Daisy and looking in her bags. She stumbled, her head turning back to the direction she and the agent headed. When they reached the edge of the park, the agent stopped, looked back at the group around Daisy, and then at Beth.

"Dr Pearce. Can you please wait here?"

"What's this about?" she demanded. "Daisy's just a lonely woman who needed a hug."

"I can't explain now," the agent replied. "Can you please wait here?"

Beth nodded and watched as the agent jogged back towards the group. He'd only taken a few steps when two of the group pointed at the tin Daisy had given her, then looked at Beth, and then turned to Daisy. Beth couldn't hear what they asked, but they leaned over the poor woman, their bodies tensed in position as they talked to Daisy. The woman cowered back, but was prevented from moving away by the agent standing behind her.

"Don't hurt her," she whispered as she watched.

The agents dispersed, one staying with Daisy as the others separated and hurried towards other people in the park. Beth saw them speak to them, then move on, and the people begin to run out of the park. The agent with Daisy dragged her away from the bench. He pulled out his cell phone and was talking rapidly as he marched the older lady towards Beth. A swift glance to the other agents, still clearing the park, and Beth felt an icy wave sweep through her.

There was a bomb in the tin Daisy had given her.

Beth turned to find shelter, but staggered as the world spun around her. The sidewalk heaved, and she fell to her knees, the impact on the concrete jarring and confusing her spinning brain further. She crouched over her knees, hands braced on the ground, as she waited for the giddiness to pass.

"Dr Pearce!"

The agent holding Daisy had reached her. She saw his shadow move on the ground beside her, folding itself as he bent over her while keeping hold of Daisy Cole.

"I'm okay," she said. "Just a bit of dizziness. I'll be fine in a minute."

"We'll get someone to help you as soon as possible," the agent replied.

"I'll be okay," Beth said, impatient now. She lifted her head to test it; no new giddiness. "I'm better already." A moment of doubt hit. "Is there a bomb in there, and I am safe here?"

"We suspect there may be, though Mrs Cole denies it. The bomb squad are on their way, and you should be safe at this distance, according to their advice."

The agent moved away, taking a silent Daisy with him. Beth rolled off her knees and onto her butt. Her head had stopped spinning, but she remained where she was. Tiny rocks bounced on the ground as her hands swept them from her clothes. The skin of her knees burned, but she didn't bother struggling to pull the jeans up to look at them. It wouldn't help, and the discomfort would pass.

She leaned back to see what was happening in the park. It was empty now, and she could see the agents hovering around the access points to prevent anyone from entering. The sound of sirens reached her, growing stronger each second. Beth turned away from the park and towards the oncoming sirens. No doubt Warren would be on his way, too.

The first vehicles to pull up were squad cars. Officers leapt out and were met by the agent who had been holding Daisy. They dispersed as Beth wondered what the agent had done with her. Was she in a car, or handcuffed somewhere? She shrugged. The morning already had so many unanswered questions, what were a few more?

Beth looked up as a shadow passed her vision, interrupting her thoughts. One of police officers had stopped in front of her.

"I'm okay," she said before he could speak.

"Let me help you up," the officer said, offering her a hand. Before she could grasp it, more cars pulled up, disgorging a mix of men and women in suits. More agents.

As Beth grabbed hold of the officer's hand a rose to her feet, a fire tender drew up, completing the blocking of the street.

"Hey," the officer called out as the first firefighter opened a door. "You guys got a paramedic? I think this lady might need help."

"I'm fine, I said," Beth snarled, pulling her hand out of the officer's hold. It would be bad enough when Warren arrived. She didn't need a fuss now. "Where do you want me to stand?"

The officer eyed her for a moment. "Behind the tender for now, please ma'am."

Beth strode off without another word. The area around the park was now full of suits and uniforms, with a mix of the casual clothes of park goers and the curious come to see what was happening. She rounded the tender and perched on the step to the driver's door. The last half an hour replayed over in her mind. The agents thought the tin Beth had been given didn't contain fruit cake, but a bomb. Was this connected to the recent bombings? Was Daisy behind it all? What had she done to become Daisy's next target?

Beth's heart raced. A hot tide, flowed by a cold one, raised goosebumps on her skin and she ran her fingers over a now damp brow. There was no dizziness, just a squeezing nausea in her gut making her bend over when she sat. A bomb? Given to her? Beth moaned as the tension in her gut twisted tighter.

"Where the hell is she?"

Warren's voice reached her, followed by hurried footsteps. She lifted her head as he rounded the tender.

"Thank God," he said, his voice rough.

Then she was in his arms, cradled and protected. The nausea subsided; she was safe. Beth slid an arm around his waist and held him. She hadn't missed the worried eyes under scowling brows, and the lines on his face. He needed comfort too.

A hand cupped her face as he looked down. "Are you all right?"

Beth mustered a little smile. "I am now." She drew a shaky breath. "Is it true? Was it a...a bomb?"

"The bomb squad have only just arrived, so we don't know yet."

"Did she want to...?"

"Beth," Warren interrupted. "Don't say it. We don't know why she wanted to meet you. It may just be coincidence."

Beth nodded, fighting down dread that had risen. She would find out eventually, but for now she needed to think the best, not the worst. Besides, Warren wasn't done yet, and she waited for him to explode.

And he did.

"What the hell were you doing here, hugging Daisy Cole for, anyway? What is it with you and finding trouble? Just when I think everything is calm, you go off and do something that lands you in danger! What were you thinking? Damn it, Beth! You have the baby to think about now! Why can't you keep yourself out of trouble?" He'd let her go during his outburst, and now gripped hold of her shoulders, as if he wanted to shake her. "It kills me every time something like this happens," he continued, his voice roughened now, and quieter as his sudden anger subsided. "It kills me."

Beth reached out for him, her heart aching at the pain in his eyes. He let go of her shoulders and pulled her hard against his chest.

"I'm sorry," she whispered, her face buried in his neck. "So very sorry."

"I know. I'm sorry too," he answered. "It's not your fault." She felt his arms stir around her, a restlessness he couldn't hide. "How is it you were here today, hugging her?" His arms relaxed as he looked at her, his brow creased over narrowed eyes.

"I loaned her twenty dollars at a gas station yesterday, and she insisted on meeting me to repay it." The scowl deepened down at her. "Who is she?" Beth asked

"Daisy Cole is the mother of the bank robber who shot and killed a man. You are connected to the case through the evidence you analysed. I think you might have been set up yesterday, that the loan was a deliberate move to get close to you." Warren sighed. "There are lots of reasons why she might want to talk to you. Why do you have to be so nice to people?"

Beth shrugged. "I'm not always nice."

"Well, you should cultivate a bit more meanness."

What? "Do you mean that?"

"No." Warren's arm tightened around her for an instant. "I don't."

"Just as well. I'd have to practise on you."

The ploy worked. Warren's scowl vanished. "Then I definitely don't want you being mean." He dropped a kiss on her lips, chasing away the chill in the body. "You look better now. I'll take you over to where the others are, and you can stay with them." A slight scowl reappeared. "I need to know you're in safe hands."

Beth nodded in agreement. She wanted to be safe, too. "As you wish."

Chapter Thirty

Burns sat back in his chair and assessed the woman sitting across from him. Her hair curled in grey and brown spirals around a lined face. Her hands rested in her lap as she returned his look, her eyes guarding her thoughts with their blankness. Burns didn't for one moment believe her mind as empty as her eyes; she was sharp and aware under the façade. Her rights had been read, her lawyer was present, and Burns already knew how the interview would go. Still, he had to work through the process.

"Mrs Cole, can you please tell me where you were between six and ten last night?"

The lawyer glanced at Daisy, and then at Burns.

"Mrs Cole?" Burns said, after a moment of silence.

"I was at home."

"Was anyone with you?"

"George."

"George Cole, your husband?"

"Yes."

"Was anyone else in the house with you?" He almost missed the flicker of light in her eyes. It disappeared as fast as it arrived.

"No," she replied.

"And what did you do last night during those hours?"

Daisy glanced at the lawyer who returned the look and nodded. "I cooked dinner, washed the dishes, and then watched television with George."

"Anything else?"

"No."

"When did you bake the cake you gave to Dr Pearce?"

Daisy smiled, irritating Burns. "I told your agents it was a cake. But no, you had to call the bomb squad to check it." She chuckled. "What idiots."

"Mrs Cole," the lawyer said, her voice quiet. Daisy looked at her and the smile died. "I baked it last week and then froze it. I took it out of the freezer last night to give to her today."

"Mrs Cole, why did you look alarmed when Dr Pearce told you she was pregnant, and why did you look at the tin the cake was in?"

"The cake has sherry in it. You're not supposed to drink alcohol when you're pregnant."

"Then why didn't you say something to Dr Pearce?"

"I figured the amount of sherry was so small it wouldn't hurt the baby."

"And you didn't want to hurt the baby."

"No."

Burns noted that Daisy had relaxed and changed topic. "Why did you target Dr Pearce?"

"What? I didn't target her. She was kind to me and I wanted to return the favour."

"But you knew that Dr Pearce is the forensic botanist who used the evidence left by your son, Jerry Cole, to lead the FBI to your nursery."

"Don't answer that," the lawyer warned Daisy.

"You knew who she was when you saw her at the gas station last night. You had seen her at the nursery, and you knew her name."

"I didn't!"

"Then why didn't you ask me who Dr Pearce is when she had only given you her first name? Not even that; a shortening of her first name?"

"Don't answer," the lawyer warned again.

"I did nothing wrong!"

Burns opened the file sitting in front of him. "Mrs Cole, can you please tell me where you were between ten and twelve noon, Monday morning just gone?"

"I was out driving."

"Where were you driving?"

"I can't remember."

Burns looked at Daisy's wide-open eyes, staring at him from across the table. The hint of curve on her lips confirmed his suspicion she was lying, but he knew that anyway. "I have a statement from a witness who saw you sitting on a park bench talking to a man the witness identified as Matthew Aitken. The witness puts the time of your meeting at approximately fifteen minutes before a bomb exploded in his truck, killing him." Burns leaned forward. "I also have a photo and an analysis of footprints found at the site of another bombing, the one that killed Reuben Dervish. What size shoes do you wear, Mrs Cole?"

"Don't answer," the lawyer rapped out.

"I didn't do it! I didn't give them a bomb, I swear!"

"Mrs Cole!"

Burns ignored the lawyer, focussing on Daisy. "Then tell me what happened, Mrs Cole."

The lawyer opened her mouth, but shut it as Daisy laid a hand on her arm, silencing her. "I saw them, I talked to them. Reuben was the first. He needed help. He wanted money to get away and go interstate. I met with him because I thought Jerry would want me to." A tear rolled down her cheek. "My Jerry was a good friend and looked out for his buddies. He would have told me to help Reuben." Daisy wiped the tear from where it rested on her jaw and sniffed. "I gave Reuben the money and a bag of food. We met in the forest, and I gave him the things and left. Then there was a loud boom. I fell over, face first. I was so scared." Burns watched Daisy wipe another tear away, willing her to continue. "I had to go back to see what had happened." Her face went white. "It was horrible. I ran back to the car and left him there." Her hand shook as she wiped another tear away. "Horrible," she whispered.

"How did he contact you?"

"He hid in the barn and called to me when I went past."

"And Aitkens?" Burns asked quietly.

"I gave him the same things as I gave Reuben; food and money." Her watery eyes met Burns'. "I swear it was only food and money. I worked it out after that. It was Jerry doing the killing. I just had to meet them, and he did the rest. It was their punishment for leading him astray, for not keeping him safe."

Burns groaned inwardly. Insanity plea coming right up. "And Dr Pearce? Why her?"

"Mrs Cole, please don't say anything," the lawyer said. It was a half-hearted plea, and one Daisy again ignored.

"Because she was a part of Jerry dying. If she hadn't led the FBI to our home, Jerry would still be alive."

"So, you wanted her to die, too," Burns said, holding back his anger. "She was just doing her job!"

"No! I didn't! I just led Jerry to her. He would have done the rest." Daisy drew a long shuddering breath. "But it was wrong. I couldn't let him hurt her." Daisy looked at Burns, her eyes suddenly bright. "She's pregnant, you know. I couldn't let Jerry kill an innocent child."

"How were you going to stop him?"

"I wanted to show Jerry she was my friend, so I talked to her."

"And the cake?"

Daisy's eyes narrowed, but she wasn't looking at him. She glared at her hands. "Jerry gave me those tins. He would buy me cookies, just because he liked the tins. The tins were a sign to him so he knew who to kill." She sniffed again. "He wouldn't like knowing he killed an innocent child."

"Enough," the lawyer said. "I want my client to see a doctor before this goes any further. There was no evidence of a bomb at the park and my client has no knowledge of explosives, or access to them. Unless you plan on charging her with giving someone a fruit cake, I suggest you let her go."

"Not yet. Daisy, where's Peter Hill?"

"I don't know."

"You knew where the others were, so I think you know where Peter is, too."

"I saw him once, right after Jerry died, but not since. He was so sad that Jerry died."

Burns could scream with frustration. This woman had contacted all the hunted robbers since the death of her son, but hadn't seen fit to report it to anyone. He sucked in a deep breath, but Daisy spoke before Burns could open his mouth.

"Jerry wouldn't want Peter dead. They were lovers. No, Jerry would keep Peter safe."

The lawyer stood up. "Charge my client, or release her."

Burns glared at her, then rose to his feet. "I'll be back," he said. He jerked his head at the agent who had sat with them during the interview, and the two of them left the room.

Burns turned right, took three strides, then opened the door and entered the adjoining observation room.

"We have to let her go."

EAD Pearce didn't respond immediately. He stood staring into the interview room, his arms folded across his chest.

"There is no hard evidence she committed the bombings," Burns said, looking for a response. "We can't keep her."

"I agree," Pearce said, not moving from his stance. "Surveillance teams are standing by to keep an eye on both the Coles." Pearce moved, dropping his arms and turning to Burns. "I'll assign additional agents to assist your search for Peter Hill."

"Thank you, sir."

"Keep me informed of the Coles' movements."

"Yes sir."

Burns stepped aside to allow Pearce to exit the room. Something close to shame sat in his chest. Pearce's wife had been targeted, and he hadn't been able to prevent it. He'd let the man down.

Pearce stopped at the doorway of the room and turned back. "Don't blame yourself, Burns. It's not your fault."

Pearce didn't wait for an answer, spinning around and striding away, leaving Burns standing bemused in the now empty room.

Warren rapped on the door of the office suite and it opened almost before his hand had dropped again. Sam opened the door wide to allow Warren in.

"She's in Sarah's office," he said.

"Thanks." His gut unravelled the knot it had been harbouring and he sighed. "Thanks for keeping an eye on her."

"Anytime."

Warren returned Sam's solemn look. "What did she tell you?"

"Enough."

"It's not over yet."

"You know where I am."

Warren nodded. "Thank you."

He left Sam and headed for Sarah's office. Sarah smiled as he walked through the door, but didn't speak, merely pointing at the small room behind hers. Beth's voice reached him, and Warren smiled as he moved to the doorway.

He stopped at the sight before him. Beth sat on the floor, her back against the wall. Logan sat in her lap, his back resting on her stomach as she read him a book. His small chubby fingers splayed on the page Beth read. An incredible, overwhelming surge of longing swept over him. This was what he wanted, this was what his soul craved. A family. His wife and a child of his own. He wanted it so much it hurt, leaving him breathless with need.

Warren drew a long, shaking breath, not fighting the emotions flooding him, but surrendering to them. Beth looked up. Her face glowed as her smile dawned and spread to her blue eyes. She robbed him of coherent thought for an instant as another wave of blinding love and longing swept through him.

"Bababa, mamababa!" Logan sang out, his arms reaching up to Warren and breaking the moment.

Beth laughed. "I think he wants you."

Warren walked over to them, bent down to kiss Beth and then lifted Logan into his arms, relishing the feel of the baby's soft weight resting on his chest.

"I consider that an honour," he responded, looking down at Logan.

"Babababa, dababa, dodododo," Logan said, staring up at him.

"I have no clue what you're saying," Warren responded.

"It's probably just as well," Sarah's voice came from behind him. "He's most likely issuing orders."

"Determined young man then? Like his mom?"

Sarah smiled, reaching out to take Logan from Warren. "I have no idea where he gets it from," she replied, the smile still in place. She turned and left the room with the baby.

Warren reached down and helped Beth to her feet and then drew her into his arms. "I can't wait until our baby is born," he said. "And I can't believe there was a time I didn't want a child." He kissed her forehead. "I want our little family so much now."

"I'm glad," Beth answered, snuggling into his chest. How he loved the way she did that. The closeness, the togetherness.

Warren paused before changing the subject, wanting to make the most of the moment. "They had to let Daisy Cole go. There is no evidence she or her husband is the bomber."

"And what does your gut tell you?" Beth asked.

"My gut tells me there is more to this than the Coles, but she… she has something to do with it. I don't know what, though." He dropped a kiss on her hair to comfort her. And him. "They'll be watched."

He felt Beth's chest expand and deflate as she sighed. "Okay," she said. "Time to go home?"

"Time to go home."

Chapter Thirty-One

George passed the cup of coffee to Daisy and sat down beside her on the old sofa on their back porch. The day was almost behind them; the sun gone and darkness creeping up with every passing second. He sat staring out past the greenhouses to the forest beyond, wanting to talk to Daisy, but not knowing what he wanted to say. What was there to talk about? The events of the day had been documented by the FBI, noted down for review by others, and they were home. It wasn't over though. Peter was still out there, somewhere. Was he the bomber, or was it someone else? Would Peter be the next one dead, or would it be one of them? George felt the weariness creeping through his limbs, the bone-tired drag of no hope of relief, and no joy in life.

He glanced across to Daisy who sat still, her cup still full of coffee in her hand, her eyes as George's had been, staring out into the darkness.

"I'm sorry," he said.

"For what?" she asked, her eyes still staring out.

"For everything."

Daisy didn't speak, and George didn't elaborate. He wasn't sure why he had apologised, but it felt like the right thing to do. Silence descended on them again as the transition from day to night completed.

"I'm glad they found me, found us," Daisy said, breaking the silence. "I couldn't have let Jerry hurt that baby. He would have been devastated if he had."

"Do you believe it's Jerry?"

Daisy turned to him. "I have to believe it's him. I didn't do it, but each one I met died. It must be Jerry. He's been with me and passed his judgement on them."

"What about Peter?"

"I haven't seen Peter."

"Doesn't mean he isn't doing it."

"I don't think he's around anymore."

"A ghost can't make a bomb and set it off."

"Maybe he's making someone else do it, someone we don't know." Daisy's eyes narrowed at him in the faint light illuminating them from the nearby kitchen window. "Is it you?"

"No, it's not me. I told you I've been going to grief counselling groups. I don't want revenge, I want... I want peace."

Daisy stared at him for another moment and then turned back to look into the darkness. "Maybe it's all over now. I'm not going to give anyone any food, or visit anyone, so Jerry won't know where to find them."

"You sought them out on purpose?"

"Yes. At first, I wanted to hurt them, but I couldn't. I baked a cake for Reuben and put rat poison in it, but I threw it away before I met him. I wasn't sure if Jerry wanted the woman, but she was the next step."

George's heart raced. "Daisy, was there anyone else on your list?"

She shrugged. "I don't know. I don't think I had a list. It was just the people who were involved in the whole thing."

George took a deep breath. "But it's over now, isn't it?"

Daisy looked down at the cup in her hand. "I hope so."

Peter lay in his makeshift hiding place under the porch, listening to the conversation going on above his head. Daisy had led him straight to the others. Reuben had welcomed him when he'd appeared after Daisy had left, and no one had seen him put the bomb in Matty's car when Matty had been talking to Daisy. He'd seen an opportunity this morning when the woman had been alone behind the fire tender for a moment. No one would have paid any attention if he put his knife to her side and told her to go with him, but he'd been thwarted by her husband before he could put his plan into action. Just as well. Daisy was right, Jerry wouldn't forgive the murder of a baby.

The husband though, he was a different matter. So much could be accomplished in one go if the head of the entire investigative division died. He would be hard to get to, but it could be done and Jerry's death would be revenged.

Peter didn't hear Daisy and George go back inside. He was too busy planning.

Chapter Thirty-Two

Warren placed the mug of steaming tea on the table beside the bed where Beth slept. He loved watching her sleep, her long brown curls tangled on the pillow, her soft lips parted, and her face at peace. As always, it didn't last. As much as he loved to watch her sleep, it always ended with him unable to resist the longing in him to touch her and see her eyes open.

He reached out and brushed a lock of hair from her shoulder. Her brows twitched and her lips curved as she opened her eyes. "Good morning," he said before leaning down to kiss her cheek. Her skin was warm and soft under his lips, and her arms reached to hold him as she turned her face so he could kiss her lips.

"Good morning," she whispered as he sat back up. Warren saw her glance at the mug. "A perfect way to wake up; a hot guy and a hot cup of tea. What more can a girl want?"

"To meet the guy for lunch today? I know it's Saturday, but I need to work this morning."

Beth stretched under the covers and then sat up. "I understand. Lunch sounds perfect. Where?"

"Clydes?" Warren said as he passed Beth her tea.

"Works for me," she replied. "Thanks for the cuppa."

"My pleasure. I need to get going."

"Okay. I'll see you at lunch. One o'clock?"

"One o'clock." Warren kissed her again. "I love you."

"I love you too."

"And try to stay out of trouble." Warren forced a smile, but the bomber was still out there.

"I'll do my best," she replied. Her brows puckered. "Do you think I'm in danger?"

"No. I suspect the remaining robber is the bomber, and he has nothing to gain by targeting you. By killing the others, he gains their share of the money stolen." He smiled, naturally this time. "Burns called about half an hour ago. A plausible lead to the suspect's whereabouts has been called in. The sighting was a fair way from here and I'm confident Burns and his agents will catch him soon. I want you to be careful though. Just don't accept packages from strangers."

"I won't." She smiled, a clear and happy smile that lit up her eyes. "You'd better get to work. I'll see you for lunch."

The false lead had been easy to do. A stolen phone bill from a trash can about a week ago, and 'Mr Yelland of Norfolk' had stopped at a payphone to say he'd seen a man matching 'that robber on the loose and was there a reward?' Peter smirked as he recalled the conversation. The information on the telephone account was enough to make him sound like the real thing, and with any luck, it would all be over before they realised what had happened.

Peter packed all he needed into a small calico shopping bag. The prepared bomb components—three sticks of dynamite, the detonator, and the timer, kept separate until the last possible moment. In a tribute to Daisy, who'd unwittingly led him to each victim, he also had a tin ready to hold the assembled device. Magnets were glued in two close rows on the lid, ready to hold it in place. Two layers of cardboard now lined the inside of the lid, negating any possible effect of the magnets on his timer. Satisfied he was as prepared as he could be, Peter assumed watch of the

FBI headquarters building, waiting for his target to arrive. Finding somewhere to observe from hadn't been easy. He'd arrived early enough to grab a park for his stolen car with its switched number plates within sight of the entrance. The area crawled with FBI agents. Peter's blond curls were now dark brown, and he'd used shoe blacking to darken his brows and the newly grown moustache as well. It made his skin smart and burn, but it had to be done. A black cap, pulled down over his face, completed the change of appearance, and Peter felt confident he would go unrecognised. The last place they would look for him was on the FBI's doorstep.

He didn't have to wait long. Pearce drew up at the entrance of the building's parking lot and waved a pass of some sort. The gate rose, and the car moved out of Peter's sight. He breathed out a long sigh of relief and smiled. All was going as planned, and he was ready for the opportunity when it arose. He flicked down the visor to reveal a photo. Jerry's sweet smile stared down at him, his chest squeezing as the fierce pain of his loss hit yet again. Never again would he see Jerry, hold him, love him. It was all gone, and soon too, so would he be. He'd wanted them all gone. He'd failed in that too. Mac was still out there, but he would never find the money, and he would never know if someone was coming for him. That gave Peter some small consolation.

Pearce didn't come out until Peter had moved the car three times. Sitting in the one place had made him jumpy, his nerves stretched taut with the anticipation and the fear of being recognised. Parking hadn't been so easy once he'd moved, and one time he had to drive around for almost half an hour before a suitable parking spot became vacant. He could only pray his target hadn't left during his absences.

When the silver nose of the Impala appeared up the ramp from the parking lot, Peter's heart started to pound.

"Settle," he whispered to himself. "Stay calm."

The heart rate didn't ease, but the tension in his muscles loosened. He started his car and pulled out into the traffic to follow Pearce.

Peter kept the silver Impala in sight, risking some changing traffic signals, but without Pearce seeming to notice. An unlucky change left him stranded on an intersection, and the nerves returned, screaming at him as the Impala vanished from sight.

Stay calm. No need to panic.

The lights changed and Peter moved down the road, following the path of his target. Two blocks further down, as he slowed for traffic, he spied Pearce climbing out the Impala, parked further down the road.

"Got you!"

Pearce walked down the street towards him. Sweat sprang up on Peter's forehead. He turned his head towards the centre console and pretended to be fiddling with the radio controls while managing to keep an eye on Pearce as he approached. Pearce passed him without glancing in his direction. Peter released a long sigh, not realising he'd been holding his breath. All was good. He kept an eye on Pearce by using his mirrors. Fortunately, the traffic had come to a complete stop, and he could watch without the fear of hitting another car. He saw Pearce stop at the entrance to Clyde's and his wife appear as if she'd been waiting at the door. They embraced and disappeared inside.

A car horn sounded behind him. The traffic had moved on and he was holding up the cars behind him. He released the brake and moved forward to find a park for his car.

He found the perfect spot; a side street with little pedestrian traffic. He opened the trunk of his car and moved the bag to the middle of the space. Using it as a screen, he took the tin and assembled the bomb. It took only a few minutes. No one passed him, let alone asked him what he was doing. Five minutes later the tin was closed and sealed, ready for delivery. This would be the hardest part.

His experience stealing cars gave him the confidence to carry out the plan. He would walk behind Pearce's car, pretending to want to cross the road. Then he would drop his keys and a handful of items he had prepared: a pen, some gum, and a few coins. It would be only reasonable to bend down to retrieve his property, some of which would have rolled under the tail of the car because he'd flick his wrist in that direction. With Pearce's car on one side, and another parked car behind that, Peter would be screened. No one would spare him a glance. It would take only a moment to extract the tin from his bag and lift it up under the car in one smooth movement. The magnets would grab onto the chassis rail, and it would be done.

Peter took the repacked bag out of the truck and sat it on the ground. He closed the lid, picked up the bag, and walked towards Pearce's car. His car keys dangled from the little finger of the hand holding the bag, ready to drop. His other hand, he thrust deep in his coat pocket, his fingers closed around the items it contained. The sweat had returned, but he couldn't bring himself to let go of anything to wipe it away.

Peter rounded the corner and his eyes lit on the silver Impala. As he strode closer, he checked the plates—it was the right car. His heart pounded, drumming in his ears. His eyes, lowered under the peak of the cap, darted from side to side as he assessed his chances.

It was now or never.

Peter headed for the gap between the cars and stepped off the sidewalk, onto the road. His little finger straightened, and the keys slid off, hitting the ground with a rattle of metal on tarmac. He stooped, reaching for them. At the same time his hand flicked the other items down, and they scattered.

"Do you need a hand there, buddy?" a voice asked from behind him.

Peter's heart leapt into his throat. He turned to see an old man with grey hair watching him. "No, thank you sir, I've got it."

The old man nodded and moved on.

Peter swallowed hard and crouched behind the car. As his left hand gathered his scattered possessions, his right hand lifted the tin out of the bag and under the car. A tiny clink told him the magnets had grabbed. He lowered his hand, allowing the magnets to take the weight of the bomb. It didn't move. Peter shoved his possessions into the bag, stood, and when the traffic parted, crossed the road.

No one stopped him, no one followed him, and no one so much as glanced at the car.

He'd done it.

Chapter Thirty-Three

Warren swallowed the last of his coffee as Beth placed her knife and fork together and patted her stomach.

"I think I'm going to explode," she said.

"Then I guess you won't want any pudding." He grinned as she blew out her cheeks and rolled her eyes.

"I couldn't eat a crumb, let alone pudding!" Her lids lowered over her eyes. "I need to go home and sleep it off."

He chuckled, enjoying her play-acting and catching her good mood. "Just don't doze off waiting for the traffic signals to change."

"Won't happen; I caught a cab here as I didn't want to spend ages looking for a car park."

"I found one without a problem."

"Well, you would. You FBI types park wherever you want."

"Not this time. I found a legal park." He reached across the table, his hand open for Beth to lay hers in it. His fingers closed around hers, squeezing gently. "Do you want me to give you a lift home?"

Before she could answer him, the buzz of her cell phone rang out from her bag.

"Hold that thought," she said as she dived her hand into the bag. She glanced at the screen and sighed. "Work," she said as she pressed the answer button and lifted the phone to her ear.

Warren leaned back in his seat and indicated to a passing waiter for the bill. Then his phone buzzed too.

"Pearce."

"Sir, Burns here. The lead this morning hasn't come through. One of the agents at the nursery said Mr Cole has been going in and out of the big barn all day, carrying things back and forth from the house. I'm heading out there now to have a chat and I was hoping you'd come with me, seeing as how he prefers you to any of us."

Warren became aware of Beth signalling him from across the table.

"Hold on a moment Burns." He lowered his phone. "What is it?"

Beth had also lowered her phone. "Call out. Can I drop you back at HQ and take the car?"

He held up a finger and lifted his phone to his ear. "Burns, can you pick me up from Clyde's in Georgetown?"

"Yes sir. Will be there in fifteen minutes."

"Good." Beth had heard his question and his response and was back on her call.

"Thank you," she said once she'd hung up. "They want me out there as soon as possible, and they're taking my kit with them."

"Where's 'out there'?"

"Just this side of Marshall."

"But you're tired."

"Not anymore." She smiled. "I'll be fine. I'll put music on—I think one of my country music albums is still in your car."

Warren closed his eyes in a moment of painful recollection. "Yes. I meant to throw it out…"

"Don't you dare!"

He opened his eyes again to meet her gaze, brimming with laughter at his reaction. "It's not worth the grief you'd give me if I did."

The waiter approached and slipped the folder with the bill onto the table. "Is there anything else I can get for you, sir? Ma'am?"

"No, thank you," Warren replied, reaching into his inner pocket for his wallet. He dropped his credit card inside the folder and the waiter bore it away.

"I should be back in time to come and get you from work."

"I can get a ride with someone or catch a cab, so don't feel you have to rush." He leaned forward. "Get an agent to drive on the way home if you feel tired. They can get a cab from there—I'll authorise it."

"I'll bear that in mind."

"Have a good day." The waiter had reappeared and handed Warren the folder again. Warren wrote on the paper inside and pocketed his card. "Shall we leave? I'll walk you to the car."

He rose from his chair and waited for Beth to join him and then followed her out of the restaurant.

Peter watched from further down the street as Pearce and his wife emerged from the restaurant and walked down the sidewalk. He followed their progress for a moment, but a group of people, led by a loud guide, strode past him and blocked his view. After straining to see around them, Peter gave up, reflecting that Pearce's car would pass his position anyway, so he would know the man had left. He relaxed back against the bricks of the building behind him, thinking over the next stage of his plan. The final act. The shotgun Peter had used for the robberies was in the trunk of his car. He would go out to the cemetery where Jerry was buried and end his life. It would all be over. Tears pricked at his eyes, blurring his vision. He wiped them away and concentrated on the passing traffic.

Another group of pedestrians moved past him. Peter panicked for an instant, his view of the road gone. A momentary gap, and he saw a flash of silver. He darted out, pushing his way through the crowd and onto the edge of the road. It was definitely Pearce's car. His shoulders slumped. It was done.

Peter turned and stepped back onto the sidewalk, almost colliding with the people walking past. A hand grabbed him.

"Watch where you're going."

"Sorry..." Peter began. His mouth dropped as horror polarised him. "What the...?"

The grip on his arm tightened painfully. Before Peter could unfreeze and react, he was swung around and his other arm grabbed, both of them pulled behind him.

"Peter Hill, you're under arrest for murder!"

Peter couldn't speak to the man arresting him, too stunned at seeing Pearce standing in front of him. A click, and he was handcuffed.

"Well spotted, Burns," Pearce said, his eyes narrowed at Peter.

"Thank you, sir. It's not often a fugitive walks into my arms like that."

Pearce's mouth curved on one side for a moment, waking Peter from his trance.

"Your car! You drove off!" he shouted, desperate to understand.

"My car? What...?"

Peter groaned as Pearce's face paled.

"What have you done to my car?" Pearce yelled, grabbing Peter by his shirt.

"It was you, it was meant for you!"

Burns pulled hard on his arms. "Is there a bomb in the car?" he shouted in Peter's ear.

"Yes!"

An arm shot around from behind Peter, gripping Pearce's wrist as his fingers closed on Peter's throat. Pearce's face, now red and contorted, his teeth gleaming white between flared lips, loomed above him.

"Sir!" Burns shouted. "Warren!"

"The car," Pearce yelled, releasing Peter and bolting.

Burns hauled Peter around and dragged him as they followed Pearce down the street. As they approached a black SUV, another man emerged.

"Take him in the back," Burns said, and pushed Peter at the man. Peter stumbled as he was shoved into the car, the man following him, and roughly fastening a seat belt around him.

Burns, now behind the wheel, pulled out into the traffic and set off after Pearce's car.

"She's heading out towards Marshall," Pearce said to Burns. He recited the plate number of his car.

Burns nodded. "Agent Modin, find out from Mr Hill exactly what he's put in the car."

A hand gripped Peter's shoulder, the finger digging in painfully.

"Three sticks of dynamite, detonator is on a timer," he volunteered. "It wasn't meant for her. Not the baby. I didn't want to hurt the baby." He struggled to breathe, panic taking over.

"How long?"

"About twenty minutes."

Pearce had a phone to his ear, Burns was on a hands free, summoning help.

"Damn it," Pearce said, dropping the phone from his ear. "She doesn't have the Blue-tooth connected and she usually puts her bag in the trunk, so she won't hear it ring. I can't reach her." The despair in Warren's voice ripped through Peter, making tears well in his eyes and spill down his cheeks.

"I didn't want to hurt the baby," he whispered.

"Where did you put the bomb?" Burns asked, pausing his phone conversation.

"It's stuck to the chassis rail under the left-hand rear of the car."

Burns relayed the information to whoever he spoke to. Pearce was staring out the windshield of the car and Burns weaved between the cars on the road.

"Idiots!" Burns hollered as a tourist bus stopped in the middle of an intersection as they approached, its way blocked by more cars. He swerved out and around the back, narrowly missing cars coming the other way.

"She had at least five minutes' head start," Pearce stated.

"We'll catch her," Burns said. "There's enough people out there now looking for her."

As Burns continued to weave through the traffic, Peter closed his eyes and prayed. *Please keep her safe, Jerry. Don't let the baby get hurt.* He'd failed. He thought he'd completed his plan so perfectly, but he'd failed. And he'd killed the baby. *Jerry, stop the bomb.*

Chapter Thirty-Four

They would have missed her if it wasn't for the sound of the explosion. As the clock ticked down, the tension in the car grew until it too became explosive.

Warren dropped his cell phone after yet another failed attempt to reach Beth. He felt sick, desperate to find her, ready to do anything, but there'd been no sign of her. She must have had an easy drive out of the city, and time was running out.

"Oh God," he whispered as he strained to see the cars in the distance ahead. "Please save her."

Clear of the city, Burns sped up, passing cars in their desperate rush to find Beth. As they approached a sign showing a comfort station on the side of the road, the whoomp of the detonation sounded.

"No!" Warren screamed, his heart shattering.

Burns stomped on the brakes, slewing the car onto a side road leading to the comfort station as smoke billowed up from behind the screening trees. They swerved into the parking lot and found a car enveloped in flames, the metal torn apart by the blast. Warren leapt out of the SUV before it stopped and raced towards the ruin of his car.

"Beth! Beth!"

Warren couldn't get close. His chest stung from the smoke as he desperately attempted to reach the wreckage. The car burned, hot metal surrounding the devastation. He saw Burns run around the car, trying to see through the flames. Numbness hit, blanking out everything—everything except Beth's voice. He could hear her sweet voice, calling his name.

"Warren!"

The numbness swept out, almost sending him reeling. He spun around, desperately hoping as his gaze searched the area. His eyes fell on the grey concrete brick of the facility block.

"Warren!"

He barely heard it, but it was real. "Beth," he yelled, and sprinted the twenty yards to the building and into the ladies' area. Crouched on the floor, her arms wrapped over her tummy, was Beth. In an instant he was beside her, holding her trembling body close, and kissing any part of her he could reach, over and over.

"I needed to pee," Beth said, her voice weak and shaking.

Burns erupted into the room. "Thank God! Is she okay?"

Warren felt her nod against his chest. "I think so," he replied.

"Emergency services are on their way," Burns said before disappearing again.

Warren slid around until he was sitting on the tiled floor with his back against the wall and Beth sitting on his lap, wrapped in his arms. They didn't speak. They didn't need to. All they needed was to exist together.

Epilogue

"Here we go," Beth growled as her face turned red again.

Warren grasped her hand and supported her right leg as the midwife on the other side did the same. He held his breath as Beth held hers, as if trying to help her push the baby out.

"Head's almost out," the obstetrician said calmly. "Beth, I want you to pant now."

Beth's eyes opened wide as she opened her mouth and panted as she'd been shown during antenatal classes. Her face lost some of its redness, but the sweat shining on her forehead and her damp curls showed the effort and hard work she'd done to get to this point.

"And head's out," the obstetrician said. Warren kept his gaze on Beth, but was aware of the obstetrician wiping over the baby's face. Beth's work wasn't finished yet, and she looked exhausted. He leaned forward and gently brushed a damp curl from her cheek. Their eyes met, and she gave him a small smile. Then her eyes opened wider.

"Here we go," she said again, and pushed.

Seconds later there was a gush, and their child was lifted onto Beth's tummy.

"Oh," she gasped, letting go of the midwife's hand to hold her baby.

Everything blurred as Warren's eyes filled with tears. Their child, their precious baby was here. He leaned down to kiss Beth's forehead.

"I love you," he croaked, his voice hampered by the incredible surge of emotion flooding through him.

A blanket appeared, seemingly from nowhere, and the baby loosely wrapped. He stared down at the tiny miracle they had created. Dark eyes stared back up, calm and serene. Warren looked up as the obstetrician nudged him.

"Do you want to cut the cord, Dad?"

Dad. He was a dad. Warren swallowed hard and accepted the scissors he was offered, cutting where the doctor pointed.

"Ooh," Beth said, looking down. "Another contraction coming."

A midwife took the baby. "Come with me, Dad," she said.

Warren squeezed Beth's hand and then followed the midwife, leaving the obstetrician to help Beth with the final stage of birth.

The midwife placed the baby on the scales. "Eight pounds, two ounces," she announced. He watched as she did a rapid assessment and then wrapped his child up in a soft blanket. "Here you go," she said, depositing the precious bundle in Warren's arms. As he felt the weight of his child settle in his arms, his world became complete.

He carried the baby back over to Beth, now resting back on the pillows, and laid the child in her arms. He slid his arm around her shoulders, enfolding her and their child in his embrace, holding his family close.

Beth smiled up at him, reaching to touch his cheek. "Are you happy?"

He smiled back. "There's nothing to describe how happy I am."

Warren moved his hand so he could stroke the soft skin of his child's cheek. "Welcome to the world, Matilda."

Connect with Alison

Website
http://alisonclifford.net

Blog
http://alisonclifford.net/alisons-blog

Facebook
http://m.facebook.com/alisoncliffordwriter